JUST A MATTER OF TIME

Dylan gingerly grasped her chin, lowered her head, and examined the spot where her head had hit the window.

"I'm . . . I'm fine. Just fine . . . Thanks," Kira stammered, and attributed her inability to speak, to the blow to the head when she'd connected with the windowpane. That had to be it. Normally she wasn't the type to go ga-ga over a handsome face.

When Kira took a step forward, Dylan grasped her arm. "And where do you think you're going?"

"I'm going after my dog, Mr. Jolivet."

Dylan paused when she called him by name. He expected anyone within a hundred-mile radius to know who he was. But she wasn't from around here.

"Do I know you?"

Kira shook her head from side to side.

"I told her who you were, Mr. Dylan," Ellis spoke up.

"Who are you?" he asked her then.

"I'm Kira Dodd," she answered, pulling her arm away.

Myra Dodd's daughter? The long-awaited-for family member had finally arrived to take Myra back. This was it. This was the opportunity he'd been waiting for. If he could just get her alone for a moment, he could begin to convince her why Myra didn't belong there. The look that she was giving him, however, told him that he would have to do some very fast talking to get her to trust him enough to listen to his reasoning.

BOOK YOUR PLACE ON OUR WEBSITE AND MAKE THE ARABESQUE ROMANCE CONNECTION!

We've created a customized website just for our very special Arabesque readers, where you can get the inside scoop on everything that's going on with Arabesque romance novels.

When you come online, you'll have the exciting opportunity to:

- View covers of upcoming books

- Learn about our future publishing schedule (listed by publication month and author)

- Find out when your favorite authors will be visiting a city near you

- Search for and order backlist books

- Check out author bios and background information

- Send e-mail to your favorite authors

- Join us in weekly chats with authors, readers and other guests

- Get writing guidelines

- AND MUCH MORE!

Visit our website at
http://www.arabesquebooks.com

NO GREATER GIFT

Geri Guillaume

BET Publications, LLC
www.msbet.com
www.arabesquebooks.com

ARABESQUE BOOKS are published by

BET Publications, LLC
c/o BET BOOKS
One BET Plaza
1900 W Place NE
Washington, D.C. 20018-1211

First Printing: November, 1999

10 9 8 7 6 5 4 3 2 1
Printed in the United States of America

Chapter One

Sleighbells ring! Are ya' listenin'?

"Maybe you didn't hear me. . . ."

Kira Dodd leaned over the ticket counter at Chicago's O'Hare airport and whispered tightly to the crisply dressed gate attendant. She spoke slowly and distinctly to compete with the airport's public address system. It was only the beginning of the holiday season, but the airport was already packed. She wanted to be certain that she was heard over the arrival and department announcements, passenger and flight crew pages, and the warble of holiday music meant to entertain the throng of passengers waiting to board their planes.

Gripping the podium until she thought her nails would gouge into it, Kira was grateful for the small obstacle. If it weren't for the podium separating them, Kira was certain that she would grab the patiently smiling attendant by the bright, polka-dot bow tie and yank her face-to-face.

"Are you listening to me? I said I've got to get on that plane."

In the lane, snow is glistenin' . . .

"I'm sorry, miss. Because of the weather, all of our flights are grounded. No one will be allowed to board the plane until the weather clears."

"When will that be?"

"We'll just have to wait and see, won't we," the attendant soothed.

"No, we won't just wait and see," Kira mimicked. "The ad in the paper said if your flights don't leave on time, you promise either to find me a seat on another airline, or refund my money. I want the seat."

"Frankly, miss, there's nothing I can do unless you're willing to take the refund." The attendant forced her most practiced, professional smile. "With this winter storm, no one is going anywhere. You're welcome to try another airline. But they'll just confirm what I've already said. In the meantime, why don't you try to relax. Get a bite to eat. Or browse through the gift shop. They're having a special on giant candy canes filled with your favorite candies."

Kira began a sarcastic retort, then clamped her mouth shut. Maybe it was true what they said about holiday stress and how it warped normally rational human beings. She changed tactics, hoping a dose of civility would undo the damage of her outburst. "Isn't there anything you can do? Check that monitor again. There's got to be something going out tonight." She leaned over the ticket counter and tried to check the flight attendant's schedule.

The flight attendant promptly splayed both hands over the list.

"Sorry. No peeking. Passenger confidentiality. Please

take a seat, ma'am. As soon as we know something we'll make an announcement. Next!" She dismissed Kira, then waved for the next in line to advance.

A beautiful sight . . .

As Kira stepped out of line, she caught her reflection in the observation window directly behind the podium. She wandered over to the window to examine herself and gave a tiny moan of dismay at the image that stared back at her. Hastily, she searched through her overstuffed overnight bag for a comb.

She'd been in such a hurry to get to the airport, she barely had time to tame her corkscrew ringlets into a loose ponytail. The pointless rush to make her flight, the jostling by thousands of other passengers in the same mood, plus her own frustrated tugs had destroyed her grooming efforts, leaving her hair in a wild, chestnut halo around her head. Worry had also given her a worn, haggard look. She rummaged in her bag again for a seldom used compact of pressed powder—though she didn't have any hope that the cocoa-tinted dusting powder could hide the shopping-cart-sized bags underneath her hazel-brown eyes.

As Kira stood by the observation window, she watched as several trucks equipped with snowplows and de-icing chemicals lumbered out to the runways. Their flashing, yellow warning lights barely cut through the mingling swirl of snow and rain.

"One, two, three, four, five . . . ," Kira counted aloud. She soon stopped counting. If the fleet of trucks heading out was any indication of how much longer she would have to wait, Kira thought she might as well take the gate attendant's suggestion. She was going to be there for a while.

We're happy tonight . . .

Kira was utterly miserable. It showed in the defeated slump of her shoulders as she leaned her head against the ice-coated glass of the observation window and cursed her own impatience. If she'd been thinking, she would have called ahead to check to see if her flight would take off as scheduled. But the thought never crossed her mind. When she'd set out, the weather had been bad, but not impossible. The snowplows were out in full force, clearing a path on the roads. It never occurred to her that there were no snowplows for the skies.

Walkin' in a Winter Wonderland!

Kira circled the waiting area, looking for an unoccupied seat. But the waiting area was filled to capacity. When her feet started to ache, she groaned aloud.

"Need a seat, sweetie?"

Kira jumped as a woman spoke suddenly at her elbow. She was seated near the end of a row of chairs thumbing through a trade magazine exposing the lives and loves of various Hollywood stars. The seat beside her was filled with sacks of festive packages covered by a well-worn camel hair coat. The woman tossed the coat over her ample lap, pushed the packages to the floor, and gestured with a broad, gapped-toothed smile at the seat.

"Thank you very much," Kira responded gratefully.

"Take a load off, sweetie. You look dead on your feet," the woman said, stretching out her own feet. She pulled off her boots, crammed them into another bag, and slid her feet into a pair of pink, faux-fur-lined house shoes. "How about a candy cane? Will that make you feel better?" She rummaged through a red-and-green-striped straw bag, then handed Kira a piece of candy.

As Kira reached for it, she started to laugh. "Isn't this precious."

"I call this little craft a Christ*moose*," the woman explained. She'd decorated the candy cane with colorful pipe cleaners bent around the candy cane to form antlers and a tiny red cotton pom-pom for the nose. Two adhesive-backed toy eyes goggled at Kira.

"All of my nieces and nephews love Auntie Margie's Christmooses. I have over two hundred of them, you know."

"Nieces and nephews?" Kira asked, her fatigued brain barely following the conversation.

"Mercy, no, child! Christ*mooses*! They're so cheerful, don't you think? They don't take any time at all to make but everyone seems to enjoy them."

"Thank you." Kira accepted the offer graciously. She peeled off the wrapper and stuck the treat into her mouth.

"Better now?" Auntie Margie asked politely.

Kira popped the sticky, sweet candy out of her mouth to say, "Yes, ma'am."

"Going home to see family?" Auntie Marge asked then.

Kira made a noncommittal sound, using the candy as an excuse not to make polite conversation.

"I have family all over the country," Auntie Marge went on. "Since I retired two years ago, I can pick up and jet off to visit them any time I want. They never know when I'm liable to turn up. So, sweetie, where are you headed?"

"Texas," Kira said through sticky lips.

"I have family there, too. My first grandson was born in Texas. You don't sound like you're from Texas. That's not where you're from, are you?"

"No, I live here in Chicago."

"I thought so. You can always tell a Yankee. No offense."

"None taken. Where are you from?" Kira asked.

"Oh, I'm from all over." Auntie Margie smiled that broad smile again. "That's why I feel at home anywhere.

I can talk to anyone. My husband, Lord rest his soul, used to say that I could talk a person to death. But I don't mean any harm. When my brain wants to know something I just pull out all of the stops and ask away. If I get too personal, you just put on the brakes and tell me to mind my own beeswax. I have to say, sweetie, that for someone who's going to see family, you don't look to pleased about it."

"I shouldn't be out here," Kira said. "To be more honest, my family. . . . my mother, actually, shouldn't be out there!" She pointed angrily toward the observation window.

"Ohhhh," Auntie Marge said sympathetically. "I see."

"No offense, Auntie Margie . . . is it? But I don't think you do," Kira said abruptly, shaking her head. She turned to watch the snow, indicating by her tightly pressed lips and angrily folded arms that she didn't feel like talking anymore.

"Guess it's time to mind my own beeswax," Auntie Marge said cheerfully and turned back to her magazine.

When a collective groan suddenly rose from the crowded waiting area, Kira spun around, looking for the source. Several passengers gathered around the monitors listing the arrivals and departures. The list of cancelled flights seemed to scroll on and on and on. Kira added her own soft sound of dismay to the rising din.

"Looks like I'd better get myself a room for the night," Auntie Marge said cheerfully. "We're not going anywhere for a while. How about you, sweetie?"

"I'm going home." Kira sighed. She then thanked Auntie Marge for the seat and the candy, and excused herself. There was nothing Kira could do tonight, she thought as she trudged back through the airport and out to the parking garage. Kira reached inside her coat pocket, fished out her keys, and was about to fit the key into the door lock when a hulking figure stepped from between a truck and a van and moved quickly toward her. Startled, Kira looked up. She glanced around, looking for a parking attendant. Another figure, dressed in a full-length leather coat and a ski mask pulled down over the face, joined the first. Kira's heart leaped to her mouth and choked off any cry of alarm she might have raised.

"Take my keys, take the car. Just leave me alone!" Kira whispered hoarsely, dropping the keys to the ground and backing away.

They continued to advance as Kira backpedaled. When she found her back pressed against another car, she berated herself for being so careless. Why hadn't she parked in an area with more lighting? Coming back to her car, would it have hurt her to accept the offer of a security escort? At the height of the holiday season, with all of its promises of peace and good tidings toward all, it didn't occur to her that she could become a crime-victim.

In a few more seconds they would be right on her. Kira sucked in her breath, tightened her fists. She didn't get a chance to test her false bravado. The area suddenly illuminated with a light so bright that she had to squint in order to see. She held up her hands to protect her eyes from the glare. Bathed in the light, their intentions exposed for all the world to see, Kira's would-be attackers suddenly fled.

"Oh, there you are, sweetie!" A familiar voice hailed her.

"Auntie Marge!" Kira called out, relief clearly evident on her face and in the pitch of her voice. "Where ... where are you?" Kira called out, peeking through her fingers.

"Mercy, let me turn this thing off." The light dimmed, then went out completely. She approached Kira, gripping the handle of a solid metal flashlight.

"Auntie Marge, what are you doing out here?"

"You dashed off so fast, you left your overnight bag in your seat."

"You brought it out to me? You didn't have to do that, Auntie Marge."

"It was no bother."

"Thank you, Auntie Marge. Thank you for everything. For the candy and for listening to me moan and complain and for scaring off those guys. . . ."

"What are you doing out here all by yourself? Don't ever, ever, ever go into a strange place unescorted. At least carry a flashlight with you, sweetie. When you're alone, check around and in your car before you get in."

Kira climbed into her car, then started the engine. "Do you want me to drop you off anywhere, Auntie Marge?" she offered.

"Now, sweetie, haven't you heard anything I've just told you? You're not supposed to give strangers a ride." Auntie Marge wagged her finger. "You go on home. I'll be all right. Besides, here's the airport security. I'll catch a ride back with them. Take care of yourself, child."

"I will," Kira said. She waited, allowing the engine to idle, as she watched Auntie Margie flag down the roving security cart and climb in; and it drove away.

Because of the weather, Kira considered pulling into the first motel parking lot she saw and riding the storm out. But the fleet of snowplows, followed by the dump trucks spewing gravel across the icy roads to improve traction, gave her the confidence and the incentive to push on. The drive that normally would have taken only forty minutes dragged for an hour an a half.

By the time she made it home, she was exhausted. Kira pulled off her hat and coat, shook the snow off them, and tossed them over the couch. She headed for the kitchen to warm a mug of milk to make hot chocolate. On the way there, she reached over and flipped the switch that started the musical chasing lights on her miniature Christmas tree to flash and *plink-plink-plink* out their repertoire of holiday music.

When the blinking light on her answering machine alerted her to three messages, Kira dove for the machine. Maybe one of the messages was her mother—letting her know that she'd escaped from that rancher and would soon be on her way home!

She stabbed at the playback button and groaned as soon as the voice began. It was Hugh. Her soon-to-be, and-I-mean-this-time, no-more-chances boyfriend.

"Hi, Kira, if you're home, pick up the phone. Come on, Kira. Pick up! It's me. Kira? Are you home? Are you just ignoring me? I know you're there, Kira. Come on, baby, don't be mad at me. We can work it out."

A few moments of silence, then the voice on the other end continued on a more conciliatory note. "Okay, maybe you're not at home. When you get back, give me a call, okay? I've got something important to talk to you about. There's something special I've got for you, Kira. Not your typical stocking stuffer, either. Something round and gold and weighing about half a carat. Sound like anything you'd be interested in? Give me a call when you get back, sweetheart."

The phone line went dead, but not before the recording picked up a high-pitched giggle and Hugh's voice warning someone in the background to keep quiet.

Kira muttered an unkind assessment of Hugh's manhood, tossed herself on the couch, and massaged her aching temples. The on-again, off-again relationship she had with Hugh had lasted for almost two years. The last time she'd spoken with Hugh, they'd argued about his tendency of looking up old girlfriends. From the background sounds on the tape, it didn't sound as if he'd taken their last conversation to heart. He certainly didn't lose any time looking for someone to take her place once she told him she might be gone for the holidays.

"It's off now," Kira said decisively, and wondered if it was too late to take back the custom-engraved pen and pencil set she'd gotten him as a Christmas present.

The tape forwarded to the next message.

"Hello, Kira, how are you doing? Oh . . . it's that stupid machine. You know how much I hate talking to these things. The least you can do is change the message so you know that you're talking to a machine and not to a real person. Anyway, I just wanted to see how you were. Are you coming over for Christmas dinner? I don't want you to spend it alone since your mother is off doing God knows what. Don't know why she picked this season of all seasons to lose her mind. She knows I can't have a family dinner without her. She's the only one who can get all the names straight when I'm passing out gifts to all of you. Anyway, give your granny a call when you get in. Love you. Good-bye. Oh, and don't forget to st—"

The machine cut her off in mid-sentence. The third message started and her grandmother's voice picked up again.

"Stupid machine! Where was I? Oh, yes. Don't forget to stop by your Aunt Galen's as soon as you get a chance. She's getting up in age, you know, and would like to see all of the nieces and nephews before she passes on. Just between you, me, and the machine, she's not really as decrepit as she makes out to be. She just likes to play on our sympathies around the holiday season because she knows we're such suckers for family. Take her a gift when you go; she'll like that. If you're stuck for ideas on what to get her, you can take her back that same fruitcake that she made for you last year. I know you haven't eaten it yet, because if you had, you would have been hospitalized with a severe case of food poisoning by now. I guess that's all. Call me when you get home, Kira. But I guess I already said that. If you w—"

The machine cut her off again, then fell silent.

"I love you, too, Granny," Kira murmured aloud. She said a small prayer of thanks that her grandmother didn't know the full extent of her mother's defection during the holidays. Members of the family knew bits and pieces of the story. Even Kira herself was not completely sure.

This was the year that Kira's mother, Myra Dodd, had chosen to retire from teaching. After thirty-five years, Myra wanted to fade from her long, illustrious teaching quietly, gracefully. No surprise parties, no grand send-offs, no special ceremonies with engraved knickknacks that would only serve to remind Myra how quickly time had passed.

During the summer months after her retirement, Myra had seemed fine. She'd spent her summer visiting other friends who'd retired, inviting them over to backyard barbecues. Right after Labor Day, however, Kira began to see signs of strain. Maybe it was all of the back-to-school reminders that had caused Myra to fall into an uncharacteristic funk.

Thinking that maybe a change of scenery would cheer her mother up, Kira and her sister Alicia had put their heads together and came up with the idea of a cruise. Seeing new places, making new friends—that would do it! Once their mother came back, she would be energized, refreshed, ready to start her new life as part of the deserved retirement.

Kira groaned aloud and put her head in her hands. It was the perfect plan. How could things have gone so terribly wrong? Her mother, the rock of stability, the essence of familial obligation, the last bastion of responsibility, had met a man! And having done so, declared in her last postcard to them that she wasn't coming back! She was going to cut her vacation cruise short and follow him back to his hometown in some little, out-of-the-way, unlikely place called Murray, Texas.

Kira did a little mental calculation. The postcard was dated the second week in November. Kira hadn't received

it, however, until the third week in November. She would
have dropped everything then if it weren't for the sense
of responsibility that she thought her mom had recklessly
abandoned. She couldn't just take off and leave at a
moment's notice. She had to make plans. She had to
inform her family and coworkers. Like her mother, Kira
was a teacher. She couldn't leave without making sure the
substitute had adequate lesson plans prepared for her and
that her students had their papers graded and returned.

The more time passed, the more time Kira secretly pan-
icked. No one wanted to swap holiday vacation days with
her. By the time she was able to arrange time off from
work, it was the first week in December. Myra had been
in the clutches of that man for at least four weeks, if not
longer. Who knew when she'd met that man? How long
he had been able to work his charms on her weakened
defenses? She hadn't heard a word from her mother since
that initial postcard.

"Hello! Hello!" the whirring sound of the answering
machine snapped her out of her fretful thoughts. "Don't
hang up! I'm here!" Kira urged. Maybe it was her mother
Myra, telling them she'd come to her senses and that she
was coming home.

"Kira, what are you doing home? I thought you'd be on
a plane to Texas by now!" It was Kira's sister Alicia.

"I tried, Ally." Kira blew out a deep sigh in frustration.
"But all of the planes are grounded because of the bad
weather."

"So what are you going to do?"

"What else can I do but wait until the weather clears?"

"But . . . but . . . ," Alicia sputtered. "But what about
Mama? Somebody's got to go after that woman before she
loses her mind and all of her savings to that cruise-ship
Casanova."

"I know that," Kira insisted. "But I can't fly out tonight."

"I'm going to go down there and get that old woman,

even if I have to flap my arms and take off myself!" Alicia threatened.

"Don't be ridiculous, Ally! You can't go. What about the baby? You try to go off now, you'll risk having that baby early at the worst possible moment." Her sister was almost eight months pregnant. Her child would be her grandmother's first great-grandchild.

"Somebody's got to go, Kira. I can't believe that she's willing to miss this." Alicia patted her swollen abdomen.

"She won't miss it," Kira said stoutly. "She still has time. You're not due for another six weeks."

"You don't have to tell me that. But who knows how long it will take to get Mama away from that man. I need my mama with me when I go into labor."

"I know. I know. And Mama knows that, too. She's just not thinking straight. And that man has probably twisted her even more. But what can I do? I can't do anything about the weather."

"Have you thought about catching a train? Or a bus? What about renting a car?"

"The roads are probably just as bad, Ally."

"You have liability insurance, don't you? Triple A?"

"Alicia!" Kira cried out in dismay.

"I don't mean to sound cold, Kira. But that's our mother out there. She shouldn't be down there, all alone, no family to protect her. . . ."

"Oh, I know where this is going. You're going to blame me for this, aren't you?"

"Did I say anything about blaming you? No, I didn't. Even though you are the one who convinced her to take that vacation."

"You pitched in. If you didn't want her to go, why didn't you say so, then?"

"If Granny finds out that we let Mother go off . . ."

"What do you mean *let*? We didn't let her go," Kira argued. "She has a mind of her own. She wanted to go."

"She wanted to go because you held out that great big carrot stick of an incentive for her. First class on the airplane, deluxe accommodations on the cruise ship, a beachside bungalow, traveler's checks. Who would turn that down? I know I wouldn't even if I weren't retired."

"Okay, okay. You don't have to rub it in," Kira complained.

"I'm sorry. I don't mean to get on your back. I'm so worried about Mama."

"I am, too. But there's nothing I can do right now. They're not letting anything off the ground until the weather clears. I waited as long as I could. It was just so depressing! All of these people crammed together."

"Poor baby. It must be a zoo at that airport . . . all those people trying to get out of town for the holidays."

"It was awful. Crowded, noisy . . ." Kira then recalled the kindness of Auntie Marge. "If it weren't for one kind soul offering me refuge against all of that insanity, I think I would have lost my mind, too."

"I'm sorry you had to go through that alone, Kira. You must be exhausted. I'll hang up and let you get some rest. We can pick up again tomorrow and decide how we want to go about this."

"Why'd you call, anyway?"

Alicia laughed and said, "I called to let Delanie leave a message on the machine for you so you'd have some good news to come back to."

Kira's face softened. "Where is my little angel? Put her on the phone."

A moment later Alicia was back on the phone calling loudly into the mouthpiece, "Are you there, Kira? I've got her. I've got the phone to Delanie's ear."

"Hello, Mama's little angel. Are you being a good girl? You're not giving Aunt Ally a hard time, are you?" Kira cooed into the phone. "You're such a good girl. Did you give her a bath before you put her to bed, Ally?"

"Of course I did. And, just like you asked, I sprinkled her with enough powder to choke a rhino."

"Good. Because we seem to be having a little flea problem."

"I warned you when I agreed to watch her for you, Kira, that if I find one flea in my house . . ."

"Don't worry, you won't. We won't stand for any nasty little bugs on us, will we, Delanie?" Kira cooed into the phone again. "That's my sweetheart."

"You ought to see her, Kira. She's as content as can be."

"That's my little girl. That's my little puppy," Kira continued. "Yes, she's such a good girl. Such a happy little puppy! Aren't you, Delanie?"

"Little? She's not fully grown yet and she's already thirty pounds."

"Such a happy, healthy puppy!" Kira laughed into the phone.

Alicia paused dramatically, then added, "I just hope Mama will be that happy down in God-knows-where Texas."

"Mama's not staying in Texas, Ally," Kira said sharply. "One way or another, I'm bringing her back here. I just don't know how I'm going to do it."

"You're going to rent a car. That's how you're going to do it," Alicia said crisply.

"I don't even know where Mama is. . . ."

"Buy a map. What's that town called again?"

"Murray," Kira supplied, making the grimace on her face convey itself by her tone. "I doubt if Murray is even on a map."

"But if the weather is as bad down there as it is up here, you'll have to drive slowly, anyway. Just keep an eye out for the road signs. You shouldn't miss it."

"And that's supposed to give me encouragement?"

"If you don't want to go, then I'll go. Somebody's got to go after Mama."

"Oh, no you don't! And risk delivering that baby at some roadside truck stop? Don't even think about it! I'm not having some beehived, gum-chewing, support-hose-wearing waitress named Nadine delivering that baby. You'd have to make her godmother then, and where would that leave me?" Kira retorted. "No, I'm the one who's got to go after her. Leave it to me, Ally. I'll get her. . . ."

Chapter Two

"Get her!"

"Watch out, now! She's trying to double back!"

"She's feinting to the left! Don't let her get around you!"

"Get that rope ready."

"Steady, now! Steady!"

"When I say 'now,' you let fly with that rope."

"If you ever get that rope around her neck, leading her back into the barn will be as easy as walking your dog."

"Watch her, now, Dylan, boy. She's a crafty, old devil with a mighty powerful kick."

"Don't I know it," Dylan Jolivet muttered as he stood in the center of the roughly circular roping pen. He rubbed his thigh and winced. He'd have one doosie of a bruise from that evil creature's well-aimed kicked.

His eyes swiveled from side to side as he tried to heed the helpful advice that came from all around him. A loosely coiled rope hung from his gloved fingers. He moved slowly on the balls of his feet, keeping a wary eye on his prey.

She'd eluded the rope three times already, ducking her head out of the way just as he'd let it fly from his fingers. Once, when he'd gotten a little too close, she'd lashed out at him with powerful legs and sent him sprawling into the dirt.

Now, after almost an hour of trying to chase the evil creature down, he'd had just about all he could take. The fact that everyone seemed to be watching him didn't help matters much. Didn't they have somewhere else to be? Why weren't they tending to their own chores? The Triple J had over fifty ranch hands and all of them were centered around the roping pen. They didn't have to stand around watching him make a fool of himself.

"She's gonna kick him again," someone prophesied. Dylan threw an irritated glance in his direction.

"Hope you got plenty of liniment, Dylan, boy. You're gonna need it by the time this day is over."

"You want to try to give me some encouragement, Baby John?" Dylan complained.

"What do you think I've been doing for the past hour and a half?"

"He doesn't need encouragement," another laughed. "He needs more practice with that rope. Let me in that pen, Dylan, boy. I'll show you how it's done."

Dylan rankled at the teasing. To add insult to injury, his own uncles were the loudest hecklers. "Boy," they'd called him. How could they still consider him a boy? He'd celebrated his twenty-seventh birthday three months ago. Standing at six foot two, Dylan topped his uncles by at least a foot. He did more than a boy's share of work around the Triple J. He was the ranch foreman in duties, if not by name.

"No thanks, Uncle Jesse. I've got to do this by myself." Dylan barely turned his head to the taunting. "Come on, baby girl. I'm not gonna hurt ya. I just want to get you in the chute so we can put our brand on ya."

He uncoiled a few feet of rope. Holding the slack in his left hand, he began to twirl the looped end in his right, letting the loop grow larger and larger. Then, with a soft grunt, he let it fly. The lasso sailed high over his head and landed evenly around her neck. Dylan let out a whoop of triumph, which quickly turned to surprise as the creature jerked her evil head, pulling him toward her. Dylan quickly let go of the rope, but not before he was pulled into the dirt again.

Dylan spat out a sizzling oath that made his uncles chastise him, then begin another chorus of laughter. The angry boil of blood in his ears couldn't drown out the laughter from his family and friends as he stood up, slapping at his jeans in disgust.

"You're going about it all wrong, *amigo*," yet another ranch hand offered. "Brute force never works with a lady."

"And just what do you expect me to do, Manolo?" Dylan shot back, spitting out a mouthful of dry dust. "Buy her some candy and flowers?"

He spat again, then winced when he noted the pinkish cast to the dust. Gingerly, he probed the inside of his cheek with his tongue to feel where he'd bitten into it.

"Try this instead!" Manolo leaned over the fence and tossed Dylan a small drawstring bag. Dylan opened it and ran his fingers through the contents.

"You want me to use this?" Dylan asked incredulously.

"*Por supuesto.* How else do you expect to catch her?"

Dylan glanced back. How else did he expect to catch her, Manolo had asked. It wasn't too far of a stretch of his imagination to expect to succeed. After all, she was just an animal—lower on the evolutionary scale than he. He was supposed to be the superior animal—the thinking man.

Dylan turned back to her with renewed determination. He'd be damned if she didn't seem to be laughing at him. With the rope still around her neck, she ducked her head several times at him. Her mouth was agape as she snapped defiantly. Dylan jumped back, not wanting to add bite marks to the bruises he already had.

"Don't let her rile you, Dylan, boy," his uncle Jesse snorted with laughter.

"Yeah, her beak is worse than her bite!" his Uncle John laughed. "Get it? Beak? Bite?"

"What's the matter, Dylan? You let the old girl get your feathers all ruffled?" Another ranch hand heckled him.

"I knew you couldn't catch her. Didn't have a wing and a prayer. Get it? Wingless? Prayerless?" Jesse laughed so hard he had to lean on his brother for support. Baby John clapped Jesse on the back and sent him tumbling off the fence where they'd perched to watch Dylan chase after the wiliest animal on the ranch.

Dylan glared at his uncles, then back at his quarry. That was it. He had had it. Enough was enough! What he wanted now was a cool drink and a hot shower. Maybe, between the two of those, he could wash away his humiliation. Couldn't they have been just a little more supportive? After all, they were family.

For over twenty years, he'd done everything they'd asked him to do. He'd done it without complaint because he knew that someday he would add his name to the dotted line that made the Triple J part his. It was all he had ever wanted.

Even as a child, he knew that here was where he belonged. Every year, when his parents asked where he wanted to go for his summer vacation, it was always the same thing. No matter how they tried to entice him with trips to various theme parks, all he ever wanted to do was visit his uncles in Texas. He suffered through the compromise of spending part of his summer with his parents on their trips and rejoiced as hard as they when they left him in the care of the Jolivet brothers.

Dylan begged to be allowed to do any small task—anything

to put him close to the animals he loved. When he was eight years old, he raked out the stables without complaint. That put him close to the horses. When he was twelve, he begged to be allowed to ride the fence line to make repairs with his uncles. That was the only way he would come to know every inch of the Jolivet seven thousand-acre spread. For his graduation present, his Uncle Jimmy had passed on to him the responsibility of making major livestock purchases.

If only Jimmy had been content to leave the responsibility of purchasing livestock in his nephew's hands, Dylan thought sourly. But Jimmy hadn't. Though he was quick to assure Dylan that he was pleased with what he'd done so far, Jimmy told Dylan that it was time for a change. Ever since he got back from that cruise, nothing had seemed the same, not even Jimmy.

Before Dylan knew what was happening, two truckloads of his uncle's *changes* were rolling onto the Triple J. Dylan followed behind the stock trailers as they lumbered through the main gate, up the driveway, and into the pens his uncle had him construct.

"What on earth ...? What has Uncle Jimmy gotten us into now?" Dylan couldn't believe his eyes. His uncle couldn't be serious. What on earth did he plan to do with these bug-eyed, vile-smelling, skinny-legged, oversized chickens?

"Well, what do you think?" Jimmy had said proudly, clapping Dylan on the back.

"I don't know what to think," Dylan replied. "Tell me that you're planning the world's biggest fricassee."

"Those aren't for cooking, Dylan, at least not all of them."

"What else were you planning to do with those ... those ..."

"Ostriches and emus," Jimmy had announced, gesturing toward the trucks. "And I plan to sell 'em."

"Tell me you're kidding, Uncle Jimmy. You've got to be. Who's going to buy those funny-looking creatures?"

"The question is, who won't buy? They're a hot commodity, Dylan, boy. Before you know it, you'll be going to your fancy, five-star restaurant and ordering emu steaks right alongside beef steaks. They say they're lower in cholesterol and just as tasty. Good for you, eh, Dylan, boy. Looks like you've been putting away more than your share of steaks these days." Jimmy feinted a punch toward Dylan's midsection and connected with a solid wall of flesh.

"I'm a growing boy." Dylan grinned at his uncle. He then looked dubiously at the trucks as the handlers drove the birds out of the trucks and into the pens. "Growing boy or not, I don't think I could bring myself to eat one of those. The day I swap a well-done steak for a chicken leg on steroids is the day I eat my own hat!"

"Food isn't all we can use those birds for, Dylan. With those animals, there's practically no waste. You just wait and see. With the hides from those birds, you'll be trading in your snakeskin boots for ostrich hide ones. And when you lay your head on your pillow at night, you'll be drifting off to sleep on emu down pillows instead of goose down."

"I'm a cowboy, Uncle Jimmy. Not a chicken boy. I'll be laughed out of Murray if I try to sell those things."

"Get used to the idea, boy. These birds are here to stay. . . ."

With his uncle's words echoing in his mind, Dylan's face twisted into a scowl. He knew good and well who was orchestrating all the changes around here. He pinned his gaze on the woman sitting contently on the front porch. Her head was buried in book. Almost as if she could feel him watching her, she marked her place with a silk ribbon and closed it, then regarded him curiously.

Rudely, and not caring whether or not she or anyone

else knew it, Dylan spun on one heel and headed for the bunkhouse. He could grab a shower and a change there and wouldn't have to face her.

He heard footsteps trailing him. Since he thought it might be *her,* he didn't turn around.

"Hold up there, boy." It was his Uncle Baby John trailing him.

"Coming to poke some more fun at me?" Dylan said sourly over his shoulder.

"Of course not. I was coming to see if you needed any help."

"I've had about all the help I can take for one day, Baby John."

"Now, Dylan, boy . . . don't be sore." When he noted how Dylan limped along, he added thoughtfully, "But I guess you can't help that, can you now? Maybe you should have taken the birdseed that Manolo offered."

"Only if it was laced with cyanide."

"You're thinking about killing off those birds, Dylan?"

"I gotta get them before they get me. I don't know if I can stand being around them anymore." The birds weren't hard to take care of. Their needs were simple. Given enough feed and water and open ground, the birds pretty much took care of themselves as long as he left them alone. But Uncle Jimmy wanted all of his livestock marked. He said they were too valuable a commodity to let any one walk off with them. So he also purchased identifying leg bands for them. Each leg band had its own transponder that emitted a low frequency signal. With the tracking equipment, he could locate the position of any bird on their thousand-acre spread. It was Dylan's job to catch the evil things and band them.

As an experiment, he thought he'd try one of the smaller birds, one of the emus; but it was too quick for him. It darted and zigzagged as if it could anticipate his every move. Then he thought he'd try a larger bird, thinking it

would be slower, not as agile. Wrong again! The evil creature was worse than the emu—having powerful legs that
sent him sprawling with a well-aimed kick. Not being able
to catch the birds, coupled with the laughter from his
uncles and coworkers, was enough for him.

Baby John grasped Dylan's shoulder and squeezed.
"Hold up there, boy. Don't say anything you're not willing
to back up later."

"No, I'm not thinking about quitting," Dylan responded
to his uncle's implied question. "I wouldn't leave the Triple J. You know that. I just don't know if I can take being
foreman to a flock of birdbrains."

"Two-winged or two-legged? What's the difference?
You've managed to do pretty well with the likes of us trying
to give you advice."

"All I had to do was listen well and do exactly the opposite of what you told me, Uncle Jesse." Dylan grinned at
his uncle. He then quickly sobered. He supposed he should
go back and give it another try. It didn't look well for the
foreman of the ranch to quit so easily. It sent a bad message
to the hands looking to him to set the example.

He rubbed his leg. But that ostrich sure could kick. It
really hurt!

"Why don't you grab something to eat," Jesse suggested,
reading his nephew's thoughts. "Take a little time to col-
lect yourself. You'll do a lot better with some of Manolo's
good cooking sticking to your ribs."

"Was I that bad?" Dylan grimaced.

"Stank like yesterday's garbage," Jesse said promptly.
Without another word, he turned and rejoined the other
hands at the roping pen. When a chorus of laughter rose
up along with a blinding cloud of dust, Dylan knew that
someone else had tried, and failed, to corner the evil creature. He was secretly glad. His uncle had entrusted the
task of banding those birds to him. He didn't want anyone
else to succeed first where he had failed. Dylan glanced

once more toward the house, at the woman who'd come to invade his home.

Myra Dodd. She was as responsible for his misery as if she had kicked him herself. She'd talked Uncle Jimmy into buying those stupid birds. It had to be her idea. His Uncle Jimmy was a rational man, without a frivolous bone in his body. He was a solid, dependable man. A pillar of the community, a deacon in the church. And now look what he'd done. He'd brought home a woman!

She had been there for almost a month, insinuating her way into every phase of Triple J business. Dylan thought sourly that Uncle Jimmy couldn't blow his nose without that woman "suggesting" the kind of tissue he should use.

From the moment they'd both arrived from the Cayman cruise, Dylan knew she would be trouble. He had an inkling that something was going on even before they showed up. He didn't believe in omens, but he trusted his gut. And his had been in knots for several days before they arrived.

The night before they arrived, he tossed and turned in his sleep, haunted by dreams that he couldn't quite recall. His restlessness made him oversleep. He didn't even say "good morning" to his uncles when he sat down to breakfast. Dylan was always the first to greet them with a hearty good morning. Eager to get the day started, he was usually the first to rouse the others from their beds. Slamming doors as he headed for the bathroom to wash the sleep from his eyes, rattling pots as he put on the first pot of coffee, turning on the radio to catch the early news or the weather report—Dylan exerted a full work day's worth of energy just getting to work.

On this particular morning, however, Dylan was strangely silent, opting for a single slice of toast and a glass of juice instead of the offered double stack of pancakes, smoked bacon, and eggs.

"*Dónde vas, patrón?*" Manolo asked.

"Out," Dylan responded curtly. He filed out of the house with barely a nod toward his uncles.

As Manolo poured coffee into to Baby John's mug, he gave him a meaningful stare. Baby John turned to Jesse and gave him a confused shrug.

"What do you suppose is eating him?" Baby John asked.

"Don't know. Never seen him like this before," Jesse returned.

Manolo nodded in agreement. "Mr. Dylan never goes off without telling us where he's going, and why, and how long he'll be gone."

"Do you think he knows?" Baby John asked, tugging at his lip. If Dylan had seen him, he would have known beyond a shadow of a doubt that something was up. Baby John always tugged on his lips when he was worried.

"He couldn't know. I've kept that postcard under locked lip and key," Jesse insisted.

"Maybe he caught you reading it . . . or heard us talking about it?" Baby John argued.

"I'm telling you, he doesn't know. And I'm not going to tell him. That's Jimmy's job. And Jimmy knows what he's doing."

He wasn't sure what he was doing, wasn't sure where he was going. He rode aimlessly across the Triple J's pasture and wondered for what seemed the thousandth time that day, "What's the matter with me?"

Dylan rode on, letting his horse pick out the familiar paths. He found himself on a ridge overlooking the main house. He would give the area one more look over, then ride back. The others were probably worried about him. He was behaving oddly, even to his own admission.

He tightened on the reins, preparing to wheel around. That's when he heard it—a slight sound at first, barely a hum in the wind. He should have dismissed it. But he couldn't. A few seconds more and the sound grew louder. Steady, hypnotic. It held him to that spot. He peered beyond the Triple J's access road to the two-lane, black-topped stretch of highway that wound past the ranch.

There! There it was. A distinct flash of midnight blue and silver chrome glinted through the trees. It was Uncle Jimmy's car. He was back. As the car pulled through the gate and up to the main house, Dylan could just make out the figures of Baby John, Jesse, and Manolo as they rushed out to greet Uncle Jimmy.

No one was more surprised than Dylan when someone else stepped out of the car, too. A woman? Uncle Jimmy had brought back a woman?

Baby John, short and squat, lead the charge out the door followed at a slower pace by the tall, rangy Jesse. Manolo, as wide as Baby John and as tall as Jesse, followed, waving his arms excitedly. Dylan saw Uncle Jimmy embrace his brothers, then clap Manolo affectionately on his back. Jimmy then placed his arm around that *woman* and drew her forward. She seemed dwarfed by all of them but not taken aback as the Jolivet clan approached her. She shook hands with Dylan's uncles and then with Manolo.

"It's exactly like you described it—only better," Myra Dodd remarked when she and Jimmy climbed out of his car. As they walked up the path leading to his home, several adjectives immediately came to mind on seeing Jimmy Jolivet's home for the first time. Quaint. Rustic. Pastoral. Myra immediately discarded those descriptions. They weren't quite right—too tame for the explosion of color and scents that greeted her as she approached the house.

Azalea bushes, still in full bloom, boasting colors from deep violet to the barest blush of pink lined the path leading to the house. The path widened to jut against the steps to the porch, which wrapped around three quarters of the house. Rose bushes staked carefully to lattice trim lined the left and right faces of the porch. Their blood-red blossoms were in fierce competition with the hues of the azalea bushes.

"Welcome to my home, Myra," Jimmy gestured grandly toward the two-story, white wood-frame house with slate blue shutters. The overhang of the porch was lined with an assortment of wind chimes that greeted her with pleasant melodies each time the wind blew. Wrought-iron patio furniture was made more comfortable with the addition of overstuffed cushions of blue and white.

She barely had time to take all of it in before Jimmy's brothers descended on her and offered her their own welcomes.

"You've made a lovely home here," Myra complimented.

"My great-grandfather built this house in 1884," Jimmy said proudly. "He built it on the site of the original house built by the first Jolivets to take the land after the house burned down. . . ."

"Or was burned down if you hear somebody else tell it," Jesse said gruffly. Jimmy cleared his throat.

"That's ancient history, Jesse. No sense in dredging it up."

Myra looked curiously from Jesse to Jimmy. When Jimmy didn't elaborate on the history of the house, Myra prodded. "How did the fire start?"

"Let's just say that back in those days, there were a few folks who didn't like the fact that while most of our folks went north after the Civil War, some of us went west," Jesse supplied.

"Ancient history is right," Myra murmured.

"Well, the Jolivets are here to stay," Jimmy said, quickly turning the subject back to more pleasant matters. "Over the years, we've made some modifications to the house. It didn't start out as a two-story. My father put on the extra level in 1945."

"To add a few amenities," Baby John supplied.

"Like running water," Manolo chimed in.

"Speaking of water and amenities, I'll be right back," Baby John said, ducking inside.

"Having electricity's been a blessing, too," Jesse said.

"And air-conditioning. I don't know how my folks lasted through these scorching Texas summers without it," Jimmy said. "I put in some of those window units myself."

"But it's nice enough to sit out now," Myra commented. She climbed the steps to the porch and perched on the edge of a porch swing made from slats of pine, varnished to show its original color, and rocked back and forth several times. "Even if it is eighty-something degrees in December."

She noted that although there were several window-unit air-conditioners intermittently studding various windows along the face of the house, there were just as many windows without them. The windows were wide open, allowing the breeze to flutter the blue-and-white gingham curtains.

"I bought the air-conditioners to bring us into the twentieth century. But we kept a lot of the old stuff, too. You'll find several pieces that were hand-hewn and pieced together by my father and his father sitting side by side."

"Mr. Jimmy made the swing you're sitting on," Manolo told her.

"It's so inviting," Myra sighed contentedly.

"I'm glad you feel that way, Myra," Jimmy said, genuinely pleased.

"You should've told us you were coming back today, Jimmy," Baby John said. He'd disappeared just long enough to bring back a tray of glasses filled with ice and a pitcher of sun tea. "We would have fixed you a special homecoming dinner for you and your guest. Here ya go, Mrs. Dodd. Take a swig of what Jolivet amenities can do for you."

"Don't go through any trouble for me," Myra said

quickly. "I don't want anyone to do any more extra work than they have to."

"I like the way she thinks," Jesse said enthusiastically, then quieted when Jimmy threw him a warning glance.

"No trouble for a guest of the Triple J," Manolo said gallantly, and bowed to her again. "I'll fix my special holiday chili con carne made with both red and green peppers for a savor that will bring tears of joy to your eyes. *¡Qué sabroso!*"

"Sounds wonderful. Is there anything I can do to help?"

"No guests in the kitchen. At least, not on the first night," Manolo said, winking at her.

"Come on, Mrs. Dodd, I'll show you to your room." Baby John took one of the suitcases. Myra stood and followed Baby John into the house. Their footsteps echoed as they crossed the oak flooring.

As Myra climbed the stairs, she ran her fingers along the railing. She smiled in genuine surprise. For a group of bachelors, they not only knew how to take care of themselves, but their guests as well. The iced tea, laced heavily with sweet sugar and tart lemons, was just the thing she needed to combat the unaccustomed heat. The meal that Manolo intended to prepare sounded more complicated than any meal she'd ever cooked without it being a special occasion.

Once inside, she was impressed by the overall appearance of the house. It was virtually spotless. Not a spec of dust anywhere—not even in the grooves of the high-gloss banister. No wisps of cobwebs hanging from the antique lighting fixtures. The carpet, though well-worn, was clean—as though it were a house rule to wipe the dust from their feet before entering.

"No hurry to come down, Myra," Jimmy called up to her. "Take some time to freshen up or take a nap. I've some things I need to catch up on. Then I'll take you on the grand tour of the place. There's a phone in your room.

You might want to call your family, too. Let them know that you've made it here all right."

Myra made a small face of reluctance. She'd purposefully avoided calling Kira and Alicia as soon as she and Jimmy made it to the airport. She knew how her daughters would react. "I'd better get plenty of rest before doing that," Myra said, squaring her shoulders. "See you in a while, Jimmy."

Jimmy gave a knowing, sympathetic nod. There was one he'd been avoiding, too. As Myra and Baby John passed out of earshot, Jimmy asked in low tones of his other brother, "Jesse, where's Dylan?"

"He took off on Lightning Blue this morning."

"Checking the fence line?"

When Jesse didn't respond, Jimmy turned to Manolo.

Manolo shrugged ambiguously. Maybe yes. Maybe no. Truth was, they didn't know what Dylan was doing.

"I thought I saw him up on the north ridge as you and Myra drove up, *patrón*. If I saw him, I know he saw us. He'll be along soon, *verdad*? If you'll excuse me, I've got a meal to prepare," Manolo made his excuse to leave the brothers alone.

"Tell me, Jesse, how'd he take the news . . . about Myra, I mean," Jimmy wanted to know.

"Can't say," Jesse said.

"Why not? Did he ask you not to?"

"Nope."

"Then what?"

"Can't say because we didn't tell him."

"You what?" Jimmy exclaimed. "But what about that postcard. Didn't you . . ."

"Nope," Jesse repeated. "Didn't give it to him. It was the kind of thing you should tell him face to face, man to man, not in a wimped-out postcard."

"You're right," Jimmy sighed. "I don't know what I was thinking. I hope he shows up soon. I was hoping to get a chance to talk to him before I introduced him to Myra. You know, to smooth the way a little bit.''

"What's the matter, Uncle Jimmy. Afraid I'll try to run your little friend away?'' Dylan called from the door.

Jesse and Jimmy spun around and shushed him in unison.

"Keep it down, boy. She's barely upstairs! She'll hear you.''

"Sorry, Uncle Jimmy. The last thing I want to do is upset your little friend. Welcome back,'' Dylan said with genuine affection, and clasped his uncle in a big bear hug.

"Her name is Myra Dodd,'' Jimmy said softly. "She's going to be staying with us for a while.''

"For how long?''

"For as long as I say,'' Jimmy snapped at him.

Dylan had gotten more than his pride stung that day. And it seemed to him that it was only getting worse. In the weeks that followed since she showed up at the Triple J, that woman had driven a wedge between him and his uncle Jimmy that seemed unremovable. He could barely talk to his uncle anymore. Not like he used to. All Jimmy had on his mind was Myra Dodd.

Somehow, he had to get that woman away from Uncle Jimmy. Couldn't he see what she was doing? Couldn't he see that she was no good for him? It was obvious that all she wanted was his money. She spent it like it was going out of style. Twice a week she was in Murray . . . shopping. And if she couldn't find what she wanted there, she went further. She was a gold digger of the worst kind!

Once Dylan tried to point that out to Jimmy. Dylan thought that his uncle was going to go ballistic. With his jaw clenched, an angry muscle ticking in his cheek, he rudely told him to mind his own business. His uncle Jimmy had never spoken to him that way.

That was it! That woman had to go.

* * *

"Come with me." After Dylan's fiasco with the birds, Jimmy Jolivet tracked his nephew down at the bunkhouse. "I want to talk to you."

"What about?"

"Don't question me, boy. Do as I tell you."

Dylan muttered a terse, "Yes, sir," then followed Jimmy into his private office.

Jimmy indicated a chair, then sat down behind a huge oak desk. He clasped his hands over her stomach, leaned back, and regarded Dylan for several seconds before speaking. "Baby John tells me you're having a hard time with those birds, Dylan. What's the problem?"

"No problem," Dylan denied. Crossing his left ankle over right thigh, he flicked an imaginary spec of dust from his boot.

"Obviously, there's something wrong. I want to know what's bothering you. You're walking around here, mad all of the time, short with the hands, half doing your work. I want to know what's eating you."

"I guess I'm having an off day," Dylan retorted.

"You watch your tone. You're not so big that I can't take a strap across your hide."

Dylan relaxed into an easy grin. His uncles had never struck him. The threat was a standard joke between all of them.

"Talk to me, Dylan," Jimmy entreated.

Dylan paused, and in doing so, reminded Jimmy that he hadn't really talked to his nephew in a long time. He'd been so wrapped up in Myra that he—

"Ohhh. . . ." The light of understanding suddenly dawned in Jimmy's eyes. "Look, son, about Myra Dodd—"

"What about her?" Dylan said tersely.

Jimmy didn't react to the obvious tension in his nephew's voice. He knew Dylan was fiercely protective of the Triple J and was only responding to what he perceived was a threat to his life here—a threat real or imagined. Jimmy intended to neutralize that threat as quickly and as effectively as possible. "Bringing Myra here has absolutely nothing to do with you."

How could he even think that? Dylan raged silently. What affected the Triple J affected him. Was he part of this family or not? Was he part of this land or not?

"Are you sure about that?" Dylan asked, his voice low and tight. "I think it has everything to do with me. Lately, Uncle Jimmy, you've been doing a lot of things that affect me."

"Everything I've ever done for you affected you, Dylan. Why should this bother you now?"

"This is different. First you go off buying those birds without consulting me. . . ." Dylan ticked off one finger.

"Hold on a minute, Dylan, boy!" Jimmy bristled in turn. "Are you forgetting who runs this ranch? Who has final say?"

"I haven't forgotten, Uncle Jimmy," Dylan backed off, realizing his mistake. His uncles had always warned him about getting too big for his britches. But they'd given him a man-sized job as foreman of the Triple J. If they didn't expect him to measure up to that expectation, why did they give him the responsibility in the first place? "Did you or did you not give me free reign in purchasing livestock?" Dylan demanded.

Jimmy settled back into his chair again, rocking slightly as he thought. Yes, he had. He'd given Dylan more and more responsibility so that he and his brothers could eventually retire.

"I'm thinking about retiring, son. Not rolling over and playing dead. Maybe I should have let you know what I was thinking when I bought those birds. But the opportunity to help the Triple J ranch out was there, so I took it. That's still part of my job."

"I just want to be sure that you still trust me to do my job."

"You know I trust you to do your job."

"And what is that, Uncle Jimmy? Just what am I supposed to be doing here?"

"You're my right-hand man, Dylan."

"So what's that *woman*'s job? Why couldn't you tell me? Or didn't you want your right hand to know what your left hand was doing?"

"Don't get smart with me, Dylan. I'm trying to talk to you like a man," Jimmy snapped.

Dylan clamped his mouth shut.

Jimmy rubbed his chin, trying to find the right words to describe how he felt about Myra. "Did it ever occur to you that maybe there's more to ranching than horses and cattle?"

And ostriches and emus, Dylan thought sullenly. He held his peace to keep from interrupting his uncle again.

"Dylan, this land has been in our family for generations. Six to be exact. You've seen the photo albums, the mementos. . . . My daddy passed it on to me and when the time comes, I'm going to pass it on to you. I put everything I had into this ranch until sometimes I think there's nothing there for me."

"What are you trying to say, Uncle Jimmy?"

"Will you just listen for a moment, Dylan! I'm trying to tell you . . . What I'm trying to say is that when all is said and done, when I put in a good day's work, and come home . . . come back here, tired and aching so much that I can hardly stand, I want . . . I want . . ." Jimmy paused, took a deep breath, and said, "I want someone there waiting for me, telling me that everything I've done was worth it."

"You know it's worth it, Uncle Jimmy," Dylan insisted. "You've kept a roof over our heads, food on the table, and money in the bank. There's not a man or woman working on this ranch who can't say that you haven't done the same for them."

"Man and woman, Dylan. That's what I'm getting at. A man gets lonely sometimes, Dylan—a loneliness that a good horse or a fertile patch of ground can't cure. Do you understand what I'm trying to tell you?"

Dylan closed his eyes. He understood all too well. As Uncle Jimmy had said, sometimes he came home too tired to breathe. Yet sometimes, when he lay in his bed, thinking about all he'd accomplished during the day, and what he expected to accomplish the next, he couldn't help thinking that there had to be more to his life than work. He was helping to build a tiny empire—but who would he share it with? Who *could* he share it with?

"Give her a chance, Dylan," Jimmy went on. "She might surprise you."

"She's your guest, Uncle Jimmy. I'll treat her accordingly."

"More than that, son. She's my heartsong."

Dylan started. This was more serious than he thought! Could he be thinking about marrying this woman? About putting her in his will?

"Right now, she's consented to be my partner in business. Give it a little time and a lot of luck, maybe, if the timing's right and the feelings grow, I can make her my life's partner. Now, I know what you're thinking. You're thinking that I'm an old fool who's gotten himself turned around by a pretty face. Myra's more than that. She's got a sharp mind and a beautiful spirit. I can't tell you how long I've looked for a woman with just those qualities, Dylan. Just like those birds, I saw a golden opportunity and I wasn't going to let it slip by me."

"You're talking about marrying this woman, Uncle Jimmy?"

"Still a little premature. We haven't talked about it. Those are just feelings that I've had on my own. I want her to get used to the idea of us being business partners, then maybe I can make her my life partner, if she'll have me."

"If? You mean, you're not certain she cares about you? Why'd you bring her here, then?"

"Because she was looking for something to fill her life as much as I was. For now, it's being part of the Triple J."

"Then it could be a temporary arrangement?" Dylan pressed.

"When I told her about you, she had some doubts about whether or not she'd be welcome here."

Dylan shifted uncomfortably in his chair. Echoes of his thoughts to drive Myra Dodd away lingered in his mind. His uncle Jimmy knew him better than he thought he did.

"We both realize her decision to come here was kind of sudden. I'm sure her own family will have something to say about it, too," Jimmy said.

Dylan's mind raced ahead. He would have to find a way to get Myra to talk about her family. Maybe he could find out where they lived, get in touch with them some kind of way. He might have a willing ally in getting her away from the Triple J. His face broke into a wide smile.

"Well, we'll just have to handle them when the time comes," Dylan said pleasantly.

Jimmy met Dylan's eyes. "Then you're okay with this? You'll make her feel welcome?"

"I'll do whatever I can," Dylan said, then added mentally, *to see that woman doesn't spend another dime of Triple J money.*

"That's my boy," Jimmy said, and took the hand that Dylan held out to him.

Chapter Three

"Let's join hands," Baby John said dramatically, drawing everyone to the dining table after Manolo announced grandly that dinner was served. "We need a special blessing. We have a lot to be thankful for this evening. Jimmy's and Dylan's reconciliation. Our lovely guest Myra. . . ."

"If you shut your mouth and let Jimmy bless this spread that Manolo set out for us, we can all eat!" Jesse said gruffly. "It's about time. I'm starving."

"Nobody's going to wolf down this food, *comprendido?*" Manolo said sternly. "I've created a work of art for dinner tonight; and you're all going to show the proper appreciation by not shoveling it into your *bocas grandes!*" Manolo then turned to Myra and said kindly, "That means big mouth, Señora Dodd."

Myra bit the inside of her cheek to keep from smiling. "Yes, I think I got the gist of what you're trying to say, Manolo. I promise to savor each mouthful before swallowing."

"As long as you don't hold up dessert," Jesse muttered

under his breath and immediately felt the swift, sharp swipe of Jimmy's foot against his shin.

Myra lowered her head quickly, thinking if they didn't sit down to eat soon, she would burst into open, uncontrollable laughter. The tone of Jimmy's voice raised both in prayer, and to cover Jesse's grunt in response to the reprimand, sobered her.

"Father, we're gathered here in your presence to give thanks for our many blessings," Jimmy began.

His prayer was brief, but honest and sincere. So much like him, Myra thought warmly. There was no excess to Jimmy Jolivet. He said what he had to say, did what he had to do, and made no excuses for either. He was direct without being abrupt, sincere without being severe. The calluses on his hands told her that he worked hard for what he had. The glint in his dark brown eyes told her that he would fight hard to keep it. Yet those same hard eyes softened whenever he beheld her. She never had to wonder what he was thinking when he looked at her. His expression was as open as the ocean which brought them together.

Not like that nephew, Myra thought, sneaking a glance through her lashes at Dylan. Though he remained polite and carefully respectful, she knew that there was more to him than he was ready to reveal. She worked around enough people who were masters at dissembling to know when she was being stonewalled. Her experience with the administrators who controlled the funding for her school honed her people skills to a fine degree. If there was any resistance to her being at the Triple J, it would come from him.

"More tortillas, Señora Dodd?" Manolo held a serving tray out to her.

Myra paused, not quite sure what to do with the pancake-like pieces of bread.

"We eat them like most folks eat biscuits," Baby John

explained. "They're made with either corn or flour and go with almost anything. Eggs and sausage in the morning for breakfast, strips of fajita meat and grilled onions for dinner . . . Take a bite after you've eaten something spicy. It cools the tongue better than water can."

"Oh." Myra nodded and placed a couple on a small plate in front of her. "Thank you."

She quickly surveyed the food that Manolo had prepared. Nothing looked dangerous enough to have to resort to a tongue-saving tortilla. Just to be safe, she tested each item by touching the tip of her tongue to the fork before taking the entire morsel into her mouth. She caught Jimmy grinning at her out of the corner of his eye. Myra shrugged and smiled back. Maybe she did look a little silly. But she'd feel worse if she had to stuff a handful of tortillas into her mouth.

When the last of the main courses were cleared away, Myra thought, *There, that wasn't so bad. Dinner conversation was lively, pleasant, without any embarrassing lags.* Even the reticent Dylan participated. All she had to do was ask about his horse, Lightning Blue. He dominated the conversation for a full fifteen minutes before Baby John changed the subject. Whatever Jimmy said to him in his office today seemed to have worked wonders.

"I hope you saved room for dessert, Señora Dodd," Manolo said.

"I don't know if I can manage another bite, Manolo. Everything was delicious. I think I overdid it."

"I'll take hers, then," Jesse offered, and scooted away before Jimmy could give him another under-the-table etiquette lesson.

"Maybe just a small bite," Myra said, pinching her fingers together. After all, Manolo had gone through all of that trouble for her benefit.

"*¡Un momento!* Be right back!" Manolo's wide, brown face beamed with pleasure.

"You just made his day, Mrs. Dodd," Baby John said. "Keep eating like that and you'll make a friend for life."

"Which won't be for long if I eat like this every night." She thought about the more than generous helpings of ground beef in the chili, the streaming, melted queso, or cheese which Jimmy called Monterey Jack, mingled with onions and peppers, and the mountain of rice. The tasty three-bean salad was doused with a vinegar, oil, and spice mixture that Myra could feel drowning her heart. "How do you do it and stay as fit as you all look?"

"No diet pills or fad drink mixes. Nothing but back-breaking labor from dawn to dusk," Jesse said, leaning back in his chair and patting his middle.

"Looks like some of us could use a few more hours in the day," Baby John teased and aimed a mock punch at his brother's paunch.

"Ta-dah!" Manolo said, bringing out a bundt-shaped cake.

Myra sniffed appreciatively. "Okay, maybe more than just a little pinch. Sorry, Jesse. You'll have to get your own. Don't skimp on the cake, Manolo. It looks delicious."

Myra's eyes traveled longingly over the gleaming white icing that streamed over the sides and dribbled onto the serving plate.

"You are the first to try this new creation before I enter it into the Christmas bazaar baking contest." Manolo cut her a generous wedge and said, "Tell me what you think. Be honest. You won't hurt my feelings."

"Manolo's won a ribbon every year since he starting baking for the annual Murray Christmas fandango," Baby John said. "Every year his concoctions get more and more elaborate. You should have seen the cheesecake he made last year."

"The topping was loaded with caramel-coated pecans, shavings of German chocolate, and red licorice." Jesse smacked his lips. "If it weren't for the name, I think he would have won the blue ribbon."

"He was robbed," Jimmy commiserated.

"*Que lástima.* Such a pity. It was a good name, *verdad?*" Manolo sighed.

"What did you call it?" Myra asked, curious. She paused in the middle of raising a forkful of cake to her mouth.

"Something that translated roughly to creamed innards of roadkill," Dylan supplied blandly.

Myra gasped and laughed aloud, "Are you serious?"

"*¡Cómo no!* Of course I was serious," Manolo said. "It took me a week to come up with just the right name."

"Well, what do you call this masterpiece?" Myra asked, raising the fork to her lips again.

"*Dulce media del fuego,*" Manolo said proudly as Myra slid the fork into her mouth.

"Myra, no!"

"Mrs. Dodd, don't!"

Jimmy and Baby John shouted simultaneously. Jimmy reached for her dessert dish and snatched it away from her. Baby John plucked the wedge-shaped server from Manolo's hands and said, "Give me that!"

Their actions startled her, making her teeth clamp down on the fork. Myra's confusion only lasted a second—for as long as it took the sweetness of the white cream icing to fade and the taste sensation of the cake's creamed filling to take its place.

Myra gasped aloud as her throat suddenly constricted. She squeezed her eyes shut tightly, allowing tears to stream freely down her cheeks. She reached for her glass of iced tea and gulped down half a glass of it before she realized her mistake.

By clenching her teeth, she'd managed to keep the feeling of a nuclear meltdown confined to her mouth and tongue. After drinking the iced tea, she carried the sensation down her throat and into her stomach. Myra was crying in earnest now—fanning her face and gasping.

It was Dylan who came to her rescue—returning her plate of untouched tortillas from the kitchen.

"Remember to chew," he said simply, his face giving no indication of how he felt about her predicament.

Myra nodded mutely, tore off a strip of tortilla, and stuffed it into her mouth.

"Chew, Myra, that's it," Jimmy urged and glared over his shoulder at Manolo. "What are you trying to do? Kill her?"

"You don't like it?" Manolo asked in genuine distress.

"I imagine most folks wouldn't think to put jalapeño peppers in a dessert," Jesse said, taking the serving knife from Baby John and cutting himself a slice of cake.

"P-p-peppers," Myra gasped. "In a cake? No, I don't imagine they would." She tore off another strip and ate it quickly. The fire in her mouth was slowly cooling to a low, fizzling flame.

"So, you don't think I should enter the cake in the contest?" Manolo asked.

Myra looked into the hopeful face and said, "Tell me, what does *dulce media del fuego* mean?"

"Sweet middle of fire," Jimmy supplied, almost sheepishly. He then said in low tones, "Sorry, Myra. If I'd known . . ."

She silenced him by laying a finger across his lips. "Manolo," she said, making an effort not to wheeze as she spoke, "I wouldn't change a thing. You go ahead and enter that cake. If it doesn't take the blue ribbon, I'll eat the whole thing myself."

"You are most kind, Señora Dodd."

"Just make sure there are plenty of tortillas around when you do," Myra added.

"Anyone else for cake?" Manolo asked, holding the dessert up for everyone's viewing.

"I'll take a slice," Baby John offered. "That is, if Jesse's left enough for us."

"I'll pass," Dylan said, backing toward the kitchen. "If you'll excuse me, I've got some more work to finish up before turning in. Good night, folks."

"Good night, Dylan," Jimmy said, pleased that Dylan was making a concerted effort to be cordial.

"Sleep tight, boy," Jesse said through a mouthful.

"See you in the morning, Dylan," Myra called after him.

"In the morning," Dylan echoed. However, he knew if they could have read his thoughts, they wouldn't have been so quick to wish him well. *See you in the morning,* she'd said. Well, he didn't expect to hear that for too much longer.

"Not much longer now, Delanie," Kira said, more to assure herself than to calm her dog. Since her conversation with her sister Alicia, she'd been on the road for three full days now. Every day she pushed herself and the rental car to the limit. In a little while, this trip into hometown hell would soon be over, Kira thought as she pressed the gas pedal down, making the little car surge forward.

"Just a few more miles . . . just a few miles . . ."

She kept repeating the phrase to push her ahead and to keep her mind alert. Though more than once she thought reluctantly that if she took the time to enjoy the view of this part of the country, she probably wouldn't have to concentrate so much on staying alert. She only stopped for the necessities, and Delanie dictated most of those. Every time she pulled off the highway to park at a scenic rest stop, Kira thought, "Oh, that's a pretty" or "I should get a picture of this."

As soon as she let herself relax, she was reminded of why she was making this trip in the first place. Then all of her anxiety came rushing back in on her.

"Mama, how and why in the world did I get you into

this? And how am I going to get you out of it? Especially if you don't want to go?" she said out loud.

She shook her head quickly, trying to amend her thinking.

"Now, Kira," she chastised herself. "It's only going to be bad if you believe it's going to be bad. Just keep thinking positive thoughts."

When she passed the road marker stating only ten more miles to Murray, her spirits picked up considerably.

"See, Delanie?" she crowed triumphantly. "I told you it wasn't going to be that bad. Just a few more miles to go."

When Kira had mapped out her route to Texas, she'd made certain to listen to the local weather report before she set out. Her trip was foolhardy enough without risking being caught in a terrible winter storm. She made certain that the car she rented was properly winterized—down to the new snow tires she insisted they put on the vehicle. Yet the further south and then west she drove, the more she started to wonder if she shouldn't have kept the extra money she'd spent—or at least, change her plan of attack for how she dressed for the weather.

The last weather report somewhere around Oklahoma said that she could expect a normal temperature of eighty-five degrees. A sweltering eighty-five degrees with a 100 percent humidity! Forget the cashmere coat, turtleneck sweaters, and woolen sweaters she'd packed. What she needed now was a cool, cotton T-shirt and a comfortable pair of shorts.

When Kira figured that she was just inches away (as the map said) from her mother, she pressed the gas pedal even harder. She might break the sound barrier, or get a ticket before getting that far, but she was close. Oh, so close! Nothing was going to stop her now!

Delanie barked once, reminding Kira that they hadn't stopped in a while.

"Not now, Delanie! We're almost there," Kira said, throwing her dog a "just be patient" glance.

She barked again, more insistently this time.

"Oh, all right! But the next time, you'd better go when I stop or you'll just have to hold it until we get where we're going."

When she passed the marker that indicated the direction of Murray, Kira pulled off the interstate onto the single-direction lane blacktop that would take her into town. She slowed to accommodate the reduced speed limit.

"Maybe it's a good time to stop, Delanie. I'll get some more gas. I was riding on the memory of fumes five miles ago."

If it weren't for Delanie's constant barking and the white-and-orange hand-painted sign that boasted of the lowest gas price in town, Kira insisted that she could have driven a little further. She put on her turn signal, though there were barely five cars on the road either coming or going, and pulled into the combined gas station and restaurant.

Once she stepped out of the air-conditioned comfort of the car and into the humid, clinging air, her system went into shock. Her first impulse was to climb back into the car and keep driving until she'd reached the south pole.

"Nope," the chatty gas station attendant told her when she mentioned her plan to keep driving, "It's a good thing you stopped here. There are no other gas stations in Murray. This is the only one and thank the good Lord it is 'cause business is real good this time of year. If you'd run out of gas, you'd been up a real creek, ma'am. The next gas station is nearly thirty miles away, on the other side of Dellville."

"I'll fill up here, then."

"Need some help with the pump? It gets a little tricky when the weather gets sticky." The attendant guffawed at his own pun.

"The sign says self-serve. I think I can handle it," Kira said pleasantly.

"Ooooh. One of those independent types. Well, I got to give you credit for that. Will there be anything else for you today? We've got a plate of holiday hash in the deli section for only two thirty-five."

Kira glanced around her then picked up a new pair of sunglasses. "No, I don't think so. But, I'll take these."

"Yes, ma'am. Good choice. They're on special." He took her credit card to pay for her purchase without a break in the conversation flowing mostly from his end. "You made a wise decision stopping here instead of Dellville. I'm full of the Christmas spirit. Everything in the store is priced for stocking stuffers. You won't find that in Delville. No, sir. I know for a certain they hike up their prices for tourists. So many of them passing through now—trying to get to their families for Christmas and New Year's Day."

"But you wouldn't do that, would you? Overcharge me during the season of giving?" Kira gave him her brightest smile.

" 'Course not, ma'am. This is the season for giving, after all. But if you'd made it on to Dellville, now I can't say what those folks over there would do. But more than one traveler has told me that their motto, plain as day, is get before you get got."

"Speaking of tourists and travelers," Kira said, too casually, "would you happen to know of one in particular. Her name is Myra Dodd. She's supposed to be staying out on a ranch somewhere around here."

"You mean Mama Dodd? You know Mama Dodd? Ain't this a small world! Everybody in Murray knows Mama Dodd! She's only been here a little while, but everybody in Murray knows and loves her. That's why we call her 'mama.' "

"Mama is right," Kira said dryly. "She's *my* mama."

"You know, I thought you looked kinda familiar. You've

got her eyes, now that I look at you closer. Yep . . . the moment you walked through the door, I knew there was something about you. You have that same look. That sweet, sophisticated look."

"I'm looking *for* her," Kira went on. "Where is she staying?"

"At the Triple J ranch."

"The Triple J," Kira repeated. "Where's that?"

"Oh, about twenty miles up that way," the gas station attendant pointed up the road. "You can't miss it. Just head up that way until you see the flashing yellow caution lights, hang a right, then go on about ten more miles. It's on your right marked by two rows of pecan trees and a big, black iron fence with the Jolivet logo—three Js linked together like so." The attendant drew the symbol into the light covering of dust on the countertop.

"Thank you."

"Don't mention it. So . . . you're Mama Dodd's daughter. Come to spend Christmas with her, are you?"

"Something like that."

"Well, welcome to Murray, Ms. Dodd." He glanced down at her credit card then smiled again. "Ms. Kira," he then amended. Kira shook her head when he pronounced her name with a long *e.*

"It's Kira," she corrected. "Sounds like Myra. Like my mother."

"Welcome to you, Ms. Kira," he said again. "Hope you enjoy the visit. Murray's a quiet little town, but I like it. Especially this time of the year. With all of the decorations and the lights . . . everybody's smiling and cheerful and full of the spirit of giving."

Full of something, Kira thought, noticing the "reduced for sale" signs on several bottles of wine and beer throughout the store.

"Oh, I don't plan to stay that long," she corrected.

"Just passing through, then?"

She nodded.

"Well, as my old granddaddy used to say, leave the world a little better than you found it. That's what Mama Dodd's gonna do if she leaves us now. Tell her I said hello, and thanks for the peach cobbler. It really hit the spot."

"Peach cobbler," Kira echoed. "I'll tell her." Kira thought she'd work the sentiment in somewhere between, *I hope you haven't signed anything* and *let's get the ho-ho-ho out of here.*

She pushed her new sunglasses onto the bridge of her nose and stepped out into the bright sunlight to get back to her car. As she approached, she noticed a group of young boys standing near the gas pump. She stopped abruptly. Memories of her near attack at the airport garage made her anxious. Kira glanced over her shoulder, trying to get the gas station attendant's attention through the wide glass front of the gas station. But he had become involved with another customer. Kira gripped her purse tighter, positioned her keys in her hand so that one key jutted between her knuckles, then lifted her head. She pinned one of the young boys with an open, defiant stare.

It seemed to work. He glanced down at his shoes and turned away. When several of the other boys spun him around and said loudly, "Go on. Ask her," Kira started to lose some of her fear.

The boy she'd glared at approached her slowly. "Pump your gas for a dollar for you, ma'am?" He couldn't have been more than thirteen or fourteen years old. He was dressed in a trendy T-shirt bearing the logos and likenesses of several famous sports heroes, wide-legged blue jeans, and a pair of high-topped tennis shoes which Kira knew for a fact cost more than a boy his age should be able to afford.

"No, thanks. I think I can handle it," Kira said quickly.

The boy looked back toward his friends and shrugged. "I told you she'd say no," he called out to them.

"Go on, Ellis," she heard one of the boys urge the one beside her. "Go on and ask her again."

"I'm not trying take advantage or anything," the boy named Ellis turned back to Kira. "It's just that me and my friends hang out around the gas station to pick up a little change during Christmastime. I'm trying to buy a present for my baby sister."

"Baby sister, huh?" Kira said suspiciously. That was a new one on her. When she was that age, buying a gift for her sister was the last thing on her mind. If anything, she spent countless days trying to figure out how she was going to convince Alicia to give up her allowance to her. Kira put her hands on her hips and stared back at the boy. "Does the guy who runs the gas station know you're doing this?"

"That guy in there? He doesn't run anything but his mouth!" Ellis laughed. Kira smiled a little in return.

"He knows I'm doing it. He's my brother Eldrick. I give him a cut of everything I make."

"How much are you charging me to pump my gas again?" Kira asked guardedly.

"Whatever you want to give, ma'am." Ellis decided not to press his luck for the whole dollar.

"I'll tell you what. Wash my windshield for me, put a little air in the tires, and I'll make it worth your while."

"For a little extra I'll walk your dog for you, too."

"Let's just see how you do with the car and then we'll negotiate from there. How does that sound?"

"Sounds like a good deal to me, ma'am."

Kira smiled ruefully. She couldn't remember the last time she'd been ma'amed so many times in one conversation. She was starting to feel a little old. Kira stood back to let Ellis do his job. As she waited, a deafening roar caught her attention. A huge truck, painted glossy black with flames blazoned on the side was speeding side by side with another huge truck painted deep purple with a yellow bolt of lightning streaking from headlight to taillight.

Both trucks had beds filled with young men and women—laughing, screaming, and cheering. They were goading each other, as the two trucks traded leads as they raced up the blacktop road. In the back of the black truck, a large, grizzled German shepherd barked furiously. Delanie's ears perked up when she heard the yowling. She gave an answering *yip-yip-yap* in return.

Kira's head turned to follow as they pulled up to a stoplight only a few feet way from her that was turning red. She watched as the driver of the black truck leaned toward the passenger window and shouted a challenge to the driver of the purple truck. The purple truck's driver shouted back—using a fair amount of profanity. Kira wrinkled her nose in distaste.

"There they go again," Ellis muttered, shaking his head as he inserted the gas nozzle into the tank and began to pump gas into Kira's car.

"Who are they?" Kira wanted to know.

"A bunch of folks who are old enough to know better," Ellis retorted. Kira raised her eyebrows in surprise. She imagined that a boy as young as Ellis would be impressed by the open display of showmanship between the two truck drivers.

The driver of the purple truck shouted, "You ain't got nothin' I can't handle even on my worst days with my *blankety-blank* three fifty engine, boy! You just take that *blankety-blank* Tonka toy and shove it up your *blankety-blank-blank* where it just might do you some *blankety* good!"

He then gunned his engine, issuing a new challenge to the driver in the black truck. The black truck's engine roared back, spewing a thick cloud of grayish-green exhaust from the tailpipe.

"Are they going to race? Right here in the middle of the street? They can't do that, can they?" Kira asked.

"They do it every time they run into each other."

"It's not running into each other that I'm worried about," Kira said, taking an involuntary step backwards.

"Go get 'em, Dylan!" One of Ellis's friends shouted and waved to get the attention of the driver of the black truck. "Eat his lunch! He can't take you!"

The driver of the black truck leaned out, grinned, and waved at Ellis's friend. He gunned his engine once more, and pumped the brakes—making the big truck surge forward.

"Don't do it, Dylan, boy. Get on about your business! Go on, get outta here!"

Another voice entered the melee. Kira watched as an elderly man in oil-stained coveralls and a weather-beaten baseball cap move slowly toward the edge of the street where the two trucks idled. He leaned his elbows against the bed of the black truck and shouted at the passengers in the back.

"You all know better than that. Get out of that truck and go on home, now. Go on! Get before I call your folks."

When a chorus of complaints rose up from the joyriders, the man slammed his hand against the side with a force that made the huge truck rattle. "You heard me. I said get on about your business!"

No more arguments. They scrambled out of the truck, leaping off the back and scattering in all directions. The man motioned for the driver of the purple truck to move along, then indicated to the driver in the black truck to pull off to the side of the road. He then leaned inside of the black truck and began to speak earnestly to the driver.

Kira saw the driver nodding—tightly, reluctantly. Kira couldn't hear everything the man was telling the driver, but the words, "Pay attention, boy! I'm trying to teach you some sense!" carried clearly across to the gas station parking lot. Kira would have paid her weight in gold to know what the older man said to the younger that replaced his look of cockiness and indifference with honest contrition. A moment later, the older man backed away from the truck and motioned for the driver to move on.

The driver in the black truck put on his right turn signal, though he was in the far left lane, and with a last, defiant squeal of tires, pulled into the parking lot of the store across from the gas station.

"Do that again and I'll take your keys away and put your truck on flat!" the man shouted after him. "See how you like running errands driving my station wagon!"

"Who was that?" Kira whispered to Ellis.

"They call that old guy Baby John," Ellis said as he placed the gas cap on Kira's car.

"Baby?" Kira echoed. Nothing about the man seemed babyish. He wasn't very tall. Maybe that's where the nickname fit. But he was powerfully built, with wide shoulders and stout legs. His booming voice carried, making Kira want to straighten up and behave even though she couldn't think of anything that she'd done wrong recently.

"He's one of the few people around here who can make Dylan behave himself," Ellis continued. "That's his nephew."

"A little wild." Kira immediately passed judgment after witnessing the truck showdown in the middle of the street.

"Not wild, just mad."

"What has he got to be mad about?" Kira wondered. She was only judging from a two-minute first impression, but it seemed to her that the young man shouldn't have a care in the world. By the look of the fancy truck he drove, he certainly had enough money not to have any financial concerns. And if the way his uncle stopped him from making an idiot out of himself was any indication of how much he was cared for, he didn't have to worry about feeling neglected.

"He'll be all right in a couple of days. He hasn't been the same since his uncle Jimmy Jolivet brought that woman home to help him run the ranch." Ellis's voice was slightly muffled as he leaned over to fill Kira's tires with air.

Kira swerved to stare at Ellis. "What did you say?" Jolivet?" That was the name her mother had mentioned in the postcard.

"This is just what I heard from my brother, but he thinks that Dylan thinks that woman's gonna cheat him out of his inheritance. He ought to know better than that. His uncle loves him."

"That woman wouldn't by any chance be Myra Dodd, would it?"

"Hey! How'd you know that?" Ellis exclaimed.

"I'm psychic," Kira said with a hint of mild sarcasm.

"Really?" This time Ellis did sound impressed. "Say, can you tell me what my dad put in that big red and silver package under the tree?"

"And ruin the surprise for you, Ellis?" Kira tsked. "I couldn't do that."

Ellis made a face and said, "All done."

"Thanks, Ellis." She reached into her wallet and handed him a crisp five-dollar bill.

"Thanks a lot, ma'am!" Ellis exclaimed.

"Merry Christmas to you," Kira said with a smile, and for the first time since the holiday season "officially" began, she truly meant the words. "And just so you'll know, Myra Dodd is my mother."

"Your mother? Hey, when you see her, tell her I said thanks for the pecan pie."

Again, Kira was surprised. Pecan pie, peach cobbler. Had her mother become a master chef suddenly?

"Just because you're Mama Dodd's daughter, for an extra five, I'll walk your dog for you. He looks like he really needs to go!"

Delanie's snout was practically pressed into the rear window as she began another chorus of barks.

"He's a she, and her name is Delanie. Make it three

dollars, and you've got a deal," Kira countered. She opened the door and reached for Delanie's leash. Quick as flash, Delanie shot through the opening and dashed into the parking lot.

"Delanie, no! You know better than that. Get back here, girl!"

"I'll get her!" Ellis offered, taking off after her.

"No, Ellis. You'll only make her run away from you," Kira warned. "She's not used to strangers."

Delanie paused only a moment to check the progress of any pursuit, gave a defiant *yip*, then took off as fast as her legs could carry her.

"Delanie, you get back here!" Kira called out. "Get back here now! Right now!"

Kira might as well have been speaking in a foreign language. Delanie completely ignored her. She was tired of being cooped up in that car. Away from familiar surroundings and her favorite toys, she was ready to vent her frustration. A good run seemed to be the perfect answer. She knew that once Kira started to run, too, she would enjoy it.

Delanie darted into the street, making Kira cry out in dismay as Delanie barely managed to avoid one of the few cars still on the road. Kira cringed as the car's tires squealed and swerved to avoid hitting her dog. The car came to a screeching halt as Kira followed after Delanie.

"Sorry! I'm so sorry!" Kira waved, passing in front of the vehicle.

When the driver leaned out of the window and shouted out a sizzling expletive, Ellis stood in the middle of the road, wagged his finger, and called out, "Merry Christmas to you, too. And you'd better watch what you say, Mr. Harcourt! That's Mama Dodd's daughter."

The driver pulled over and stepped out of the car. Kira wasn't sure if he was planning to help her catch Delanie or give Ellis a sound thrashing for his impudence. She grabbed Ellis by the elbow and pulled him.

"Come on. We'd better catch her before she gets lost."

Delanie sprinted across the street, running under several parked cars and trucks. When she got to the black truck, she looked up at the German shepherd, snapped once, then took off. Delanie looked over her shoulder to see if the dog would respond to her invitation to play. The shepherd strained against his leash, which was loosely wrapped around a spare tire on the back of the truck. His barks echoed up and down the street. Kira only gave a cursory glance at the dog before skirting around the truck. In that instant of taking her eyes off of Delanie, her dog darted around the corner of the building and out of sight.

"Delanie, heel!" Kira used her most threatening voice, but she didn't know what she would do to punish Delanie if she didn't obey. And at the moment, it didn't look as if she would.

The shepherd leaned against his leash, pacing frantically from side to side until he worked the leash loose from the tire. His huge paws hung onto the side of the truck as he scrambled over the edge.

Chapter Four

"Mr. Dylan, I think you'd better see about your dog. Those kids out there have got Keeper all stirred up!"

The store manager pointed through the huge glass storefront as Dylan's dog leaped to the sidewalk and ran after a poodle, of all things.

Dylan turned toward the window and muttered, "If I told those kids once, I've told them a thousand times not to tease him."

"Out of the way!" Ellis shouted, and shoved Kira out of the path of the huge shepherd barreling toward them. Ellis slammed Kira against the storefront window, making it rattle. Flakes of spray-on snow sprinkled down on her as Kira gasped and grabbed the back of her head.

Dylan dropped the fifty pound bag of dog food he'd purchased and rushed outside. He propelled himself around the corner by grasping the door and slinging himself around. Kira didn't realize she'd sank to the sidewalk until she felt two wide gloved hands grasping her by the shoulders and pulling her to her feet.

"You kids know better than to . . . ," Dylan began, then stopped in mid-sentence. This wasn't one of the local kids. This wasn't a kid at all—though it was no surprise to him why he'd thought so at first. When he'd first caught sight of her through the store window, she and Ellis stood at the same height. Ellis had just turned thirteen and had yet to hit his growth spurt. The "kid" sprinting beside Ellis was only as tall as he was because of the shock of corkscrew, light-brown hair that added the extra inch that put her even with Ellis.

When Dylan's hands grasped the "kid's" shoulders, he'd expected to feel bones with taunt, ready-to-sprout skin stretched over them. But even through his gloves, he felt her softness. He felt her rounded shoulders give way to the insistent pressure of his fingers as he lifted her from the sidewalk. He was surprised she didn't wince as his hands dropped to his sides.

"Ma'am, are you all right?"

Kira looked into the face of owner of the black truck. She nodded mutely, unable to take her eyes from the lean face that was more rugged than handsome. It was a face marked by deeply set lines and oddly slanting shadows. Sepia-toned crevices carved out high cheekbones and defined the borders of a wide, hard mouth.

"Are you sure you're okay?" He continued when she didn't respond. "You're not bleeding, are you?"

His voice was deep and softly marked by the drawl that she and her sister Alicia had poked fun at. But this was no laughing matter. The timbre of this man's voice did something to her, made her feel all quivery inside. When he directed her to lower her head so that he could examine it, Kira immediately obeyed. Forgotten was the car she'd left behind, the search for her mother, and the chase after Delanie.

There were few voices that she could honestly admit could hold her at rapt attention—and those had been entertainers. James Earl Jones, Avery Brooks, Barry White—all known for the deeply resonant quality of their voices. But those men were trained to use their voices for just that effect. How did this hometown homeboy come by such a talent?

Mindful of the fact that this wasn't a child but a grown woman, Dylan gingerly grasped Kira's chin, lowered her head, and examined the spot where her head had hit the window. Some of the spray-on snow had flaked onto the area. A small lump was forming, but no blood.

"I'm ... I'm fine. Just fine. ... Thanks," Kira stammered, and attributed her inability to speak to the blow to the head when she'd connected with the windowpane. That had to be it. There had to be a physiological, if not logical, reason why she was behaving like a starstruck teenager.

Normally she wasn't the type to go *ga-ga* over a handsome face. She lowered her eyes, finding herself nose to chest. *Or a great body,* she silently amended. Though, if she were the kind of person who was suckered in by purely physical appearances, she figured that this was as good a body as any to start admiring. The man who'd stopped to help her was simply dressed in well-worn faded jeans and a white, short-sleeved shirt. It was as plain an outfit as anyone could find. But Kira found herself wondering if, somehow, this small-town wonder couldn't have worn this same ensemble parading up and down a glitzy, glamorous fashion show runway. Designers from New York or Paris would kill for a male model with one-tenth of his effortless appeal.

"There she is!" Ellis grasped Kira's arm and tried to pull her away from Dylan's grasp. "There they both are." Ellis pointed to the shepherd and the poodle as they sniffed at one other and began another chorus of ear-splitting howls.

"Delanie, you stop that noise!" Kira ordered.

Dylan spun around, "Keeper! Come here, boy. Get over here."

Keeper circled around Delanie, then suddenly began to sniff in an area that Kira had hoped he wouldn't be interested in—especially since she had planned to have Delanie and another pedigreed poodle mate at the beginning of the new year.

"Is that your dog?" Kira asked, moving quickly to intercept the dogs.

Dylan picked up on the implication immediately. "Is that yours?" he countered.

"Somebody do something or we're going to be up to our ears in mongrels," Ellis warned. "What would you call a shepherd and poodle mix anyway? Shoodles? Pepherds?

"Pooples," Dylan supplied, then winked at Ellis. The young boy grinned in return, having forgotten his caustic comment regarding Dylan's driving performance earlier that afternoon.

"That's not funny," Kira scolded. "Delanie, where are you going?" she cried out as her dog darted under what appeared to be an abandoned building. The shepherd was close behind her.

"Don't just stand there!" Kira grasped Dylan by the arm and propelled him forward. "Do something!"

"And just what do you expect me to do?"

"Go after them."

"And do what?" Dylan said, his face twisted into an amused smile.

"Stop them!" Kira insisted.

"Oh, no! Not me," Dylan replied, laughter bubbling toward the surface. "I'm not coming between them. I think we ought to just let nature take its course."

"There's nothing natural about a mangy, over-sexed shepherd and a pedigreed poodle," Kira snapped. "Now you get in there and call off your dog."

"Ma'am, I'm not crawling under that house after them.

It's been my experience that they'll come out when they're good and ready."

"But what if they get stuck . . . under the house I mean!" Kira exclaimed. "She could get hurt. She doesn't know what she's doing."

"They've got nature and instinct to help them out. They don't need me."

"Oh, this is ridiculous!" Kira snapped. "You mean you're just going to stand there and let them—"

"Yes, ma'am, I am," Dylan interrupted.

"Well, I'm not," Kira said, lifting her chin. When Kira took a step forward, Dylan grasped her arm. "And just where do you think you're going?"

"I'm going after my dog, Mr. Jolivet."

Dylan paused when she called him by name. He expected anyone within a hundred-mile radius to know who he was. But she wasn't from around here. That much was obvious. She stuck out as easily as if someone had painted a sign on her in big, bright letters—Up North. He knew that the moment she opened her mouth to speak. Foreign to this part of Texas, but somehow familiar. In fact everything about this woman seemed familiar—from the way she spoke, to the way she looked, and the way she carried herself.

"Do I know you?"

Kira shook her head from side to side.

"I told her who you were, Mr. Dylan," Ellis spoke up. "We watched you and Hank try to drag strip down Main Street."

"Who are you?" he asked her then.

"I'm Kira Dodd," she answered, pulling her arm away.

"Mama Dodd's daughter," Ellis supplied.

Myra Dodd's daughter? The long-awaited-for family member had finally arrived to take Myra back. This was it. This was the opportunity he'd been waiting for. If he could just get her alone for a moment, he could begin to convince her why Myra didn't belong there. The look that she was giving him, however, told him that he would have to do some very fast talking to get her to trust him enough to listen to his reasoning. So far things hadn't gone well. He hadn't made a good first impression with that drag-strip stunt. And now she'd accused him of being responsible for the actions of her own dog.

"If you'll excuse me, I'm going after my dog," Kira said abruptly.

"You can't go in there," Dylan insisted. He couldn't let her go under there. What if she got hurt? What kind of impression would that make?

"Watch me!" Kira retorted.

"The building says 'condemned' for a reason. You go crawling around under there and you're likely to get hurt."

"I'm not going to leave her to that ... that ... that hound."

"Keeper won't hurt that floppy mop with teeth," Dylan said derisively.

"You bet he won't. I'm not going to give him the chance. I'm going to get my dog."

Kira squatted near the opening where Delanie and Keeper had squeezed through. The foundation of the house was resting on large, gray cinder blocks. There was barely enough room for the dogs to squeeze under. But Kira was determined that she wouldn't leave until she had Delanie safely in her arms again.

"Ellis, there's a flashlight in the trunk of my car. Would you bring it back to me, please?" She tossed him the keys.

Ellis looked to Dylan for direction. Dylan shrugged, giving Ellis no indication whether he thought he should go after the flashlight or stay.

"Maybe you shouldn't go under there, Ms. Dodd." Ellis hesitated. "Maybe you should call the animal control people, or the SPCA, the fire department, or something. Don't go under there."

"I can't wait. By the time someone gets here the damage will have been done."

"Yes, ma'am," Ellis said dubiously.

"If you come right back, without you and your friends trying to take the car for a joyride, there'll be another five in it for you," Kira promised.

"Yes, ma'am!" Ellis repeated with more enthusiasm.

"I can't let you do this, Ms. Dodd," Dylan said, as Ellis sprinted for the gas station.

"You don't have a choice," she retorted, her voice echoing as she peered under the house. Moments later, Ellis returned, carrying the flashlight.

"Do you want me to go with you, Ms. Dodd?" Ellis offered as Kira shown the light under the house. Noting the debris and fallen planks from what should have been the house's foundation, Kira gulped silently then said, "No, Ellis. I think you'd be better off staying behind. Keep an eye on my car for me, will you?"

"Yes, ma'am. I sure will."

She glanced over her shoulder at Dylan. He gave a negative shake of his head, one final warning to her.

"Never mind. I'll do it myself," Kira muttered through clenched teeth. She bent down on all fours and started to scoot under the house. Dylan knelt down beside her and called out, "You shouldn't be doing this, Ms. Dodd."

"Thanks for the encouragement," she called back. Shining the light with one hand and pushing aside debris with the other, she inched along the ground.

"Delanie? Here, girl! Come to mama!" She called out. She thought she heard her dog's distinctive bark far back and to the right of her. She scooted along the ground in that direction, repressing a shudder of disgust when her hand made contact with something soft, squishy, and smelly. Kira wiped her hand on her pants leg, then went on.

"Do you think she'll be all right, Mr. Dylan?" Ellis looked

worriedly at the older man for assurance. "What if there are snakes under there? Or rats? My brother told me that sometimes wild dogs hide out in old buildings to get out of the cold."

"What cold? It's eighty-something degrees out here!" Dylan retorted.

"Then maybe they want to get out of the heat. It doesn't matter. You still shouldn't have let her go off by herself."

"Like the lady said, I didn't have a choice."

"If Mama Dodd finds out you let something to happen to her . . ." Ellis's voice trailed off meaningfully.

Dylan swore softly. "Oh, all right! You get to the car like she told you. I'll be out in a minute."

He had a more difficult time of squeezing his broad frame under the house. With a grunt of mingled pain and irritation, he wormed his way along the path Kira had taken.

"Ms. Dodd?" he called out. He could see the glow from her flashlight, but could barely make out her form.

"Over here!" Kira called out. "I think I can hear our dogs, but I can't see them."

Dylan pulled himself along by digging his elbows into the ground. He pulled himself up nearly parallel with Kira, panting slightly for the effort.

"Whew!" he whistled. "What's that smell?"

"You don't want to know," she said, shining the light on him and noting the same stains on his shirt as she had on her hand.

"Where are they?" he then asked her.

"Somewhere over there. There's too much trash in the way—broken soda bottles, concrete blocks, some rotted two-by-fours . . ." She took a cursory inventory of the area.

"Let me see that," Dylan said, taking the flashlight from her. "Hang on. I'll be back in a minute."

"Wait, I'm coming, too," Kira protested.

"I said wait here!" he snapped. "If I move the wrong two-by-four, we could both wind up like pancakes."

"Hurry up. It's creepy under here," Kira complained.

"Yes, Dylan, I'll be careful. Thanks for being so concerned, Ms. Dodd," Dylan said nastily, as he inched away from her.

"Ow! Watch it!" Kira snapped when Dylan's boot grazed her shoulder.

Ahead, he could hear their dogs. At least he thought the dogs belonged to them. Judging from the area littered with old bones, scraps of blanket, and a torn flea collar or two, he couldn't be sure. He thought he heard Keeper's rapid panting and Delanie's soft snuffling. A few feet more, and he could see them, too. He swept the light across the area, wondering how he was going to get to them.

"Hey, I see'em!" Dylan turned his head and called back to Kira.

"You can see them? Are they all right?"

Dylan shone the light on the dogs again.

"They're ... they're fine," he said, and bit his lip to keep from laughing.

"What are they doing?" Kira demanded.

"You don't want to know!" He returned, and burst out laughing at Kira's squawk of indignation.

"You mean it's too late?" she called to him.

"No, ma'am. I'd say we're too early. I told you we should have waited," he reminded her.

"Can you reach them?"

"No, I don't think so," Dylan replied, backing away from them.

"Do you mean that or are you trying to give your dog a break?"

"Hey! What is that supposed to mean?" Dylan said with righteous indignation.

"You know exactly what I mean," Kira retorted.

"My dog doesn't *need* your dog, you know. There are

plenty of other female dogs around here who would give their eyeteeth for a chance with Keeper. Your dog ought to consider herself lucky that Keeper even gave her a second look.''

"If looking was all he'd done, we wouldn't be in this mess!'' Kira snapped, then gave a frustrated "Ooh!'' when her hands landed in another unsavory pile.

"Let's get out of here before you start sprouting like a mushroom. Here ... take this.'' Dylan handed her the flashlight and indicated a direction to get out. "Head that way.''

"But what about Delanie?''

"Give them a few more minutes. I promise you, they'll be out.''

Dylan followed closely, keeping his eyes trained on the subtle sway of Kira's bottom as she crawled away from him. "Get your mind out of the gutter, Dylan,'' he muttered to himself, then wondered what other thoughts could he expect to have crawling around in this muck.

Kira lowered herself to squeeze through, then cried out as she flattened to the ground.

"What is it?'' Dylan rose up to investigate, then quickly lowered his head when it grazed against a rotted floor beam. He was thankful for the baseball cap he wore; otherwise he figured he'd be picking splinters out of his scalp for the next three days.

"I think I'm caught on something,'' Kira said, reaching behind her.

"Pass me the flashlight again.''

She snaked her arms around her, until she felt Dylan's gloved hand touch hers.

"Your belt,'' Dylan told her, shining the light against her back. "It's caught on a piece of something—something metal, I think. I'll see if I can work it loose.''

Setting the light aside, he moved next to her, flipped his cap around, then rolled onto his side. Resting one hand against her back, Dylan slid the other along her spine until he found a tear in her shirt. Kira tensed. She wasn't sure whether it was in anticipation of the painful sting of the area where she was caught, or the unintentional caress of Dylan's hand on her back.

"Kira," he said softly, peeling aside the shirt to examine the area.

"What is it? What do you see?" She tried to crane her neck around to see.

"When was the last time you had a tetanus shot?"

"I don't know. . . . I think I had a booster shot when I was in high school? Why?"

"You'd better get another one soon. You've got a nasty cut back here."

"How bad is it?"

"It's not deep, but I don't want you to take any chances. Something sliced through your shirt and it's caught in your belt. Give me a minute, and I'll cut you loose."

She heard him slide a utility knife from its sheath on his belt.

"Suck it in," he warned and grinned when Kira took a deep breath. "I've got to cut through the shirt to get a better look at where you're caught." He then hooked the knife under her belt and began to saw. The knife sliced through the thin leather belt as easily as it had the shirt she wore. When he got to her pants, he warned, "Don't move a muscle."

He pinched the material, trying to draw it away from her skin, and made a tiny incision. When Kira heard the material rip, she cried out, "Not my new pants!"

"Sorry, Ms. Dodd, couldn't be helped," Dylan gave a low chuckle.

"You'd better not be enjoying this, Dylan Jolivet," Kira warned.

"Now what possible pleasure could I take in gawking at a woman's bottom?" he said snidely.

"That's not funny."

"Do you hear me laughing?" He retorted, biting his lip again to keep himself from ruining his assertion. "Now, don't move. I think I can bend the metal away from you. Otherwise you'll just get caught again when your . . . uh . . . that is, when you try to get the rest of you through."

"If I get out of this without flaying myself alive, it's no more sweets for me," Kira promised herself.

"Okay, now try to pull yourself out. Be careful."

"You don't have to tell me twice," Kira replied, dragging herself free. Once she was out into the fresh air and sunshine, she took deep, gulping breaths. She then bent down and peered at Dylan's dust-streaked face peeking out from under the house.

"What about you? You won't be able to get out without cutting yourself to shreds."

"I'm going to work my way around to the other side where we came in. I'll meet you over there."

Kira nodded, then said softly. "Be careful, okay?"

"Oh, so now you're worried about me?" Dylan teased.

"I meant don't lose my flashlight," Kira shot back. She stood up, tried to dust herself off, then gave up. Nothing short of a fire hose would get those stains off. She hurried around to the other side of the house, then crouched down to peer under it.

"Mr. Jolivet," she called out to him. "Are you all right?"

"Just peachy," Dylan muttered. He flicked the flashlight on and off a couple of times to help her locate him.

"Can you hurry it up, Mr. Jolivet," Kira said, glancing at her watch. Every minute she'd spent in Murray was another minute that *that man* her mama had met on the cruise would have to convince her to give up her savings to him.

"I'm going as fast as I can!" Dylan called out irritably, then continued under his breath, "Just the kind of day I look forward to. Can't believe I'm doing this, crawling around in the muck. And for what? It isn't even my dog I'm worried about. But, no! I've got to try and rescue a little flirty, floppy mop with teeth who'll probably wind up giving old Keeper more grief than it's worth for what he's getting. . . ."

Dylan skirted around an old cardboard box that had been dragged under the house who-knew-when and by who-knew-what. As he shoved against a fallen beam to clear it from his path, his foot slid into the soft ground and landed against the cardboard. It gave way, but not before he heard the plaintive whelps of a litter of puppies that had taken refuge in the box.

He spun around to get a better look. Four or five spotted puppies whined and scrambled to get out of the way.

"What is this place? A swinging hot spot for hounds?" he said aloud, chuckling to himself. "No wonder Keeper and that mop were so eager to get here."

The puppies were barely six weeks old. Their fat, round bodies were held up by fur-clad stubby legs. He smiled, thinking that these little puppies would bring a smile to some kid's face on Christmas morning. He started to inch toward them. They were all so tiny, he could stuff them in his shirt and . . .

Dylan didn't get a chance to complete the thought. He'd only taken half a crawl toward them when a growl, deep and menacing, sounded very close to him.

"Keeper?" He called out, hoping against hope that it was his dog. He flicked the light on again and waved it across the area where he thought the sounds were coming from. Glaring out from underneath the flap of the cardboard box were two huge yellowish eyes. When Dylan shone the light on her, the dog blinked and lowered her eyes.

"Uh-oh," Dylan groaned. "Sorry, Mama. I didn't mean it. You can keep your babies."

The mother of the puppies crouched low and inched

her way toward him. Dylan knew he only had seconds. It wouldn't take long for the dog to get used to the flashlight even after being in the dark. He slid backwards, trying to talk in low, soothing tones.

"I'm not gonna hurt you, Mama. All I want to do is get out of here. See? I'm on my way. That's a girl. Just take it nice and easy, and I promise I'll be out of your hair quicker than you say 'Doggie, Doggie, where's your bone. . . .' "

"Hey! Are you coming out of there or not?" Kira demanded, laying down flat on the ground and pushing her head under the house.

"Kira! What do you think you're doing? Get out of here!" Dylan snapped, indicating with jerk of his head toward the angry mother hound.

Thinking there was a new threat to her puppies, the mother hound sprang toward the opening as Kira cried out and tried to get out of the way.

"Oh, no you don't!"

Dylan rolled over and grasped the hound's hind legs, dragging her back as she lunged for Kira. The hound twisted and bared her fangs. She snapped at Dylan, barely missing his forearm. She twisted again, whipping her head around to go for the other arm. Instinctively, Dylan brought his hand up to shield his exposed face and throat.

The mother hound snapped down. Her fangs connected with the heavy, dark metal of the flashlight. Still whipping her head, she somehow managed to flip the beam off. Her growls grew in intensity, then the offending light was no longer a bother to her sensitive eyes.

Dylan began to struggle in earnest, now, too. He didn't want to hurt the mama. After all, she was only doing what came naturally to her—protecting her territory. But remaining pain-free came naturally to Dylan, too. If he could avoid hurting Kira or getting hurt himself, he would. But it didn't look as if the mama was going to cooperate.

He still had the angry mama by the hind legs. At any

moment she'd realize that the hold he currently had on her wasn't enough to be a threat. She wasn't going to stop until she could no longer smell him or she could get a good whiff of his cold, stiffening carcass.

She let go of the flashlight, twisted, and lunged at him again. Again, Dylan brought the flashlight up. He didn't want to hurt her, but the light had a will of its own. It grazed her soundly across the muzzle, making her cry out. Still, she didn't give up. She snapped again and again. Each time, her teeth connected with the cold, slick, metal handle.

"Keeper! Keeper, get out here! Now!"

Dylan almost lost his hold on the hound when he turned in surprise at the sound of Kira's voice.

"I thought I told you to—"

"Shut up!" Kira snapped, dragging herself under the house again. "Can't you see I'm trying to rescue you! Keeper! Delanie! Drop what you're doing and get out here now."

Kira couldn't see exactly see them, but she heard them. Delanie's high-pitched bark was nearly drowned out by Keeper's deeper answering one. The shepherd shot out of his hiding place and loped toward the mother hound. Delanie followed closely behind, barking and snarling as if she could present a back-up threat to Keeper's warning.

The mother hound released her grip on the flashlight and issued an obvious warning to the new intruders.

"Go on!" Dylan whispered tightly to Kira. "Get out of here while she's got her mind and teeth on something else."

"If she hurts my Delanie . . . ," Kira began.

"Will you get moving!" he urged her.

Kira backed out, reaching for Dylan. "Give me your hand!"

She grasped both hands and leaned back with all of her weight. She hauled him from the underside of the house.

Once he was clear, Dylan leaned down and whistled for Keeper. Seconds later, Keeper hauled his shaggy body from underneath. Delanie followed, shaking out her previously well-groomed coat as casually as if she'd just taken a bubble bath.

"Good dog! Good boy," Dylan said, leaning over to stroke his dog.

When Delanie pranced up to Kira for the same affection, Kira put her hands on her hips and said severely, "Don't go looking at me with those big brown eyes. You should be ashamed of yourself! You little Jezebel!"

"Don't be too hard on her, Ms. Dodd," Dylan teased. "After all, we got ourselves into that trouble. They were doing just fine without us."

"Well, at least you didn't say I told you so," Kira said ungraciously.

"That was next," he retorted, handing her the flashlight. "Thanks for the flashlight. I think it saved my life."

Kira's eyes fastened on the teeth marks on the flashlight's handle. Her gaze then traveled to Dylan's shredded glove and the bright red blood stain where more than one bite had found its mark.

"Good heavens! Are you all right!" Kira cried out, clutching his hand and examining it.

Dylan shrugged. He hadn't had time to think about it. He'd been too concerned with keeping his throat from being ripped out to worry about what he'd originally thought were a few scratches on his hand. When she started to peel off the glove, he jerked his hand away.

"Don't do that," he said sharply.

"Does it hurt?" Kira asked sympathetically.

"Like the dickens," he admitted. But it wasn't the dog bite that sent a sharp sensation shooting up his arm. It was the concerned touch of Kira Dodd's hand against his that had him tingling. She'd forgotten that she was supposed to be mad at him for allowing his dog and hers to meet and mate. She'd forgotten that he belonged to the family she suspected of taking advantage of her mother. The only thing that mattered to her now was that he was hurt and needed attention.

"Let me see that hand," Kira demanded, using the same tone of voice used to cower the kindergarten kids she'd taught.

"It doesn't hurt much," Dylan grumbled. He relented and allowed her to examine him as he protested, "A little antiseptic and it'll be good as new."

"You're the one who's going to need the shot now," Kira warned, gingerly turning the hand over on one side and then the other. "What if that dog had rabies or something?"

"It wasn't rabies. It was babies," Dylan corrected. "She was just trying to protect her puppies."

"What puppies?"

"When I was crawling out, I accidentally kicked over a box where she'd stashed a litter of puppies."

"Poor things! We can't leave them under there like that. They could starve," Kira said sympathetically.

"They're not going to starve," Dylan was quick to contradict her. "From what I could tell before the mama nearly mauled me, they looked pretty fat and healthy."

"We can't leave them under the house. What if some other, bigger dogs decide to make them a snack?"

"Dogs don't eat other dogs," Dylan said, scowling at her.

"Oh, no? So, where did the phrase 'dog eat dog' come from?" Kira argued.

"I don't care where it came from!" He threw up his hands in resignation, winced, then grabbed his now-throbbing, injured hand. "If you even think of going back there after them . . ." Dylan threatened.

"Not me," Kira began, staring meaningfully up at him.

"Oh, no you don't! Or me, for that matter. Let sleeping

dogs lie . . . and I don't care where that phrase came from, either. I'm not going back under there and neither are you."

"But—"

"But nothing. You got your dog back. I've done more than my share of Good Samaritan work for the season."

"But—" Kira began again.

"Ah!" He held up his good hand in front of her face. "I don't want to hear it."

She blew out a frustrated breath, then conceded, "I guess you're right."

"I know I am."

Kira grabbed Delanie's leash. "You don't have to sound so self-righteous about it. Come on, Delanie. Let's go." She turned on one heel and strode toward the gas station.

"Come on, boy," Dylan whistled to his dog. "We've still got errands to run." It wasn't until he'd retrieved his purchases at the store, when he caught sight of Kira climbing into her car across the street, that the abruptness of her departure hit him.

So that was Mama Dodd's daughter. As far as making a good impression, he felt confident in saying that he'd missed the first opportunity. He could have recovered by offering to escort her out to the Triple J if he'd been thinking on his feet. He'd let that opportunity pass, also, when he'd let her walk away from him.

"Strike two," he muttered. He had one more chance— one more chance to gain her as an ally of getting Myra Dodd away from Uncle Jimmy. Ally? No, not an ally. That was too chummy. More like an unwilling partner in crime. That would be more like it. She'd been nothing but antagonistic since they met. Was it his fault that their dogs hit it off when they couldn't?

"Ungrateful little troublemaker," Dylan muttered. After all he'd done for her, she didn't even say "thank you."

Chapter Five

"Thank you, Ellis," Kira said as she took the keys from him. "Thanks for all of your trouble."

"It was no trouble, Ms. Dodd," Ellis said, eagerly accepting the five dollars she'd promised him as a reward for his vigil over the car. "But it looks like you ran into some. What happened to you? Did you get into a fight or something?" Ellis said, eyeing her from head to foot.

"No, I didn't get into a fight. I was trying to rescue Delanie. She and that German shepherd ... Well, never mind about that. Thanks again. And I hope you have a merry Christmas."

"It's a lot merrier thanks to you." Ellis grinned at her and held up the bills. "Don't forget to say hello to your mama for me."

"I won't forget," Kira promised as she climbed into the car and started the engine. Waving good-bye to Ellis, she pulled away from the gas station. Kira then pointed the rental car in the direction of the Triple J.

Maybe it was curiosity that made her look back. Or maybe

it was instinct. She felt as if she was being watched. She glanced into the rearview mirror and swept the area with her eyes, trying to figure out what had given her that impression. It didn't take Kira long to figure it out. Standing beside the big, black truck, she found Dylan Jolivet staring intensely after her. He leaned back against the truck, his arms folded across his chest. Keeper sat on his haunches next to him, his long red tongue hanging from the side of his mouth as he panted.

As she pulled away from them, she watched as Dylan slapped the bed of the truck, indicating to Keeper to climb up. Keeper scrambled up, then turned to lick at the dried mud on his master's cheek. Dylan laughed and pushed the dog away.

So vivid was the image of the man and his dog that Kira almost thought she heard the scratch of Keeper's claws against the metal bed, almost felt the warm, rough wetness of his tongue against her cheek when Keeper kissed Dylan. When Dylan rubbed affectionately over his dog's head, Kira could almost feel the supple leather of his gloved hand pass over her own head.

She bit her lip, vividly remembering the tingling of the senses she'd felt when Dylan touched her—from the first time he'd held her to examine her head to the last time when he'd run his hand along her spine just before cutting her loose from the jagged metal under that old house. Even through the gloves, she'd felt the tenderness in his touch. It was a touch that knew how to soothe, knew how to save. Though it was as embarrassing a situation as she'd ever want to be in, she felt an odd reluctance once he took his hand away.

"Maybe I ought to have my head examined if I keep thinking there's any snowball's chance in hell for me and that hometown homeboy," she said aloud. Delanie barked in response.

"You're not supposed to agree with me. Besides, what

do you know? You were just as suckered in by that rugged, rough, and ready charm as I was. How could you, Delanie? How could you! I thought you were saving yourself?"

Delanie whined forlornly and lay her head down on her slender paws. Grinning, Kira turned her head over her shoulder and asked, "By the way, how was he?"

"She's on her way, Myra!"

Jimmy stood at the front door, peering through the screen. At any moment, he expected to see Myra's daughter tearing up the road—all fired up and ready to kidnap her mother, if necessary, to take her back to Chicago.

"How do you know?" Myra asked.

"I got a call from Dylan. He says he ran into her in Murray."

"He was sure it was Kira?"

Jimmy smiled as Dylan's description of Kira came to mind. Except for the part of her being "as welcome as a plague of locusts," Jimmy thought that he might as well have described Myra, for all the similarity mother and daughter had.

"Let me see if I can give his description of her and keep it clean." Jimmy chuckled.

"Oh, my. . . ." Myra joined him at the door. "I knew she'd be upset. I should have called her sooner. Maybe then I could have saved her a trip down here. I got in touch with Ally but she told me that Kira had already set out. I knew she'd be furious. Did Dylan say how mad she was?"

"She was pretty worked up," Jimmy said soberly, then broke into a wide grin. "But not entirely about you. According to Dylan, you hardly came up in the conversation at all."

"Then what was she so hot about?"

Jimmy winked broadly and said, "What do you think got

your daughter hot under the collar? After all, Dylan being the man he is . . . a Jolivet and all . . .''

"No!" Myra gasped. "Don't tell me it was over Dylan?!" Myra laughed a little in return. "Oh, no! It couldn't be!"

"And why not?" Jimmy sounded wounded for Dylan's sake. "My nephew's the catch of the county, I'll have you know. Most women around here would . . ." Jimmy began.

"Oh, I can almost guess what most women around here would do." Myra raised her eyebrows at him. "I saw how they looked at him when we were making those Christmas care basket deliveries around town. I'm sure more than a few of them offered to give him a goody or two in return."

"Then you know the kind of effect he has on women," Jimmy said smugly.

"Not my Kira," Myra denied, shaking her head.

"Why? What's wrong with her?"

"There's nothing wrong with her!" Myra said quickly. "Why would you assume that something was wrong with her just because she isn't ready to rip off her clothes and dance the hoochie-koochie to catch your nephew?"

"Calm down, Myra, I didn't mean to suggest anything. I just meant . . ."

"Maybe you meant to say that she's too levelheaded to fall for that charm that runs through the Jolivet males." Myra raised up on tiptoe and planted a soft kiss on the tip of Jimmy's nose.

"Is that what drew you to me, Myra?"

"Like a bee to a blossom," she replied promptly. "And the more I got to know you, the more I knew that I'd made the right choice." Her expression suddenly hardened. "Kira already has a boyfriend. They've been dating on and off for a couple of years."

Jimmy glanced down at Myra and noted her tight-lipped expression. "It doesn't sound like you approve."

"It's not my place to approve or disapprove. Kira's a grown woman—capable of making her own decisions."

"But you don't like him?" Jimmy insisted.

"I can't stand the two-timing jerk!" Myra fumed. "He's sleazy and slimy and thinks he knows everything when he doesn't know diddly! He's made her cry just one time too many. I know I would rest a lot easier if she told that jerk when and where he could jump in the lake."

"Maybe if your daughter and Dylan . . . ," Jimmy began hopefully. He knew he was grasping at straws. But if she did take a liking to him, that would take so much of the pressure off of him and Myra. She and Dylan would be so busy romancing each other, they wouldn't have time to focus on him and Myra.

"Oh, Jimmy. We can't gamble on Cupid like that. Like I said, Dylan just isn't Kira's type. I know my daughter. Speaking of which, here she comes. There she is! Kira! Hello! Hello, sweetheart!"

She waved as Kira's rental car passed through the Triple J's gate and headed up the horseshoe-shaped drive. Myra was smiling, obviously pleased to see her daughter. But Jimmy was certain he saw clouds pass over her eyes for just a fraction of a second. There was only one reason why Myra's daughter would have traveled all this way—and it wasn't to hang mistletoe.

If anyone was about to be hung, it would be him, he thought ruefully. He was, after all, the man responsible for taking her mother away at the one time of year when family should be together. But Myra was family, he thought fiercely. She didn't carry his name—yet. But she was his just the same. It was only a matter of time before it was all official. When he looked into her eyes, he knew there was no other woman for him.

There were a million subtle clues that let him know that there was none other. He knew by the way he smiled whenever she said his name. How he loved to hear the sound of his name coming from her lips. He knew it by the way his pulse raced every time she took his hand in hers, or when she smoothed her hand over his forehead whenever it crinkled in worry. With her around, those moments of worry seemed less and less now. He was almost starting to believe that with Myra by his side, he need not ever worry again. He was convinced that there was nothing he couldn't solve with the love of this woman holding him up—keeping him strong.

He took a deep breath, preparing himself for whatever— that is, whoever—may come. From what Myra had told him, her daughter was a very determined woman. Myra told him more than once that whatever she put her mind to, she accomplished. If she couldn't be convinced to let Myra stay on the Triple J, then she could prove quite an obstacle to their happiness.

Jimmy wrapped an arm around Myra for comfort as much as for courage. He didn't want to come between her and her daughter. On the other hand, he wasn't quite prepared to let her go without a fight, either.

Myra flew outside with her arms outstretched. Kira didn't even bother shutting off the engine. She threw open the car door and ran to greet her mother. Seeing them both together, Jimmy was struck by how alike the women were. Seeing them from a distance, he could easily mistake them for sisters. They had the same slender frame. They both stood a little over five feet. They had the same thick, coiling mass of light-brown hair, the same wide, hazelish eyes, the same wide, full mouth—quick to laugh, just as quick to lash out.

At the moment, both were using their mobile mouths to talk a mile a minute—laughing, crying, scolding. Finally, gasping for breath, Myra held her daughter away from her and cried out, "Kira, what one earth happened to you?"

"Delanie got away from me and I had to chase after her."

"Dylan, the gentleman that he is, helped to get her dog back," Jimmy said, pushing the screen door open and stepping out onto the porch. He couldn't wait on Cupid. He had to give it his own best shot to keep Kira Dodd out of his business.

"Kira, I'd like you to meet a very special friend of mine. This is James Jolivet. He's one of the owners of the Triple J ranch," Myra made the introduction.

Kira fixed as warm a smile as she could muster on her face and held her hand out to Jimmy. Yes, she was afraid that this man had hoodwinked her mother. But maybe it wasn't too late to control the damage. If she had any hope at all of getting her mother to come back to Chicago, it wouldn't help her cause to alienate him.

"How do you do, Mr. Jolivet," she said, climbing the stairs to meet him.

"My friends call me Jimmy," he said automatically. Then, in a lower tone, "I'm hoping that you'll feel comfortable enough to do that soon."

Kira smiled a smile that promised nothing but also managed to put him strangely at ease. At least she wasn't snarling at him. He had been prepared for the worst, ready to launch into a grand speech he'd prepared in his defense. He'd even stuffed an extra handkerchief in his pocket in case Kira's verbal attack left Myra in distressed tears. Looking at this diminutive version of Myra before him, covered in mud, beaming at the sight of her mother, and talking a mile a minute to get the details of Myra's cruise, he didn't know why he had worried. It was obvious she was pleased to see Myra. There wasn't a harsh word between them. Everything was going to be all right!

"No offense, Ms. Kira, but you look like you could do with a hot meal and a nice, warm bath," Jimmy offered.

"No offense, Mr. Jolivet ... uh ... Mr. Jimmy"—Kira took her cue from the way Ellis had addressed Dylan—"everything here in Murray is hot," Kira said, fanning her face. After climbing out of the air-conditioned comfort of the car, the heat was starting to get to her again.

"Why don't you come on inside. We've got a room ready for you, though I know you don't plan on putting it to use for long. I'll take your bags up." Jimmy headed for the car. He reached inside to pull the key from the ignition, then drew back with a terse expletive when Delanie leaped at him—snarling and snapping for all she was worth.

"Delanie, bad puppy. Bad, bad puppy! No biting the host. Come here, girl. You don't mind if I take my dog up with me, do you, Mr. Jimmy?"

"No. She's more than welcome to stay with you, Ms. Kira. Though I'm not sure how Keeper is going to take to having a strange dog in the house."

"Oh, I wouldn't worry about him," Kira said, putting her hands on her hips. "I'm sure Delanie and Keeper will get along just fine. They've already been introduced. That's how I met your nephew in the first place. That's how I got to be in this state." Kira gestured at her clothes.

"Sounds like a whopper of a story in the making," Jimmy said. He opened the trunk and withdrew two overnight bags. "You can entertain us all over dinner tonight."

"How long were you planning to stay, Kira?" Myra asked, wrapping her arm around her daughter.

"I don't know," Kira said honestly. As Jimmy passed ahead of them, she whispered to Myra, "I guess that depends a lot on you, Mama. You know why I'm here, don't you. I'm here to take you back with me."

"You can make this visit a really short one if you go ahead and accept the fact that here is where I want to be. I don't want to leave."

"But everyone expects you to be home for Christmas," Kira objected.

"This is my home now," Myra insisted, a little too loudly for Kira. Out of the corner of her eye, she watched as Jimmy paused for just a fraction of a second. Kira thought she actually saw his back straighten. If he had any doubts of Myra's heart and where it wanted to be, he didn't now.

Kira opened her mouth, then shut it again as a familiar rattling caught her attention. Myra turned around, too.

"Dylan's back," Myra said unnecessarily. Kira knew as soon as she saw the black truck pull up right behind hers.

"I'm not in the way, am I? Do I need to move my car?" Kira paused before going inside.

"No, of course not. If you were really in the way, he'd just roll right over you in that monster truck of his," Myra teased.

Kira stiffened. "He'd better not. It's a rental. Tiny dents and dings from flying highway gravel I can explain. Anything deeper than that and it comes out of my pocket. So that nephew of yours had better be heavier on the brakes than he is on the gas."

"Oh, don't listen to that. She's just kidding you, Ms. Kira," Jimmy said quickly, nudging Myra. He was serious about fanning any sparks, real or imagined, between Kira and Dylan. Myra's little joke was smudging the pristine image he was trying to paint of his nephew. "Dylan is a very good driver."

Kira made a noncommittal sound. She wondered if Dylan had ever performed one of his drag-strip stunts in front of his uncle Jimmy.

"Of course he's a good driver," Myra returned. "He drove me all around Murray when I'd created some Christmas care baskets to distribute around town."

"Oh, that reminds me. I'm supposed to tell you thanks from Eldrick, the gas station attendant, and his little brother Ellis. They really enjoyed the pies."

"Well, they're more than welcome," Myra said, pleasantly surprised.

"Since when did you become Susie Homemaker? If they didn't come already cooked, or at least frozen and precut, you didn't bake pies for us."

"I have extra time on my hands now."

"Oh, yeah . . . like the haircut you gave yourself," Kira reminded her mother of her first retirement experiment.

"I see you made it all right," Dylan said as he approached them. "You should have waited, Ms. Dodd. I would have escorted you out here."

"You didn't have to do that. I took up enough of your time when you went after Delanie," Kira returned.

"Whew!" Jimmy said, noting the stains on Dylan's clothes. "You want to hang out downwind from us, Dylan, boy?" Jimmy quickly realized his mistake. He was just as bad as Myra when it came to killing the mood. "That is, if you get started now, you might get presentable enough for dinner."

Kira coughed delicately and tugged at her clothes. "I guess that goes for me, too."

"Come on, Kira. I'll show you to your room. Take all the time you need. Dinner is at seven," Myra told her.

Dinner was going to be a strange affair. Dylan felt the "oddness" in the atmosphere the moment he stepped into the formal dining room. It had been a while since the family had taken a meal in this room. It was generally only used for holiday gatherings, special meetings from various ranching organizations or committees they belonged to, or when trying to impress a potential addition to the family, as the case seemed to be tonight.

Dylan's eyes were drawn immediately to the freshly cut flowers forming the centerpiece of the cherry wood Queen-Anne style dining table. The table sat ten comfortably. Elaborately folded cloth napkins replaced the usual dinner's paper napkins. Crystal stemware gleamed in the light of the chandelier hanging above the table.

As he circled the table, he let out a low whistle. Three forks? Three distinct courses! And the plates, saucers, and cups . . . all of them matching . . . not a cartoon character or bargain mail-order dish in the entire setup.

"I think I'm underdressed," he muttered, stuffing his hands into the back pockets of the fresh pair of jeans he'd tossed on after his brief shower. He'd meant to take a long, leisurely one to wash away the embarrassment of being chastised by his uncle in public and his near mauling underneath that old house. But after competing with Kira Dodd for the bulk of the hot water when she drew a full tub for a bubble bath, he cut his own shower short. Seeing the lengths his family had gone through for Kira Dodd's arrival, he spun around, with intentions of changing into something a little more formal. As he did so he nearly ran into Baby John on his way out of the room.

"Where are you off to in such a hurry?" Baby John called after him.

"To air out my tux. I think we're dining with royalty tonight," Dylan retorted.

Baby John glanced at the table and grinned. "Now, I wonder who Jimmy's trying to impress? Can't be Myra. He's already got her heart locked up tight. Must be the other Dodd woman."

Dylan dropped his voice. "Do you think it'll work?"

Baby John shrugged. "You know more about her than we do. You met her in town. What do you think?"

Dylan shrugged in return and said, "I was too busy trying not to get my throat ripped out to worry about impressing anybody."

"Oh, yeah, Ellis told me that you and Ms. Dodd went exploring."

"Exploring, hell," Dylan replied with a snort of derision. "That woman and her fool dog nearly got me killed."

Baby John winced at the venom in Dylan's expression. "You be on your best behavior tonight, Dylan."

"Who, me?" Dylan spread his hands across his chest

and put on his most innocent expression. "You know me, Baby John."

"That's right, I do know you. I know how you feel about the Triple J and I know what you think about Myra. That's why I'm warning you. Don't mess this up for Jimmy. He's convinced that Myra is his true chance for happiness. He'll do anything to make sure that woman's just as happy for coming here as he is for bringing her here."

"I knew all of this was for her."

"That's right. If Jimmy has to lay out a line of sweet talk for Myra's daughter from here to the moon, he'll do it. And he'll make sure we're all along for the ride when he does."

"I wouldn't dream of ruining Uncle Jimmy's chances of happiness. You know I only want the best for him." Dylan smiled, but Baby John heard the edge in his voice.

"I know you do, son. We all do. I'm just running my mouth. Nervous, I guess. With all of this fancy froufrou that Manolo's set out, I'm afraid of doing something to embarrass myself . . . and Jimmy."

"You won't, Baby John," Dylan said, squeezing the older man's shoulder. "I know you won't."

"Thanks for the vote of confidence, Dylan, boy. So, what do you think? You think I should put on a tie?" Baby John asked as he buttoned the top button of his shirt. "What about the fancy string tie with the silver coin clip that Jimmy bought for me on that last business trip to San Antonio? How about this shirt? Does this shirt go with these pants? Maybe I ought to change into my Sunday suit?"

Dylan joined is his thumb and forefinger together to give the "okay" sign. "You look fine, Baby John. Just fine. I wouldn't change a thing." But inside, Dylan seethed. What was it about having women in the house that suddenly made all the men stupid when it came to dressing themselves?

* * *

Kira didn't know why it was taking her so long to dress. It wasn't as if she had an expansive selection to chose from. The clothes she'd crammed into her overnight bags were geared for the harsh weather she'd just left. Once she'd hit the warmer weather in the south, she picked up a few things at a discount clothing outlet mall—a couple of short-sleeved cotton blouses, a denim skirt, and a pair of light canvas shoes.

Laying out everything on her bed, Kira mixed and matched until she came up with what she thought would get her through tonight's dinner. Maybe, if she talked fast and furious, she could convince her mother to pack her bags tonight. They could be on the road by morning, and she wouldn't have to worry about what to wear to dinner tomorrow.

Kira stepped into the denim skirt, the only dressy blouse she'd brought with her, and a pair of leather, flat-soled shoes. She lamented the loss of the matching leather belt which Dylan had to slice in order to free her from the house.

She paused while dressing. The shock of everything that had happened to her that afternoon finally settled in. No wonder she was on edge. Since when did she treat having a knife within inches of her backside like it happened every day? That man had actually put a knife within inches of her body! Even more unsettling than that, he'd put his hands on her. A strange man. A strange hand. Her body unwillingly responded with shivers to the memory of his hand along her backside.

Even though Dylan was a perfect stranger, she hadn't balked when he placed his hand lightly against her back. Why she didn't react negatively, she was still trying to figure out. After all, she was in a strange town, in an awkward situation. When he touched her, she should have made enough of a fuss to make him think twice about ever touching her again. Instead, she'd relaxed under his touch. Maybe it was the fact that he was trying to help her that put her at ease. But Kira had a sneaking suspicion that it was something more than that. She spun around and surveyed what she thought would have been his view of her derriere. She let out an involuntary groan.

"That's it," she said, shaking her head. "No matter how tempting, no holiday goodies for me. No wonder I got stuck under that house!"

Kira turned around again. Facing herself in the mirror, she smoothed her hands over the denim skirt. It was a little shorter than she remembered it being when she'd bought it. She had been in such a hurry to get into the bargain store and get out again, that she hadn't bothered trying it on. The tag said it was the size she usually wore; and the price, marked 75 percent reduced, was definitely right. When she snatched it off of the rack, she wasn't worried about flair or fashion—only functionality.

It was a simple skirt, cream-colored with tan stitching around the pockets. She topped it with a dark, brown silk blouse and a long strand of faux pearls that her boyfriend Hugh had given her as an apology for one of his lapses in fidelity.

"Ex-boyfriend," she corrected, remembering that she'd told herself that she was officially going to break up with him again as soon as she made it back to Chicago.

Kira quickly twisted up her hair into a tight coil and clipped it into place with a gold and pearl barrette.

"Kira? Are you ready to go down to dinner?" Myra rapped on the door and stuck her head in. "It's almost seven."

"I'll be down in a minute, Mama," Kira said, lightly dusting powder over her nose, chin, and forehead. She then applied a muted earth-tone lipstick as Myra stepped in and closed the door behind her. As Myra stood regarding Kira, her eyes misted. Kira met her mother's gaze in the mirror and turned to face her.

"What is it? What's wrong, Mama?"

"Nothing," Myra said, shaking her head. "Nothing's wrong."

"Something is wrong," Kira insisted after hearing the quiver in Myra's voice. "What is it?"

"Oh, I was just thinking . . . remembering . . ."

Myra moved slowly and sat on the bed. She patted the covers next to her, indicating to Kira to sit down. "Do you remember the time you were eight years old and you were helping me to get dressed to go out."

"To your and Daddy's anniversary dinner," Kira finished for her. She started to smile, too. "You were wearing the blue dress, the one with all of the fluffy layers that made it stand out to here." Kira exaggerated by extending both of her arms as far as they would go.

"And why was I wearing the puffy blue dress?" Myra prompted. Kira started to laugh.

"Because just minutes before, I'd gotten into your lipstick and managed to get it all over the white one you were going to wear—the white slinky one with the leg slit all the way up to there." Kira drew an imaginary line from her ankle to her navel. "You had little red kiss prints all over your dress. I thought you were going to kill me!"

"You don't know how close I came to it," Myra confessed. "You really tried my patience that night, Kira."

"Why didn't you spank me?"

"All I could think was you were my little girl—my only little girl at the time. That was before Ally was born."

"Come to think of it," Kira said, her eyes twinkling, "Ally was born almost nine months to the day of your ten-year anniversary. You and Daddy must have had some kind of wonderful party."

"Don't get saucy with me, little missy. I didn't spank you

then for playing dress up with my makeup. I can still make up for lost time."

"How could you even think of spanking me? I was so cute."

"You know I didn't have the heart to punish you. You were my baby. And you were only going to be eight years old once. I'd never have that moment again. After I got over the panic of figuring out what I was going to wear, I made a major decision about how I was going to handle that evening. I could make you miserable by punishing you and myself miserable for feeling guilty about what I'd done, or I could make the most of it."

"So you decided to make the most of it?"

"Do you remember how relieved you felt when you knew I wasn't going to punish you?"

"I remember," Kira said softly.

"And do you remember how happy you felt when I let you stay in the room with me?"

"You even asked me to help you get ready."

"I knew how much you wanted to stay, Kira. Knowing that made you happy, I would have suffered a thousand little red kisses to see that smile on your face when I told you that you didn't have to leave the room. Seeing you getting ready to go down to dinner tonight—"

"Made you think of a way to get your point across," Kira retorted. "You don't want me to try to convince you to come back to Chicago with me." She stood up and moved away from her mother.

"Kira, wait. That's not why I started reminiscing. You're giving me credit for being a lot more creative than I am."

"You have to admit that the little trip down memory lane fits perfectly with your wanting to stay here with that Jolivet person."

"His name is Jimmy," Myra said crisply. "And you ought to show a little more respect when talking about him, Kira.

He's opened his heart and his home to me. I care for him, Kira. I care very much."

"You don't even know him. You just met the man! You don't know anything about him. He could be a swindler for all you know, ready to cheat you out of every cent you own."

"So that's what's bothering you. The money? I'd gladly give it to him if he asked me, Kira."

"Mama!"

"He hasn't asked me, Kira. He hasn't asked me for a dime."

"But you said you were going to be business partners."

"I came to him with the idea."

"That's the mark of good con man, Mama. He makes you think it's all your idea."

"Jimmy is not a con man, Kira. If you gave him half a chance, you'd see that."

"Between my half knowing him and your half knowing him, that should pretty well flesh out the picture," Kira snapped. "I swear, Mama, since you've retired, I think you've left your common sense back at the job."

"Now you listen to me, Kira Dodd, and listen carefully," Myra's voice hardened. "I'm a grown woman. What I do or don't do with my life, with my money, is my business."

"I'm just trying to—"

"I said be quiet and listen! You're wrong about Jimmy. He's a kind, decent, hard-working man."

"But it's barely been a month. How do you—"

"Your father and I knew each other only a month before we knew we were right for each other. And if the Good Lord hadn't taken him from me, we'd still be together."

"Is . . . is that the way you feel about Mr. Jolivet, Mama?" Kira asked in awe. "I didn't know."

"Some people take years to figure out what they want, Kira. Not so with me." Myra grasped her daughter by the shoulders and squeezed. "You don't have to accept Jimmy and his family if you don't want to, Kira. This is my life. My choice."

"I can't leave knowing that you might be making the biggest mistake of your life, Mama. I have to try to make you see that. I wouldn't be a daughter worth anything if I didn't try."

"I know that. But I'm not leaving now. I've made some commitments, some things I want to follow through on. Make this one promise to me. Give me two weeks. Give me two weeks without trying to get me to go back with you."

"To give Mr. Jimmy Jolivet time to get all the ink dry on the papers you've probably signed?" Kira said suspiciously.

"Kira, don't be so hard-hearted! He's not like that. If you gave him a chance, you'd see that. Take that time to get to know Jimmy and his family. See what a vital part I've become in the running of this ranch. See for yourself what I mean to the people of Murray and what they mean to me. If, after two weeks, you aren't convinced that I'm needed here and that I need to be here, then you can wheedle, cajole, and convince to your heart's content. I'll listen to every argument you can throw at me why I should go back."

"But that's not guaranteeing that you'll go back with me," Kira objected.

"No, it isn't. But I promise that I'll listen to you without cutting you off. Is it a deal?"

"Two weeks before I can even begin to try to convince you? But that might put me here for Christmas, too."

Myra smiled enigmatically. "Maybe."

"The whole point is to get you back home before then, Mama."

"That's not going to happen. Two weeks of peace or you go back by yourself tomorrow. That's my final offer."

"Something tells me that I shouldn't go through with this," Kira hedged, chewing her lip in indecision.

"But you are."

"What makes you so sure, Mama?"

"Because you're my daughter," Myra said, kissing her on the cheek. "And you're not one to back down from a golden opportunity to say, 'I told you so.'"

Kira laughed again and kissed her mother in return.

"Come on, sweetheart. I think we've kept them waiting long enough."

"All right," Kira relented. "You've got two weeks."

Chapter Six

"So, Miss Kira, how do you like our little town?" Jimmy asked after the conversation lulled for the first time that evening. Inwardly he berated himself for not being able to think of something more creative to say to Myra Dodd's daughter. He'd been trying to think of ways to draw her out all evening—wanting to know if she'd be willing to listen to him before insisting Myra go back to Chicago with her. She'd lulled him into a false sense of security when she arrived that afternoon—full of energy, open smiles, and pleasant conversation. But when she came down to dinner tonight, she was different. "Subdued" was the only word he could think of to describe her behavior.

Kira remained conspicuously quiet during dinner. She didn't exactly ignore the lively dinner conversation valiantly held by Jimmy, Myra, and Baby John, but she didn't initiate any, either. The fact that Jesse seldom talked during dinner and Dylan was also silent made for a very strained dinner. Each time she ventured to add to the conversation, she made obvious eye contact with Myra first. It was as awkward as when Myra had tested each dish before eating the night Manolo had surprised her with that *dulce media del fuego* cake.

Jimmy thought he could attribute part of Kira's reticence to the closed-door conversation she had with her mother. At one point during the conversation he could hear their voices raised excitedly, but he couldn't make out any details of the conversation. He would have given his eyeteeth to know what they'd been talking about so long upstairs before dinner. He'd passed by Kira's room once during that time, hoping to catch a whisper or two. He stood with a stack of clean bath towels in his hand, ready to give the excuse of good old Texas hospitality should they come out and catch him trying to eavesdrop. But before he could press his ear to the door, Baby John caught him first and dragged him away—confusing him with talk of tuxes and ties.

"I really haven't seen enough of it to give an honest opinion," Kira said evasively.

"If you like, tomorrow Jesse and I could give you the grand tour," Baby John suggested.

"Any time you got a spare fifteen minutes," Jesse snorted.

"Jimmy told me you didn't bring any luggage worth mentioning with you. Maybe you could get in a little shopping while you're in town. It is the holiday season, you know," Baby John went on.

"Every shop on the strip has raised its prices one hundred fifty percent so that they mark off twenty-five to make you think you're getting a bargain," Jesse said sarcastically.

"Thanks, but I think I've done all the shopping I need to do," Kira replied.

"Kira will only be with us for a little while," Myra put in. "And then *she's* going back to Chicago."

She said it pleasantly enough, but Kira knew by the firm set of Myra's mouth that she was letting everyone at the table know that she had no intention of going back with her.

Kira opened her mouth to protest, then thought better of it. She stuck a forkful of salad into her mouth. With the crunchiness of the lettuce, tomatoes, and garbanzo beans, she could grind out her anger and disappointment without making it obvious.

"If you don't feel like shopping, how about a tour of the ranch? That'll take more than fifteen minutes, I know," Baby John said smugly. "You could ride around for fifteen days and still not see all there is to see around here."

Kira paused with the fork midway to her mouth. "I had no idea that—"

"That the Triple J was such a spread? Yes, ma'am!" Jimmy said enthusiastically. He thought he saw an impressed glimmer in Kira's eyes. He would jump at the chance to make her see that his ranch wasn't a rinky-dink operation. The empire that had been passed on to him, and which he would pass on would grow and continue to grow as long as he had breath in his body. That's exactly why he was diversifying in the animals that Dylan found such a hard time coping with.

He glanced over at his nephew. Come to think of it, he'd been unusually quiet this evening, too. Jimmy glanced at Dylan's plate. He'd hardly touched a thing. That wasn't like him. With so much restless energy penned inside of him, Jimmy sometimes thought that Dylan had to eat twice his weight just to keep up with the demands of his body.

"We just bought a piece of property a couple of months back. On it, there's a small lake fed by a spring. The water's so clear, you see straight to the bottom. It's good and cold. A cure for whatever ails you," Baby John continued.

"That's something I would like to see," Kira said honestly.

For the first time that evening, Jimmy seemed to relax. He leaned back in his chair and said decisively, "A tour it is, then. Just as soon as the morning's chores are out of the way.''

"Can you be ready to ride by seven, Kira?" Dylan spoke up without prompting for the first time that evening.

"Ride? You mean on a horse? Oh, I don't know about that . . . ," Kira started to renege on the offer for a tour.

"Kira's never been on a horse in her life!" Myra laughed.

"Oh, like you have," Kira scoffed, then thought about it. Her mother had been here for several weeks. In addition to learning to bake, what else had these Jolivet men convinced her to try?

"I'll put her on Sun Morning. She won't be too frisky," Dylan said.

"I thought she was due to foal soon?" Jesse asked.

"I had her checked out by the vet. She'll be all right as long as we keep her at an easy walk. She's been stabled for a while. I think the exercise will do her some good."

"Are you sure?" Kira asked, glancing hesitantly at her mother.

"I'm sure," Dylan said firmly, drawing her attention back to him. Baby John had given him the opening he needed to get Kira Dodd alone. Once he had her away from the others, he would have no trouble convincing her to get her mother away from the Triple J.

"Seven o'clock. I'll be ready," she said, then used an interest in her dessert as an excuse to break eye contact.

"You won't be too tired?" he asked solicitously. Step one to gaining her trust was making her believe he cared for her welfare.

"I think I can manage to stay up another hour or two. I know life in the big city can't compare to the nonstop, madcap, hurly-burly of good old Murray, Texas. But I'll do my best," Kira replied smugly.

"I'll try to keep it down to a dull roar," Dylan said silkily. She wasn't going to make it easy for him to pretend to like her.

Baby John placed his thumb and forefinger between his teeth and whistled sharply. He then formed a T with his hands and said, "Time out, you two. Save some of that energy for the ride!"

Jimmy threw back his head and burst into relieved laughter. So Cupid had beaten him to the punch after all. Judging by the way Dylan was glowering across the table at Kira and she was glaring back, Jimmy knew beyond a shadow of a doubt that everything was going to be all right.

Something was definitely wrong.

Kira opened her eyes to a feeling of dread and apprehension. She wasn't where she was supposed to be. This wasn't her apartment. This wasn't even Chicago! There was too much sunshine slanting into the room. And the last she remembered of her home, the sun was obscured by an ice storm.

No, she wasn't in Chicago anymore. She sniffed deeply. She would never wake up to the smell of hot homemade blueberry pancakes.

"They're holding her here with food, that's what they're doing," Kira muttered aloud. She had to admit, it was a sound tactic. Everything smelled so delicious to her. Her stomach rumbled in agreement.

She then leaned over, searching for a pair of slippers. When she heard the soft breathing of Delanie under the bed, she smiled and said, "Good morning, my precious!"

Kira peered over the edge of the bed, calling softly to her dog. Her smile quickly faded as she cried out, "You!"

She grasped her slipper and flung it under the bed. "Get out of here, you . . . you . . . fleabitten, four-legged furball!"

Her aim was far off the mark, but it was enough to disturb Keeper's light doze as he curled himself protectively around Delanie.

"Did you hear me?" Kira cried, reaching for another shoe. "I said get out!"

Keeper yawned and stretched, undaunted by Kira's threatening posture. He raised his head and stared at her with huge blinking eyes, then laid his head on his paws again.

Kira leaped out of bed and stormed to the door. She could hear voices coming from the kitchen. With shoe still in hand, she took the stairs two at a time and burst in on breakfast.

"He's at it again!" Kira shouted, waving the slipper at Dylan as he stood at the kitchen sink, rinsing his plate of the last vestiges of breakfast.

"Who's at what again?"

"That dog of yours!"

"What about him?"

"He's upstairs . . . in my room!"

"Well, there's no accounting for taste," Dylan quipped.

"Get him out of there," Kira said through clenched teeth.

"What's he doing? He didn't tear up anything, did he? Or do a naughty on the rug?"

"He's lying next to my Delanie! Who knows what they've been doing all night under there?"

Dylan grinned at her. "Well, why shouldn't they be together? They've had a wedding and honeymoon all in one afternoon. I say leave the happy couple be."

"Dylan," Baby John said, in quiet warning. "If Ms. Dodd doesn't want Keeper hanging around her dog, then get him out of there. She's our guest."

Kira flashed Dylan a "so there!" look as he passed her. Dylan had the strangest, strongest urge to stick his tongue out at her in a childish display. The look she was giving him was so smug, so self-confident, that he would have done anything to shock that look right off of her face. The second urge to hit him was stronger, but nothing close to childish. He wondered what she would have done if he had grabbed her by those haughty shoulders, pulled him to her, and planted a wide smacking kiss right on her prissy lips? He stepped quickly away from her before he gave in to the impulse.

He stood at the bottom of the stairs, put two fingers between his teeth, and whistled. Seconds later, Keeper came barreling down the stairs. He stopped at Dylan's side and nudged his hand, demanding to be petted. Delanie stood at the head of the stairs. When Kira flashed her a stern look, she turned around and retreated into the room with a soft whimper that spoke volumes.

"Ready to start the day, old boy?" Dylan said affectionately, obliging by stroking his dog.

"What time is it?" Kira wanted to know.

Dylan checked his watch. "Six-thirty."

"Six-thirty?"

From the look of the kitchen and the fully-dressed occupants, excluding herself, Kira guessed that everyone must have been up for at least an hour.

"You're still up for that ride, Ms. Kira?" Baby John asked.

Kira took a longing look at the stack of pancakes that Myra had set aside for her. She'd promised Dylan that she'd be ready to ride by seven. She wouldn't make it if she had to stop to eat. And a stack like that just couldn't be rushed through.

"Maybe she shouldn't go. She's probably worn out from the long drive," Myra made an excuse for Kira.

"And all of the excitement yesterday," Baby John added.

"Another day, then," Dylan said, then shrugged. His expression gave no indication how he felt about her backing out. He then cursed himself for being so acquiescent. Was he trying to get rid of her or wasn't he?

"Go on, Kira, and get dressed. I'll warm your breakfast for you," Myra offered.

* * *

It didn't take long for Kira to shower, dress, and join her mother at the table. Myra sat with a huge mug of coffee held in her hands. Spread on the table and around the kitchen counters were bolts of bright material.

"What are you doing? Don't tell me you've become a seamstress in your spare time, too?" Kira asked, sitting down. She sniffed appreciatively and said a brief blessing of thanks for the breakfast.

"Not quite. But I did volunteer to help out. This is one of the commitments I was talking about. I'm helping with costumes for the annual Murray Christmas pageant."

"Christmas pageant. As in a play?"

"More than a play. The entire town gets involved. Jimmy tells me that the entire town is decorated to look like ancient Bethlehem. The two who are chosen to play Joseph and Mary move through the town—"

"On a donkey?"

"Or a horse if there isn't one available."

"I don't believe it!" Kira laughed.

"What's so unbelievable about that? I think it's wonderful for an entire town to get involved with such a wonderful story. I'm proud to be a part of it."

"Everything is wonderful to you these days," Kira said irritably. She softened her barb by adding, "Like these pancakes."

"Manolo taught me," Myra said proudly.

"Why am I not surprised? So who's the lucky couple this year?"

Myra shrugged. "They're still holding tryouts. There are still a few parts that haven't been filled."

Too bad we won't be around to find out, Kira thought. If she had her say and her way, she and Myra would be halfway to Chicago before the ink dried on the script pages.

As if Myra read her thoughts, she said, "It's almost worth

hanging around an extra week or two just to see who gets what."

Kira pursed her lips to object, then changed her mind. She'd promised her mother two full weeks without trying to sway her. She'd stick to that promise if she had to staple her lips shut to do it.

"So, what do you think of this?" Myra asked, holding up a swatch of vibrant red cloth against Kira.

"For what? The whore of Babylon?"

"Okay, maybe that was a little flashy. What about this?" Myra tried a striped white and blue against her. "You know, you ought to try out for a part in the pageant, Kira."

"Who, me? I don't think so. I'm no actress."

"I didn't say you had to have talent."

"Gee, thank you so much, Mama. If I had any notions of stepping out on the stage, you've killed it with that comment."

"Sorry, sweetheart. Now, what do you think of this one?"

"What do you think, Dylan? Do you think she'll like it?"

Baby John stood back and admired his handiwork. He'd gotten the keys to Kira's rental car from Myra and drove it around to the bunkhouse out of sight. He spent most of the morning washing, vacuuming, and polishing the road-trip dust off it until it gleamed.

"What's there not to like?" Dylan replied absently. He took his mare Sun Morning out of her stall and brushed her until her coat shone, as well. He patted her swollen belly and placed his ear to her side.

"How're ya doing in there, little fella? Ready to come out yet?"

"Any day now," Baby John said knowingly. "You're sure she's all right to ride?"

"Don't worry," Dylan said with a snort. "We're not going

anywhere. I knew that Mama Dodd's daughter would back out.''

"I'm surprised. She doesn't seem like the kind of woman who'd back down from anything.''

"How would you know? You've only known her for a day. Less than a day. What do we know about her at all?'' Dylan challenged.

"I know she's her mother's daughter and Myra's got more spirit than most.''

"If I didn't know better, Baby John, I'd say you've got a thing for Mama Dodd yourself.''

"I admire the woman. I don't mind admitting that. But that's as far as it goes. She loves Jimmy.''

Only because she got to him first, Dylan thought sourly. He supposed that any of the Jolivets would have done, if they'd agreed to set her up for life. His fingers convulsed around the brush and in Sun Morning's long mane. When she whinnied in protest, Dylan patted her side and murmured, "Sorry, girl.''

Baby John didn't miss the exchange.

"Easy on the brushing, boy! What in the world's gotten into you?''

"Nothing,'' Dylan muttered and moved around to the other side of the horse to avoid his uncle's gaze.

"Something's wrong. Why don't you tell me what's on your mind? You know you can talk to me. You can always talk to me.''

"I know that, Baby John,'' Dylan insisted. "When there's something to tell, I will. You'll be the first to know.'' Dylan thought to himself that then the rest of the world would know. He loved his uncle, and wouldn't hurt his feelings for a million Triple J ranches. But the fact remained that Baby John liked to talk. If he even hinted that he wanted Myra and that daughter of hers off of the ranch and out of their lives, the entire world would know before the end of the day.

Thinking that he was helping, Baby John would only make matters worse. Like last night. Baby John had the best intentions in the world when he suggested that tour of the ranch. But Kira had backed out, making Dylan miss out on yet another opportunity to talk to her. And when she came downstairs this morning, spitting fire because Keeper was in her room, Baby John had taken her side— giving her more fuel for her snobbery. If he kept alienating the woman, he'd have to rethink his plans.

Dylan had gone to dinner last night hoping that Kira Dodd would be all fired up, ready to drag Myra back to Chicago by her hair, if necessary. He thought all he had to do was sit back and wait for her to work on her mother, wear her down, and make her feel guilty for leaving them— at Christmas, of all times! Myra would be so upset, maybe break down in tears. And that would make Jimmy upset.

All Dylan had to do was get Uncle Jimmy alone to have a heart-to-heart talk with him. He would remind Uncle Jimmy that if he really loved Myra, he wouldn't want to see her upset. He'd do the right thing. He'd let her go. If you truly loved someone, if holding them meant hurting them, weren't you supposed to let go? Then that would have been the end of that. He'd come off looking like the good guy because he was so supportive and understanding of Uncle Jimmy's needs. And Kira would be the bad guy because she'd raised such a stink about Myra staying there.

But she wasn't like that at all. She was calm, quiet. He hated to admit it, but she seemed almost cowed. He almost didn't recognize her. The woman who came down to dinner was not the woman who'd confronted him back in Murray. The woman back in Murray was . . . well . . . covered from head to toe in muck that stunk to high heaven, for one thing. But she was proud, and resourceful, and brave. And more than a little nutty, he added. What kind of a crackpot would crawl under a condemned building after a dog?

When it hit him that he was just as nutty for following after her, he involuntarily jerked on Sun Morning's mane again. She stomped her foot and blew out a *whoosh* of warning breath.

"Sorry," Dylan repeated. He sneaked a peek at Baby John and found his uncle, blowing his breath on the rearview mirror, then polishing it with his sleeve. Dylan rolled is eyes in mild disgust, then went back to brushing his horse absently. He groomed her because it was his job to do so. Normally it would have been a pleasure to take care of his horse. Today, however, his mind was far away from his present task. His thoughts were centered on the house. To be more honest, they were centered on someone in the house—Kira Dodd.

Who did she think she was, coming down to dinner so meek and mild-mannered? How dare she leave all of the responsibility of breaking up Jimmy and Myra to him? If she was going to be any use to him at all, she was going to have to get with the program. And in order to get her on his side, he had to get her away from Myra and Jimmy.

"All done!" Baby John said proudly. "That ought to put a sparkle in those pretty brown eyes."

"Hazel," Dylan corrected. "More golden than brown."

Baby John grinned at him. "I suppose you're the expert, having been so close to her."

"We weren't that close," Dylan denied.

"Give it time. You will be," Baby John predicted.

"What are you trying to do? Ruin my day?" Dylan griped.

"Come on now, Dylan. Don't tell me that you didn't notice all of those special qualities that a man is supposed to notice in a woman. Those eyes, that hair, that body! Boy, if I were just twenty-five years younger . . ."

"Like I told you before, Baby John, I was too busy—"

"I know, I know. You were trying not to get your throat ripped out by that dog. But before you crawled under that house, while you were being mauled, and after you came out smelling less than a rose, you're trying to tell me that in all of that time, you didn't give that woman a second look?''

Dylan laughed, somewhat sheepishly, then said, "Of course I looked. I'm not blind.''

"Ah-hah! I knew it!''

"But that's all I did! Once I found out who she was, it was all over from there. I completely lost interest in her.''

"Uh-huh,'' Baby John said, completely unconvinced.

"It's true!''

"I'm getting a little too old to start believing in fairy tales now, Dylan, Boy.''

"You think I'm trying to pull one over on you?''

"Or yourself.'' Baby John pointed an accusing finger at his nephew. "It's as plain as the nose on your face, boy. I give it one week before she gets a ring through that very same nose, leading you around as easily as you do that dog of yours.''

Dylan snorted in derision, shook his head, then turned back to grooming his horse. Okay, so he wasn't being entirely truthful. He *was* interested in Kira Dodd. But not for the reason that Baby John thought. Let him go ahead and think that he wanted Kira. Maybe, in his blundering effort to play Cupid, he could come up with some creative ways of getting him and Kira alone. That's the only way he could think of to have that talk with her without being interrupted. If he knew that Dylan wanted to get next to Kira so that they could double team Uncle Jimmy and Myra, he wouldn't be so quick to try to push them together.

Kira pushed her plate away from her and patted her stomach appreciatively.

"I have to admit, Mama, being out here certainly has done wonders for your cooking skills.''

"Thanks . . . I think.''

"So what do you do now?"

Myra shrugged. "Usually by this time I'm helping Jimmy with the paperwork."

"What kind of paperwork?"

"Sorting out receipts of sale for livestock, making sure property taxes are up to date, tracking payroll for all of the employees—all the administrative aspects of running a ranch. You know, Kira, the more I think about it, the more I see how much like running a school district it is."

"Only it's not the taxpayers who are footing the bill, Mama."

"What are you trying to say, Kira?"

"I want to know who writes out the checks."

"He does, of course. Between Jimmy and Dylan, they know best how to allocate funds to keep the ranch running smoothly."

"You don't have to . . . uh . . . contribute to the fund?" Kira didn't want to suggest it. She knew it would make her mother angry; but she had to know. She had to know if all of her worry over her mother's financial future was justified.

"You ought to be ashamed of yourself for thinking that Jimmy is milking me. Yes, I occasionally make deposits into his account. But he's made it clear that they're loans. The money goes back into my account as soon it becomes available. And with interest. So, you see, I'm making money by helping out."

"It's your money," Kira said sullenly. "You can do what you want with it."

"Thank you for giving me permission to handle what I worked thirty-five years for," Myra retorted.

"Mama, I don't want to fight with you," Kira said earnestly. "I promised you that I'd behave. If you have to help Mr. Jimmy with his work, go on. I can find something to do until this afternoon. Maybe by then Dylan will be ready to take me on that ride."

"Not if you keep insulting him and throwing shoes at his dog," Myra suggested.

"That mongrel defiled my Delanie. She's ruined."

"She seems happier for her ruination." Myra laughed.

"Oh, Mama! Not you, too!"

"You have to admit, Kira. It is pretty funny."

"It is not!"

"You're taking this way too hard, sweetheart."

"I had plans for her—big plans. I had a breeder already lined up for her. Do you know what I could have gotten for purebred, pedigreed, poodle puppies?"

"No-ooo," Myra replied. "But can you say that ten times fast? That's got to be worth something."

Kira made a face, then burst out laughing as well. "Oh, Mama!"

"I'll tell you what. Jimmy can handle the paperwork one day without me. Why don't we go into Murray and go shopping. I think you could use some cooler clothes. It's supposed to stay in the eighties through Christmas."

"I'm not planning to be here that long," Kira needlessly reminded her mother.

"Then let's go pick up some souvenirs. I'm sure Ally will get a kick out of anything you bring back. Pick up something nice for the baby."

"Ally!" Kira gasped, slapping her head. "I didn't even call her to let her know that I made it okay. She must be going out of her mind by now."

"Give her a call now. I need to wrap up a few things here and then I'll be ready to go to town with you."

"I'll drive. I want to get my car checked out by a mechanic before I make the drive back to Chicago."

"By the way, I didn't want to tell you because I wanted it to be a surprise," Myra began.

"What's that?"

"I let Baby John have your keys."

"What does he want with my keys?"

"I told you. He's planning a surprise for you. Now go on and call your sister. I'll be ready in a little bit."

"Just a little bit more spit and polish and the car will be perfect." Baby John stood back and admired his handiwork.

"You spit one more time and I'll staple your mouth shut myself," Dylan warned.

"I just want Ms Dodd to feel like she's welcome. Come on. Want to take a little joyride with me while I drive the car back up to the house?"

"No thanks. I've got to catch up to Hank. We're supposed to be checking the signals on those modified leg bands Uncle Jimmy had me to put on his breeder birds. He doesn't want those birds running loose on the open pasture without a way to track them."

"Then I can drive you down to the bunkhouse."

"You're determined to get me in that car, aren't you?"

"Why not? We can snoop through the glove box while we're at it."

"Now, why would I want to do that?" Dylan asked suspiciously.

"I don't know," Baby John shrugged. "Find out more about her."

"Why don't you just ask her what you want to know?"

"Some things a woman won't tell you no matter how many times and in how many ways you ask. The only way to find out is to sift through her things. It's not likely that I'll get to peek in her purse—that's where you can really find what a woman is like—by what she considers important enough to lug around with her all day. If I can't get into her bag, I can get into the next, best thing—the car!"

"And you don't think that's invading her privacy?"

"Of course it is."

"But you don't have a problem with that," Dylan insisted.

"I have a problem with not knowing a thing about someone who very well might be part of the family one day. She didn't tell us much last night, so—"

"You don't need to know anything about her, Baby John. She's not sticking around long enough for us to get attached. By the time we get used to the sound of her voice she'll be out of here. All of that effort to get to know her will be wasted."

Baby John pinned Dylan with a hard stare. "So, you're saying we shouldn't look?"

"No. I'm saying just make sure you put everything back like you found it. We don't want her going away mad." *Just going away*, Dylan added mentally.

"Come on. Climb in. I'll drive while you look through her stuff."

"Oh, no you don't! I'll drive and you snoop."

"Chicken!" Baby John accused.

Dylan clucked in agreement as he climbed behind the steering wheel. "One thing we can say about her—she has good taste in cars. Not too flashy, plenty of creature comforts." His fingers gripped the wood-trimmed steering wheel and ran along the high-gloss, woodgrain dashboard. "Lots of power under the hood, too—V–8 engine, fuel-injected. Man, I'll bet she made this baby fly over the highway."

Baby John pulled out a stack of compact disks. "She likes jazz, too. The real thing—not that alternative, watered-down stuff. Look at this ... Marsalis, Coltrane, Whalum, Parker ... gotta love a lady who knows her Bird."

"How do you know those are hers? This is a rental car, Baby John. Those could be anybody's CDs," Dylan scoffed.

Baby John opened up the glove box and pulled out a map that had the route from Chicago to Murray highlighted. Baby John then whistled under his breath.

"What is it? What did you find?"

"Look at this. Do you see this!" Baby John waved the map at him.

"So? It's just a map."

"So! What do you mean 'so'? It's a map that's been used and folded back the right way. All the original creases in the proper direction. How many people do you know who can do that?"

"Or even want to," Dylan replied. He pulled the car around to the bunkhouse and blew the horn twice to signal his arrival.

"About time you dragged your carcass down here, lazy-bones!" Hank Darvin, the assistant foreman of the Triple J, greeted Dylan from the entrance of the bunkhouse. "I was just about to get started without you."

"Yeah, you're always 'just about' to start work," Baby John retorted. "If it weren't for me keeping a close eye on you, you loud-mouthed, flat-footed goldbrick, you'd be 'just about' all day."

Hank laughed a loud, raucous laugh that never failed to startle the livestock whenever he was around. That laugh coming from Hank's broad, barreled chest coupled with his tendency to wave his bear-sized arms when he was excited sometimes made him more of a liability than an asset when it came to working with skittish animals.

Dylan remembered once that Uncle Jimmy had forbidden Hank ever to laugh on the Triple J again. If it weren't for the fact that Hank's laugh had once saved Uncle Jimmy's hide by startling a bull that was about to charge, Dylan was sure that he would never have heard Hank laugh again.

"Is that what we're chasing those oversized pea hens in? A little fancy for your tastes, Dylan. I thought you'd be a truck man until the day you died."

"I'm not cruising around in this thing. This was Baby John's idea of a joyride." Dylan quickly distanced himself from the luxury car.

"I don't know. It might be kind of fun tearing up some of the back roads in this little mama. What's she got under the hood?" Hank ran his hand over the car's smooth finish.

"Hey! Keep your grubby mitts off. I spent over an hour scrubbing the dust from over four states off Miss Kira's car!" Baby John protested.

"Oooh-la-la! Miss Kira, is it?" Hank laughed again, sending several of the penned ostriches fleeing to the far side of the yard.

"Have you got the gear?" Dylan asked abruptly, not wanting to think how many of the animals they were supposed to check had just scurried to the far side of the yard. That meant he would have to get into the pen and drive them back again. His leg immediately started to throb at the memory of his first encounter with the big birds.

"Yeah . . . yeah, sure. Sitting right next to the door," Hank said absently. He was circling Kira's car, eyeing it appreciatively.

"I'll load it up on your truck. Let's see if we can drive the birds back to this end. If not, we'll have to make do out in the open," Dylan said. Hank's truck was parked just on the inside of the pen. Since the birds had already scattered to the far side of the fenced area, he felt confident that he could get the gear, toss it into the bed of the truck, and lock the gate before any of them escaped. All he had to do was keep Hank laughing.

"Yeah . . . yeah, sure," Hank repeated, waving Dylan along. He said low under his breath to Baby John, "I sure would like to know what this baby does on the open road."

Baby John immediately caught the gist of the gleam in Hank's eye. He began to reach for the door that Dylan had left ajar when he'd gotten out, but Hank's bulk was deceiving. He slipped quickly into the driver's seat of Kira's car, stepped on the gas, and yanked on the gearshift before Baby John's fingers clasped onto the door handle to pull it toward him. Hank peeled out into the ostrich pen with a roar of the engine and a squeal of tires.

"Here, chick, chick, chickies!" Hank shouted. "Get your *blankety-blank, blank, blank* tail feathers back over here, you stinkin' *blankety-blank blanks!*

"What the . . ." Dylan dropped the gear to the floor of the bunkhouse and grimaced when a shower of sparks flew from the expensive, electronic sensor equipment. *Oh, well,* he thought in resignation. He thought he could forget seeing a dime of his paycheck if he had to replace the equipment. More sparks and the smell of burnt components made him shrug again. Or the next paycheck! From the sounds coming from Hank in Kira's rental car, he may never see another paycheck again, he thought.

He sprinted to the ostrich pens just in time to see Hank disappear over a low dip in the open pasture. He heard tires squeal again as Hank cut the wheel sharply to come up on the opposite side. He came up so fast over the edge that Dylan was certain that, for a fraction of time the little car was airborne.

When the car hit the ground, it fishtailed as it tried to right itself. Hank gunned the engine again, driving up thick clumps of sod. He did several 360s before turning the nose of the car to the open pasture again. He blew his horn several times, driving the birds in one direction, then the other. The roar of the engine became a faint hum.

Dylan climbed up on the fence, shielded his eyes with his hands, and tried to catch sight of Hank and Baby John again. Nothing. For several minutes, all he heard was the rushing of the wind, broken only by the occasional sounds of a horse's whinny or a cow's low. Dylan checked his watch. Five minutes passed, then ten. After twenty minutes ticked away, Dylan shrugged and figured he might as well do something constructive with his time. He checked the water and feed bins. He gathered up the tracking equipment and surveyed the damage.

"Uncle Jimmy is going to flay me alive," he said aloud. "Maybe if I throw myself on the mercy of Myra's court, he might let me live long enough to regret ever laying eyes on those birds." Well, there went his morning. Maybe he would be free to take Kira Dodd for an afternoon ride, after all. He'd better make it a good one. When Uncle Jimmy found out that he let Hank run those birds, it would be his last. He resumed his spot on the fence, propping his face on his fists as he waited.

Just when Dylan thought that Hank must have taken that car all the way back to Illinois, he heard Hank blowing the horn for all he was worth. He couldn't see him just yet. What caught his attention first was the flock of ostriches that came barreling toward him at top speed.

Dylan leaped from the fence and scrambled to close the gate. The birds slowed, milling around the troughs where Dylan had refreshed their feed and water. A few minutes later, Hank drove slowly toward him. Every so often he tapped the horn, keeping the birds close to the feeding troughs.

Hank shut off the engine, climbed out, then tossed Dylan the keys.

"I don't want them," Dylan said. "Baby John is driving the car back up the house for Miss Dodd."

Baby John climbed out, too. He was tugging on his lower lip.

Uh-oh. Dylan knew what that meant. Something was wrong. It wasn't just the fact that the bright, shiny car was covered from headlight to taillight in thick, cloying mud and grass. That could be easily corrected with a water hose and another round of spit and polish.

"I'm not driving this car anywhere near that house," Baby John said, backing away.

"What's the matter, Baby John? Scared to face Miss Dodd? Like you said, a woman who can fold maps and listens to jazz can't be all that bad," Dylan teased.

"This car ain't going nowhere for a while," Hank said, and laughed longer and harder than Dylan had ever heard him laugh. When the birds scattered again, Dylan threw up his hands in mild disgust. Hank continued to laugh, wiping tears from his eyes. Dylan became suspicious. Nothing was that funny. It couldn't be. Not the way Baby John was worrying his lip.

"Why not?" Dylan said tightly.

"For starters, I think when we went over that patch about a mile that way"—Baby John pointed—"I think we twisted the rear axle . . . just a little . . . I think."

"Uh-oh," Dylan said aloud this time.

"We wouldn't have had trouble getting over that last ridge if it weren't for the transmission slipping a little. . . ."

"You ruined the transmission, too?" Dylan snapped. "What were you thinking?"

"Well, we wouldn't have had trouble with the transmission if we hadn't tried to get away from that bird that turned on us. Nearly kicked out the window, it did! If Hank hadn't cut the wheel when he had, it would have gotten me in the head. Yes, sir. It sure would have. Instead, it just put a nice little dent in the door. Nothing to worry about. Art's Garage and Repair Shop can pound that out in no time," Baby John explained.

"I don't believe this! I don't believe it. You wouldn't let me and Hank run our trucks down Main Street, one little tiny drag up the road and back again, but it's perfectly all right for you to go tearing up the countryside in a car that doesn't even belong to you. What were you thinking, Baby John?" Dylan ranted at his uncle.

Baby John could look only at Hank and shrug.

Dylan started to pass the keys back to his uncle, but Baby John pulled at his lower lip again. "Uh, Dylan . . . I was hoping that you could take the car into town, pull it with your truck, and get Art to take a look at it. While you're gone, I could take Kira on that ride . . . you know, keep her occupied while they knock out some of the dents, straighten the axle, and replace the transmission.''

''Oh, sure,'' Dylan said snidely, ''And while he's at it, he can add a new finish and reupholster the seats. Knowing Art, he'll even throw in one of those pine-scented air fresheners for free.''

''You think?'' Hank put in.

''Shut up,'' Dylan snapped, walking around the car and shaking his head at the damage. After a heavily exhaled breath, he said firmly, ''No, sir. I'm not going to do it. It's bad enough that you got me to snoop through her personal things. . . .''

''I didn't push you,'' Baby John said in his defense. ''You were just as curious to know.''

When Dylan glared at him, he fell silent. ''Voyeurism is one thing. Vandalism is another. If you think I'm going to sit back and let you try a patch job on that woman's car and try to pass it off, you're crazy. I'm not going to do it.''

''Look, Dylan, boy, she likes you. I know she does. You go on ahead and take her on that ride this afternoon. I'll pull the car into town myself. By the time Art gets finished with it, it'll be good as new. Better than new.''

''I'm not going to do it, Baby John. And I'm not going to let you do it, either. You take that car back up the house and 'fess up. There's no way you can hide something like this. No way. If you try, you'll only make it worse.''

''But—''

''Ah!'' Dylan held up his hand. ''I don't want to hear it.''

Chapter Seven

"I just heard Baby John pull up with your car, Kira. Let's go." Myra stuck her head into the family room where Kira had chosen to make the call to her sister.

"Okay . . . okay. . . ." Kira was saying her final good-byes. She waved to her mother to indicate that she'd heard her, then finished with the conversation. "I will. You take care of yourself, Ally. Tell Granny and Aunt Galen that I miss them." She then held the phone out to her mother.

"Mama, it's Ally. She wants to talk to you."

Myra bit her lip indecisively until Kira thrust the phone at her insistently. "Talk to your daughter. She misses you."

"I know," Myra said, apologetically. She pressed the phone to her ear. "Hello, sweetheart. . . ."

Kira smiled sweetly, but inside she was crowing triumphantly. She'd promised her mother that she wouldn't try to talk her into going back to Chicago with her. At least, not for a while. But Alicia hadn't made that promise. Myra knew that. The first sentiment out of Ally's mouth, after expressing how much she missed her mother, was a demand to know when she was coming home.

"I don't know, dear. I'm pretty settled here," Myra said patiently, throwing Kira an 'I'll-get-you-for-this' look. Kira shrugged innocently and turned away before her mother could see her satisfied grin.

Kira had insisted that Ally press her mother for information. She told her to be firm, to use every trick in the book to get Myra to say when she was coming back.

"Maybe I should suddenly start having contractions over the phone," Ally had teased before Myra entered the room.

"Let me hear you moan," Kira suggested.

"Kira! Tell me you were just kidding."

"I'm not. I'm desperate. This is war, Ally. You don't know the hold these men have over her."

"Men? What kind of men? What kind of hold? Just what's going on down there, Kira? Has Mama gotten involved in some kind of cult?"

"No . . . heavens, no! Nothing like that. Everybody seems perfectly normal. Nice to the extreme. It's a family-owned ranch run by three brothers and their nephew. There's Jimmy Jolivet—he's the one that Mama met on the cruise, and his brothers Jesse and Baby John."

"So what kind of a hold do they have over her?"

"They're keeping her here with kindness! Everybody is so polite, it's sickening. 'Yes, Miss Myra' this and 'Yes, Miss Myra' that. She's got them eating out of her hands. Literally! Did you know that Mama is baking peach pies and blueberry pancakes from scratch?"

"Our mother?"

"Yes, our mother. I wouldn't have believed it until some perfect strangers came up to me in town and asked me to thank her for them."

"Oh, Kira, you're so gullible. It had to be a setup. They knew you were coming. You probably stuck out like a sore thumb. That's how they knew to pump you up."

"They were for real, Ally. They really like her. That's why I feel like a bad guy for her asking her to leave them. When I tried to mention going back to Chicago, she made me promise that I wouldn't say another word about it for two weeks. My hands are tied, Ally. I'm stuck here. I'm not going back without her and she won't listen to a word of common sense from me. But that doesn't mean you can't work on her . . . Oh, here she comes. Work your magic, sister. And I'll do what I can from this end."

It was at that moment when Myra insisted that she heard Baby John drive up in the car. Kira quickly changed the subject; but Myra wasn't fooled. It wouldn't be Kira if she didn't try another way to make her see her way. Kira just didn't give up.

Once Kira handed her the phone, Myra fielded the questions as best she could from Alicia. She waited for Alicia to use the baby as a leverage to get her to come back. The best she could do was promise that she would be there for the baby's birth. After all, it would make her a first-time grandmother.

Kira fumed. That baby wasn't due for at least another month. By that time, Jimmy Jolivet would have his hooks so far into Myra, she would be surprised if they were celebrating the birth of Ally's baby and the marriage of Jimmy and Myra at the same time.

"I've got to run now, Ally," Myra said. "Tell everyone that I said hello, and not to worry. I'm perfectly fine."

"It just won't be Christmas without you, Mama," Alicia complained.

"Of course it will," Myra said stoutly. "As long as I'm in your heart, I'll be there."

"I just don't understand why you don't want to—" Alicia began.

"Ally, I've really got to be going now," Myra interrupted. "I'll give you a call later this evening. I promise. You take care of yourself, sweetheart, and tell that husband of yours I said I love him dearly, too."

"I will, Mama," Alicia sighed.

"Bye, now!"

"Good-bye. Tell Kira I'll talk to her later."

"So will I," Myra said, glaring at her daughter. Kira raised her eyebrows again, feigning complete innocence, then sauntered out to the front porch with Myra trailing behind her.

"Double team me, will you?" she began.

"What are you talking about, Mama? I didn't do anything. It's just your imagina . . ." Kira's voice trailed off abruptly when she caught sight of her car. She stood on the front porch with her hands covering her mouth to choke off the strangled cry she made at the sight of it.

Myra pulled up short behind her with a startled, "Oh! Oh, my! Oh, my . . . my . . . my . . ."

"My car!" Kira managed to exclaim, taking the stairs two at a time until she was inches away from it. "What did you do to my car?"

Baby John stood by the door on the driver's side. With a sopping wet shining rag, he tried to swipe at some of the dried mud on the hood and windshield. To avoid Kira's accusing gaze, he peered closely at one of the stains and thought in chagrin, *I don't think that's mud. . . .*

Dylan stood by the passenger door. Baby John had convinced him to come back to the house with him so he wouldn't have to face the Dodd women alone. Safety in numbers, Baby John had said, and Dylan had retorted, "You mean misery loves company."

Kira circled at the car in shocked silence. When she got around to the passenger's side and saw the huge dent in the door, she let out a fresh cry of dismay.

"It's not as bad as it looks," Dylan said lamely. She turned to him and stared. The look in her eyes was so openly angry, so accusing, that Dylan had a hard time

An important message from the ARABESQUE Editor

Dear Arabesque Reader,

Because you've chosen to read one of our Arabesque romance novels, we'd like to say "thank you"! And, as a special way to thank you, we've selected four more of the books you love so well to send you for only $1.99.

Please enjoy them with our compliments, and thank you for continuing to enjoy Arabesque...the soul of romance.

Karen R. Thomas

Karen Thomas
Senior Editor,
Arabesque Romance Novels

3 QUICK STEPS
TO RECEIVE YOUR "THANK YOU" GIFT
FROM THE EDITOR

Send back this card and you'll receive 4 Arabesque novels!
These books have a combined cover price of $20.00 or more,
but they are yours to keep for a mere $1.99.

There's no catch. You're under no obligation to buy anything.
We charge only $1.99 for the books (plus $1.50 for shipping
and handling). And you don't have to make a minimum
number of purchases—not even one!

We hope that after receiving your books you'll want to
remain an Arabesque subscriber. But the choice is yours to
continue or cancel, anytime at all! So why not take us up on
our invitation to receive 4 Arabesque Romance Novels, with
no risk of any kind. You'll be glad you did!

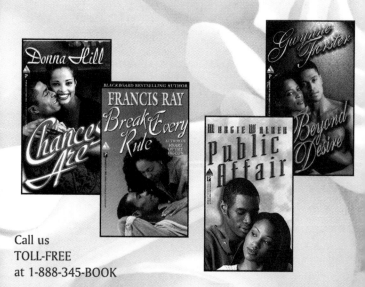

Call us
TOLL-FREE
at 1-888-345-BOOK

THE EDITOR'S "THANK YOU" GIFT INCLUDES:
4 books delivered for only $1.99 (plus $1.50 for shipping and handling)

FREE newsletter, Arabesque Romance News, filled with author interviews, book previews, special offers, and more!

No risks or obligations. You're free to cancel whenever you wish . . . with no questions asked.

BOOK CERTIFICATE

Yes! Please send me 4 Arabesque books for $1.99 (+ $1.50 for shipping & handling). I understand I am under no obligation to purchase any books, as explained on the back of this card.

Name _____

Address _____ Apt. _____

City _____ State _____ Zip _____

Telephone ( ) _____

Signature _____

Offer limited to one per household and not valid to current subscribers. All orders subject to approval. Terms, offer, & price subject to change. Offer valid in U.S. only.

ANH9A

Thank you!

Accepting the four introductory books for $1.99 (+ $1.50 for shipping & handling) places you under no obligation to buy anything. You may keep the books and return the shipping statement marked "cancel". If you do not cancel, about a month later we will send 4 additional Arabesque novels, and bill you a preferred subscriber's price of just $4.00 per title (plus a small shipping and handling fee). That's $16.00 for all 4 books for a savings of 25% off the publisher's price. You may cancel at any time, but if you choose to continue, every month we'll send you 4 more books, which you may either purchase at the preferred discount price. . . or return to us and cancel your subscription.

THE ARABESQUE ROMANCE CLUB
c/o ZEBRA HOME SUBSCRIPTION SERVICE, INC.
120 BRIGHTON ROAD
P.O. BOX 5214
CLIFTON, NEW JERSEY 07015-5214

AFFIX
STAMP
HERE

meeting her gaze. He held it for as long as he could, then shifted uncomfortably.

"What happened to my car?" Kira asked slowly, distinctly, through clenched teeth.

"Well, you see, it all started when . . ." Baby John began, then fell silent when Kira turned her burning gaze to him. She ignored Baby John and choked out, "Did you do this, Dylan? To get back at me for giving your dog the boot?"

"What?" Dylan sputtered. He splayed his hands across his chest, "You think I'm responsible for . . . you think that I could have . . . that I . . ."

Kira didn't give him the chance to explain. She spun sharply on her heel and darted back up the stairs.

"Baby John!" Dylan protested, "tell her!"

"Miss Kira, wait!" Baby John called after her.

Myra pressed her lips tightly together and held up her hand to silence him.

"Mama Dodd, I didn't do it." When his protest fell on Kira's deaf ears, Dylan tried to plead his case to the mother.

"We'll talk about it later," Myra replied gently as she headed inside to comfort her daughter.

It was called Southern Comfort. But as Dylan held the bottle in his hand, he couldn't imagine why anyone would willingly pour the amber liquid that tasted as appealing as battery acid down his throat—especially over a woman he'd only known for a day. Two days and a night, he then corrected. He slipped the bottle back into the dusty, seldom-used hiding place and closed up the line shack with a mental note to make sure the next occupants would have more of a selection than a half-empty bottle of whisky and some pinto beans to nourish them while they performed their watch duties. He then climbed back onto his horse to continue to check the condition of the next section of fence.

So far the fence line along this border of the Triple J looked clear. It wouldn't need a crew to come to pull the scrub brush aside for at least another month. Then again, he already knew that—having worked the crew that cleared this same section of fence line a few weeks ago. But he had to tell his uncle something when he'd taken off from the house at a breakneck pace. He had to tell him something to keeping from pulling that lower lip clean off of his head with worry.

"Don't worry, Kira. Everything's going to be all right," Myra urged, stroking her daughter's head. "It was an accident. It could have happened to anybody."

"Accident?" Kira returned sarcastically. "Two cars smashing into each other is an accident. Having a bird the size of a small car smash into you is . . . is . . . unbelievable!"

"It's not that bad. I checked," Myra said, crossing her fingers and saying a prayer against the slight stretch of the truth. "Baby John explained how it happened. He's really sorry. He's already taken the car to be looked at by the best mechanic in town."

"With all of the tractors and trucks and goodness knows what else they've got on this place, why'd they have to use my car to go chasing after their stupid birds?"

"They were just having fun, sweetheart."

"At my expense!"

"No . . . not really," Myra corrected. "Baby John promises to pay for whatever it takes to get the car running as good as new."

"What if they can't?"

"Relax, Kira! It'll be all right."

"Maybe I overreacted just a little. But you can't blame me. It just took me by surprise, that's all."

"Not quite the surprise I had in store of you when I suggested we go shopping," Myra admitted.

"Good, because I was starting to worry about you, Mama. If that's your idea of a pleasant surprise, I was going to have you committed," Kira teased.

"Their hearts were in the right places. Just not their heads."

"I could have killed him!" Kira cried out, reaching out and strangling the open air as if she had the guilty party within her grasp.

"Him?" Myra echoed, raising an eyebrow at her daughter.

Kira then amended sheepishly, "I meant them. All three of them, of course. They were all to blame—uncle, nephew, and their hired help."

"You came down pretty hard on Dylan, Kira, accusing him like you did."

"He was closest. I guess that's why I let loose on him first."

"I know you two didn't meet under the best possible conditions, but that was no reason to tear into him like that. I think you owe him an apology."

Kira groaned aloud. She didn't want to face him. "You do it, Mama. Tell him that I admit I was wrong for yelling at him like that."

"You tell him," Myra countered, prodding at her daughter with her finger.

"He won't want to listen to me after I acted like such a hard-hearted witch this morning."

"How do you know?"

"I just have a feeling." Kira shrugged helplessly.

"And so do I," Myra said cryptically. She'd had a feeling about those two the moment Jimmy had informed him that Kira and Dylan had already met in Murray.

"What do I say to him, Mama?"

"You'll think of something."

"I'll try. But it won't be pretty. I'm not good at apologizing."

"Well, you can't hide out here all day, Kira. It's too

pretty a day to be cooped up. Why don't you go outside for a while. Clear your head. Maybe you can think of how you're going to apologize to Dylan.''

Kira leaned over and whistled for her dog. "Come on, Delanie. Let's soak up some of this warm December sunshine. You'd better enjoy it now. You won't get much more of this before we go home.''

"Oh, Dylan, you're home!'' Myra caught him as he headed toward the kitchen to fix a snack. "I didn't expect you back so soon.'' Again, Myra crossed her fingers against the slight stretch of the truth. She'd practically camped out, waiting for him to return.

"The fences were in better shape than I thought,'' Dylan mumbled in response.

"Do you have a minute to talk?'' she asked, trailing him as he headed for the kitchen.

"Sure. What do you want to talk about?''

"Actually, it's not me that needs to talk. It's Kira.''

"Is that so?'' Dylan said nodding tightly. "About what?''

"I think it'll be better if I let her explain in her own way.''

"Where is her highness?'' Dylan asked, glancing up the stairs as if he expected to see Kira standing there, glaring down at him.

"Out walking Delanie, I think.''

"Is Keeper with them?'' Dylan asked.

"No, I don't think so. If he was, I would have heard it from *her highness* by now. I think she's walking down by the emu pens.''

"All right, then. I'll go down and have a little chat with her.'' He started to leave, but Myra grasped his arm.

"I just wanted you to know, Dylan, that Kira may not show it, but she does feel terrible about blowing up at you this morning.''

"I'm not looking for an apology, Mama Dodd," Dylan said truthfully. *I'm looking to run that little, wide-eyed, smart-mouthed troublemaker away from here,* he thought grimly.

"Try to catch them if you can, *chiquita*! Just try!" Manolo laughed as he watched Kira try to scoop a fuzzy brown emu chick into her hands. She darted around a small area that was fenced in by wire mesh.

"These little devils are fast!" Kira gasped, resting the palms of her hands on her knees. "Every time I think I'm getting close, they slip right between my fingers."

It didn't help that Delanie paced at the entrance of the pen, barking and snarling at the birds she could see and smell but was not allowed to sample.

"Maybe this will entice them to come to you, no?" Manolo handed Kira a bag filled with a mixture of grain and dried fruit.

"There isn't anything gross in here, like dried grasshoppers or chopped-up earthworms, is there? I want to know before I stick my hand in the bag." Kira hesitated.

Manolo shrugged enigmatically. "You want the chicks to come to you? You've got to give them what they want."

"Here, chick, chick, chick!" Kira said dubiously as she reached into the bag, then spread a handful of the mixture on the ground. "Come and get it! Or should I say, here emu chick, emu chick, emu chick!"

"Not very easy on the tongue," Manolo mused. "*Me pienso que . . .* that is, I think you'd better stick to chick, *angelita.*"

Kira knelt down, spreading the seeds closer and closer to her. Gradually a few of the bolder emu chicks ventured around her. She reached out, with her hand barely hovering over the nearest one, and waited patiently.

That's how Dylan found her as he walked up and stood

beside Manolo. Her back was to him so he could observe her unnoticed. Manolo, too, held his hand up for silence.

"How's she doing?" Dylan asked softly, indicating the emu cage with a point of his chin.

"See for yourself," Manolo whispered in turn.

"Come on, little chickies," Kira murmured. "I'm not going to hurt you. That's it . . . just a little bit closer . . . a little bit closer."

When one overly curious chick brushed against her outstretched hand and didn't dart away, Kira carefully set the bag aside to free her other hand. Moving barely a fraction of an inch at a time, she brought that hand into position, then clasped the bird between her cupped hands.

The emu chick chirped once or twice and squirmed, giving Kira the impression that it wasn't so much hurt or surprised as it was making that noise to let her know that he wouldn't allow her to catch him without a token struggle.

"I did it!" Kira crowed, spinning around to show off her prize to Manolo. "I caught him!"

When she saw Dylan standing next to him she started in surprise, dropping her hard won emu chick in the process.

Where did he come from? How long had he been standing there? She wondered. She'd been so busy playing with the emu chicks that she hadn't practiced her apology.

Dylan leaned against the fence. "Your mother said you wanted to talk to me."

"She did?" Kira stalled. What could she say to him? Sorry for thinking you're a jerk? Sorry for thinking you care so little about other people's property? If she'd been thinking clearly she would have realized that none of that was true. He'd proven that he cared by his willingness to risk his own safety. Not only had he crawled around under an abandoned building for a dog that didn't belong to him, but he'd risked being bitten to save her from the same fate. Did that say selfish? Unfeeling?

"Yes, she did. Do you?" Dylan pressed, when she didn't continue.

"No, I don't *want* to," she admitted openly. "But I think we have to."

"So talk."

"In here?" Kira gave a nervous little laugh.

"Nobody in there but you chickens," he replied caustically. Even Manolo chuckled.

"You think you're so funny," Kira retorted as she stood and dusted off her jeans.

Dylan opened the door of the pen a crack and allowed her to slip through. As she passed him, he again found himself marveling at how small she was. She looked as fragile as the baby chick she'd held in her hands. He wondered how she ever survived and thrived in a city as notoriously hard as Chicago. A city that big should have swallowed her.

Picturing her in that environment evoked in him protective feelings that threatened to smother the anger against her that he kept boiling just beneath the surface. He clenched his jaw, steeling himself against any weakening of his position. He couldn't forget that she'd come down here, in all her big city toughness, to dupe what she must consider small-time hicks.

"Walk with me," he said tersely, indicating a path that lead past the emu pens, on to the larger birds.

They walked for several yards without saying a word. Kira with her hands clasped behind her back and Dylan with his hands tucked into his back pockets took a roundabout stroll by the bird pens to the stable where he kept the pregnant mare.

Kira waited a heartbeat before jumping in with an explanation of her behavior. "I didn't mean it, you know . . . all that stuff I said this morning about . . . you know . . . the car and the birds . . . and you know the rest. Are you going to make me say it?"

"Call me a stickler, but I like my apologies to sound like apologies."

"I'm not good at making apologies," Kira complained.

"But you are good at making accusations," he countered.

"No, I'm not. Usually I try to avoid confrontations." Kira thought about Hugh and how many times she'd broken up with him in her mind.

"You could have fooled me."

"I admit I was upset about my car, but I shouldn't have blamed you. It wasn't your fault."

"Then why did you blame me?"

"Like I told my mom, you were the closest thing to me."

"That's not good enough, Kira. I want to know what was going on in your head. What did I ever do to you to make you so mad at me?"

Kira shrugged and said, "You're a Jolivet." As if that would explain everything. Dylan shook his head uncomprehendingly. Around here, that name stood for something— respect, prosperity, generosity.

"And?" he prompted.

"Up until a few weeks ago, I'd never heard of you," she went on. "I had absolutely no reason at all to resent the sound of that name."

"And now you do?"

"All right, if you're going to make me say it . . . if it weren't for your uncle, my mother would be back home by now . . . back where she belongs! It's almost Christmas, for goodness' sake. She should be with her family. But she isn't, she's here . . . making a new life, a new family away from us. That's why I can't stand the sound of your name. It's all your uncle's fault."

Kira expected him to blow up at her, to say something rude or scathing to defend his family. Instead he remained still and silently regarding her. When he didn't speak, Kira went on in a more conciliatory tone. "I know that sounds mean. But I can't help the way that I feel, Dylan." She stepped away and leaned her elbows onto the fence.

Dylan rested his hand lightly on her shoulder. She tensed, jerking away from him.

"I'm just trying to warn you not to get too close, Kira," he said in exasperation. "Some of those birds get pretty nasty if they think you're a threat."

"Sort of like some humans I know," she replied, glancing up at him.

"All right, so I haven't been the perfect host, either," he admitted. "But my reasons are just as good as yours. I don't like the name Dodd any more than you like mine. Do you think I like having some strange woman taking over things, changing things, spending my uncle's money?"

"What do you mean *his* money?" Kira spun around. "Your uncle's spending her money."

"Woman, you've got to be out of your mind. Take a look at this place. Do you think we need your mother's money? A teacher's salary?" Dylan scoffed.

"My mother was a district administrator," Kira said proudly, lifting her chin.

"Which I'm sure paid enough to put her in the lap of luxury."

"My mother has a smart head for business. She made her own money, Dylan Jolivet."

"That cruise was the perfect opportunity to make and take more."

"Are you calling my mother a gold digger?" Kira accused.

"Are you calling my uncle a swindler?" Dylan countered, towering over her.

"I've been calling you for twenty minutes," Jimmy interrupted, suddenly stepping between them. Myra had warned him that those two might need a referee by now and had sent him after them. Jimmy cursed himself. He should have set out sooner. He'd hoped that by leaving them alone together, Cupid would work its magic. The way these two were acting, he supposed it was just the wrong season. Cupid must have flown further south for the winter.

Dylan took a step away from Kira, his clenched jaw moving spasmodically. Kira folded her arms across her heaving chest.

"What is it, Uncle Jimmy?" Dylan asked, barely turning his head to address his uncle.

"I could use a hand with putting up the lights, Dylan."

"I thought Uncle Jesse was supposed to . . ." Dylan began, then stopped abruptly when Jimmy threw him a reproving look. Grown man or not, when he issued an order, either directly or indirectly, he expected it to be followed.

"Yes, sir," Dylan replied.

"It takes all three of you to put up a couple of strands of lights?" Kira asked incredulously.

"It's more than a couple of strands, Ms. Dodd. More like a couple of thousand," Jimmy explained.

"Why so many?"

"There's a lot of open land around here. We want to make sure Santa Claus can find us when he's making his midnight run," Jimmy said with a straight face. Kira turned a startled glance to Dylan.

"That's what we tell the children who visit us during the annual Christmas pageant. Every year for about ten years running the Triple J hosts a party for all of the area children. It's gotten so big, we're passing out presents to needy children from over five counties," Dylan elaborated.

"No wonder Mama is so intent on staying," Kira murmured. "The thought of helping so so many children . . ."

"We could sure use your help Christmas Eve, too, Ms. Dodd," Jimmy encouraged.

Kira smiled wanly and said, "Maybe. We'll see." Without a backward glance at Dylan, she nodded at Jimmy and started for the house. Dylan shook his head, grinding his teeth.

Once she was out of earshot, he turned to Jimmy. "Why are you still trying to make her welcome? Did you hear what that woman said about you, Uncle Jimmy?"

"Yes, I did," Jimmy said simply, and said nothing else. He didn't have to. If he'd heard what Kira had said, then he'd also heard what Dylan had said. He couldn't take back those words. He couldn't convince Uncle Jimmy now that he was on his side. All he could do was sit back and wait for the inevitable to happen.

It was bound to happen. With his foul mood and the distracting thoughts of Kira Dodd to affect his aim, Dylan missed a nail and slammed his thumb with the small hammer as he tacked the last row of a strand of lights across the porch. His resulting yowl brought Kira and Myra to the door.

"What did you do to maim yourself this time?" Kira called out to him. When she saw Dylan grasping the same hand that the angry mother hound had bitten, her first impulse was to tend to it immediately. Then she remembered how Dylan felt about her mother—and all of her maternal instincts dissipated.

"Are you all right, Dylan?" Myra asked in concern. Dylan nodded tightly, afraid that if he opened his mouth that he would swear a blue streak and embarrass himself.

"Kira, get some ice and a towel," Myra directed.

"No, that's all right. I'll take care of it," Dylan said tersely. He bent his thumb experimentally. It would be sore for several days to come, but it wasn't broken. "You can go on and do what you were doing." From the immediate way Kira turned from the door when he refused her help, it was obvious to him that she wasn't too concerned about his welfare. So much for the season of caring for one's fellow man, he grumbled.

"Are you sure?" Myra asked.

"I'm fine," Dylan said, using the excuse of checking another strand of lights to turn away from her. Jimmy wasn't fooled by the gesture. When Myra retreated back into the house, he said harshly, "Would it have hurt you to let her take a look at it, Dylan?"

"It hurts like hell now, Uncle Jimmy," Dylan retorted. "I'm a big boy. I can tend to my own boo-boos. I don't need the Dodds hovering over me."

"They were only trying to help."

"Yes, I could see the milk of human kindness flowing all over that Kira Dodd."

Jimmy paused, wondering which hurt his nephew more—the slam from the hammer or the slam of the door when Kira turned away from him.

"We'll let Ms. Dodd have the honor of turning on the first lights for the first phase of Operation Labor of Love," Jimmy said dramatically. Myra rolled her eyes. She wished Jimmy would just let it go. Kira and Dylan weren't going to go for each other. Pushing them together in the hope that they would accept how she and Jimmy felt about each other wasn't going to work. It had been two days since Jimmy told her about the argument he'd stumbled on between Dylan and Kira. In two days, those two had chosen to ignore each other completely. Now that everyone had gathered to see the first lighting, it was even more obvious that what those two needed was space.

Jimmy, Jesse, and Dylan had attached the last light strand in the afternoon, but waited until nightfall to drag everyone outside to witness the lighting event. Kira looked up at the house. She could see vague outlines of the dark, green strands against the white house—but nothing that would cause the obvious excitement and expectation written on the faces of the family members and of several of the ranch hands who'd gathered up at the house to watch.

"This is just a trial run, mind you," Baby John warned her. "This is only a small sample of what's going to be when we finish running lights through the yard, over the nativity scene that we always put up by the front gate and across the bunkhouse." He handed Kira the switch box that was attached to a heavy-duty orange extension cord, attached in turn to the multiple strands of lights surrounding the Jolivet home.

She stood on the path leading to the house, several feet away from the porch, staring up at the house. Behind her Jimmy stood with his arm around Myra. Jesse and Manolo sat on a fence overlooking the yard. Dylan hung back with several of the other hands, pointing to areas in the darkness where Kira could not see but were of interest to the others for some reason.

"Shouldn't there be a drumroll or something?" she teased. Someone started to beat two sticks against the fence as she called loudly, "Here we go!"

She flipped the switch Jimmy indicated, then nearly dropped the switch box in surprise when the air was suddenly aglow with twinkling, flashing, chasing lights in almost every color imaginable. Kira's mouth dropped open to join in the chorus of oohs and ahhs from the pleased onlookers. She didn't know what she was expecting after all of their hammering, shouting, and rewiring; but it certainly wasn't this. It was beautiful, whimsical, and awe-inspiring all at the same time. Everywhere she looked, her eyes were treated to a feast of festivity—from traditional to trend-setting.

On her left, stretched across a wire frame leading from the house to the emu chick pens, she saw Santa's sleigh flying through a sky of swirling snowflakes and stars. Across the front porch was a stand of multicolored lights that glowed steadily. In the area just before the door to the entrance to the porch, small red, green, and white lights wound around a wire frame in the shape of a holly wreath and mistletoe. On the roof of the house, Kira saw an angel blowing a trumpet blast heralding the birth of the baby savior. She then pointed to the switch box. "What's this button for?"

"Some of the lights are musical," Baby John explained. "That switch mutes or activates them."

"Can I?" she asked, her hand hovering over the button.

"I don't think you should—" Dylan began to object, but Baby John cut in enthusiastically, "Sure, go right head. This is supposed to be a trial run, isn't it? Let's go for broke."

Kira pressed the button, then laughed in gleeful wonder when the air filled with the amplified sound of a synthesized orchestra playing a medley of traditional holiday music.

"This is *soooo* cool!" Kira exclaimed, spinning around to get the full effect of all of the lights and music. She felt as if she were child, experiencing her first carousel ride. "You guys are geniuses!" she declared, and on impulse gave Baby John a forgiving hug. Baby John grinned and told her, "You think so? Well, we're just getting warmed up, Ms. Dodd!"

Kira couldn't imagine what more could be done to improve the display. She handed the switch box back to Baby John who made a tiny adjustment to the brightness level.

"I think we should cut them off now, Baby John," Dylan said, then endured a chorus of disappointed "awww!" from the onlookers. "Show's over, folks. We still have some tinkering to do before it's all perfect."

"Need some more help? I'm no electrical engineer, but I think I can replace a burned-out bulb or two," Kira asked as a beginning of a truce. If she could be a part of this spectacular display, it would soothe some of her wounded feelings from their argument.

"No, I think we've got it covered," Dylan turned her peace offering down. He wasn't quite ready to forgive and forget.

"Oh, okay, just thought that I'd ask," Kira said pleasantly enough. But Myra knew by the barely perceptible sag in her daughter's shoulders that she was disappointed.

"It's very tricky electrical work, Ms. Dodd," Jimmy said solicitously. "All of that climbing and wiring and stuff. Dylan just wants to make sure you don't get hurt."

"Uh-huh," Kira said, unconvinced. She folded her arms and regarded Dylan dubiously.

"It's true," Baby John ad-libbed when Dylan remained silent.

Kira threw up her hands. Everybody wanted to tell her what Dylan thought except Dylan. She started for the house; she'd had enough. She'd made an apology, in her own uncomfortable way, and he'd turned it down. She didn't need to be hit in the head with a ton of bricks. He'd made up his mind to hate her and her mother and she couldn't change that. As she headed up the walk, she heard Dylan tell his uncle, "You'd better shut it down, Baby John. I'm starting to smell the lights."

"Maybe we've got a bad bulb or two somewhere," Baby John muttered.

As Kira passed under the lights of the holly wreath, she thought she heard sizzling, then a distinctive pop!

"Ouch!" she cried out, grasping her cheek where glass shards from an exploding bulb had grazed her. "What the—"

"Get out of the way," Dylan said brusquely, hustling her aside when instead of moving away, she glanced up at the fizzling wreath.

"Shut it off, Baby John," Jimmy insisted when another bulb popped, then another.

Dylan reached up and disconnected the nearest cord that supplied power to the lights encircling the porch. The lights bordering the porch dimmed.

"Show's over," Jesse said, indicating for everyone to scatter.

As Kira swiped at the thin trail of blood on her cheek, Dylan turned from disconnecting the lights to ask, "Are you all right?"

"It's just a scratch."

"Let me see."

"Don't bother," her tone hardened. Why should he pretend to care now? He ignored her and stepped closer to examine her face.

"Mira, patrón!" Manolo called out and pointed. "Look where you are."

Jimmy glanced at Myra and grinned. Baby John whispered loud enough for those still standing around to hear, "Look out, folks. They're standing under the mistletoe."

"Go on, Dylan, boy! Give the girl a kiss!" Hank shouted, and laughed.

Kira felt as if she wanted to sink into the ground. She glanced at Dylan and thought for a fraction of a second that she read in his eyes he was actually considering it.

"In your dreams!" she retorted, and ducked into the house to escape the chorus of laughter that followed.

Chapter Eight

Kira fell asleep as soon as her head hit the pillow. For the previous several days, she'd stayed up late with Myra, making baked goods, sewing costumes, and wrapping presents for needy children. Well into two in the morning, she dragged her body up the flight of stairs and fell face forward into bed. But, she always managed to wake up on her own without prodding from her mother or her alarm clock. Maybe it had something to do with the smell of freshly brewed coffee and homemade biscuits dripping with butter and thick maple syrup wafting up from the kitchen, tickling her nose, and causing her to sniff deeply. Or maybe it was the sound of doors slamming, shower water splashing, and the radio blasting to the local weather report.

Kira's eyelids fluttered open. The room was still pitch black. The sun wasn't even up! Yet by the sounds of activity coming through her open window, she could tell that several others were already up and had been for some time.

She threw on a robe over her pajamas and drifted over

to the window. On the east horizon, the first rays of sunlight were just beginning to touch the sky, painting streaks of pink and gold across the wisps of clouds hovering low. Closer to her, the sky was still dark with a smattering of stars still winking at her.

She leaned further out the window, trying to catch a glimpse of the cause of the activity going on below her. She could hear excited shouts, and the roar of several engines. Moments later, a line of trucks and men and women on horses came barreling out of the stable and bunkhouse for the Triple J. They cut across the property line and disappeared into a line of trees beyond her sight. By now the sun was rising higher, casting a golden glow over the entire yard.

Kira leaned further out the window, unmindful of the early morning chill, to say a final good-bye to the waning moon and the fading stars.

"Who are you supposed to be? Juliet?"

She started at the intrusion on her morning reflection, bumping her head against the window sash. Rubbing her head with one hand and drawing her robe around her with the other, she stared down into Dylan's amused expression. He stood with his hands on his hips, openly laughing at Kira's distress.

She didn't know which bothered her more—the fact that he'd caught her star gazing or the fact that, for a moment, when she heard his voice, she felt her heart pound as erratically as the fabled Juliet's must have when she found her beloved Romeo lingering outside of her balcony window.

"Juliet was a child who didn't know any better than to let a hormonal adolescent within a hundred yards of her bedroom," Kira replied.

Dylan gave her a half smile and said, "You don't have to worry about me, Juliet. I'm a long way from being an adolescent."

But not from being hormonal? was a question both were conveniently rescued from addressing by the arrival of a dust-covered late model Chevy as it came racing up the drive. The driver blew the horn and shouted, "Come on, lazybones, let's go!"

"On my way!" Dylan called back, hefting a saddle over his shoulder to rest on his back.

"What's going on?" Kira asked.

Dylan turned to the driver and said, "Hold on a sec, Hank."

He then walked until he was directly under Kira's window. "You mean what's all the nonstop, madcap, hurly-burly all about?" He couldn't resist the urge to tease her about the comment she'd made the first night she arrived on the Triple J. "We got wind of a herd of wild horses on the far side of the ranch. We're going to check them out. If they haven't been branded yet, and Baby John doesn't think they have, it's a free for all."

"Oh, well, good luck. Happy hunting, or whatever it is you say when you go off to do your ranching thing."

"What a way to start a mornin'," Hank commented, staring up at Kira's window. "Tell me, Dylan. Does Mama Dodd's daughter always parade around the house in her jammies?"

"I wouldn't know," Dylan said stiffly.

"Might give me more of a reason to accept Manolo's offers to eat up at the big house. If she's half the woman Mama Dodd is, I'd say it would be worth it to find out, don't you, lazybones?"

"Would you just drive, Hank? The horses will be halfway to another county before you get moving," Dylan snapped.

"I wonder if Ms. Dodd would like to come along?" Hank mused aloud. Dylan started to retort, "forget it!" The last thing he needed was for a handful of "hormonal adolescents," as Kira called them, squabbling over who would be the one to keep an eye on her. Then again, Dylan thought as he stroked his chin, he could easily solve that debate by being the one to keep her himself. That should head off any trouble. Now if only he could keep his wits about him while he was watching out for her. So far he hadn't been too successful with keeping his emotions on an even keel. She had an annoying habit of getting under his skin.

Last night was the perfect example of how he seesawed when it came to her. He had been furious with her for accusing Uncle Jimmy of being a swindler. Yet, when he thought that she was in trouble, when the thought that Baby John's rigged lights could hurt her, he'd rushed to her defense. It didn't take his uncle's not-so-subtle reminders that he was standing under the mistletoe. He was the one who framed that design. Though it hadn't occurred to him that he and she would ever be under there at the same time. The way they were dancing around each other for the past few days, it was a wonder they wound up in the same hemisphere at the same time.

Then he realized that the more he fought with her, the closer it drove Jimmy and Myra—and that wouldn't do at all. No, he'd have to try to make peace with Kira. It wasn't enough that she didn't want Myra with Jimmy any more than he did. He wanted her on his side, standing side by side, in a united effort to break them up. He thought a friendly peck on the cheek would do that trick. It would convince her that he was sorry they'd quarreled. But it didn't turn out that way. Instead, she rejected him. She'd run back to her room like a scared rabbit.

"Hold up a minute, Hank," Dylan said, opening the door and leaping out. It was time to draw the rabbit out of her bolting hole.

"Now you're talkin'!" Hank said enthusiastically. Dylan ignored him and sprinted up to Kira's window. He scooped up a handful of small stones and flung them at Kira's window.

"Hey, Juliet!" he shouted, knowing that if the rocks didn't get her attention, the shouting would. Kira flung the window open and said acidly, "I know you ranch people are supposed to get up with the dawn, but do you have to wake up the dead when you do?"

Dylan made a face at her. She couldn't have gone back to sleep that fast. Then again, judging by the rumpled robe and the tousled hair, she just might have crawled back under the covers. He paused with his hand still raised as if to make another stone toss, as the image of Kira, with that mane of wild hair she tried too hard to tame with that demure braid came to his mind.

"What do you want?" she demanded when he didn't speak but only stared, openly appraising her.

"Be down in here in five minutes, Juliet, and you can go."

"Are you kidding?" Kira gasped.

"Now you've got four minutes and forty-five seconds," Dylan responded, tapping his watch for emphasis.

Kira ducked back in and slammed the window shut, but not before Dylan saw the pleased glow of her smile. Did that mean she was ready to make up now? The look she gave him when she thought he was going to kiss her told him that she had at least another full day's hostility inside of her.

Kira leaped into a pair of jeans and a sleeveless cotton shirt while brushing her teeth and splashing cold water on her face. A barrette clipped most of her hair out of the way. She was struggling into her tennis shoes as she hopped down the stairs.

Myra stood at the bottom of the stairs. She'd heard Dylan shout the impromptu invitation and was there waiting with a napkin filled with biscuits and a cup of barely cooled coffee. She also held an oversized plaid shirt in her hands, saying, "It's a little chilly in the mornings around here. But by the time the sun rises, you won't need it."

"Thanks, Mama," Kira said breathlessly, cramming a syrupy biscuit into her mouth and gulping down as much of the coffee as her tongue could stand. She came out of the house still licking syrup from her fingers. Dylan averted his eyes, pretending to be more concerned with the condition of his watch than of the sticky condition of Kira's fingers as her tongue moved over them.

"Ready!" Kira said, breathlessly.

"Not yet," he retorted. With gloved fingers, he brushed the crumbs from around her mouth and chin. Kira complained, meeting his gaze with a mixture of annoyance and amusement.

"Now you're ready. And with fifteen seconds to spare," Dylan teased her.

"Have fun, Kira! And try to stay out of the way." Myra planted a kiss on her daughter's cheek.

"Don't worry, Mama Dodd. I won't let anything happen to her," Dylan promised.

Hank stepped out of the truck and moved to shake Kira's hand.

"Hank Darvin," he introduced himself.

"I know you." Kira gave him a mock glare.

Hank guffawed, causing Kira to wince at the rude disturbance on such a serene morning. "Sorry about your car, ma'am. We're gettin' it taken care of. We'll have that *blankety-blank* roadster back on the road in no time."

"I hope I didn't hold you up too much," Kira apologized.

"Being late does have its advantages," Hank said, smiling broadly at her.

"Let's go," Dylan broke in. "I'll ride shotgun." He held the door open for her and allowed her to climb in first. Kira took the cue from Dylan and climbed into the rear of the truck where an extended cab held a comfortably padded bench seat. Hank kept his eyes trained on her jean-clad bottom as she did so until Dylan snapped the seat back into place with more force than necessary. Hank's grin faded slightly. He shrugged. Couldn't blame a man for trying.

"Strap yourself in good and tight, Ms. Dodd! Here we go!" Hank shouted, revved the engine, then peeled off down the road with a wild whoop that made Kira's ears ring in the confines of the cab.

"So, what's the word on how many horses were sighted?" Dylan asked.

"The nearest Baby John could tell, we could be looking at as many as fifty or sixty wild mustangs with a smattering of domesticated horses mixed in."

"If we could get those back, I know more than a few ranchers who'd be grateful."

"I heard that Harcourt is offering up to two hundred for every horse returned," Hank said. "No questions asked when they're returned."

"Do you have a problem with rustlers?" Kira asked, feeling a little foolish for using a term she'd heard only in Western movies.

"What operation doesn't? It's the curse of having so much area to cover," Dylan supplied.

"We've got line shacks set up at ten-mile intervals. We figure on a clear day, that's the most a person could see and get to a given spot in time to stop anybody they do find where they don't belong," Hank continued. "But . . ."

"But what?"

"But we can't keep every shack filled, twenty-four hours a day, seven days a week, three hundred sixty-five days out of the year. Sometimes we have to pull the manpower where it's most needed."

"Like when you're chasing wild horses?" Kira asked. She leaned between the two seats and asked, "With so much open space you claim the Triple J covers, how do you plan to catch so many horses to see which ones belongs where?"

"We're going to try to pin them in at Ritter's Cut, Ms. Dodd," Hank supplied.

"Ritter's Cut? What's that?"

"You know that spring that Uncle Jimmy told you about?" Dylan added. Kira nodded.

"It's surrounded on two sides by walls of steep rock and scrub brush. There's a narrow path between the walls where runoff from the lake and the spring eventually winds underground again. There's barely enough room for one horse to go through that pass. They'd have to be half mountain goat to get up the sides."

"And if that's the case, we don't want 'em," Hank added with his characteristic guffaw.

"We're going to try to drive them through the wide end and weed them out through the narrow end," Dylan continued.

"Pretty slick." Kira nodded in approval.

"Not a bad plan if I do say so myself."

"Don't let pretty boy here take all of the credit. Molly was the one who suggested not to try to push them all the way back the horse pens."

"Molly?" Kira turned a curious gaze to Dylan, who shifted uncomfortably.

"One of the ranch hands," Hank continued, enjoying the pained look on Dylan's face.

"Duncan Bell's oldest daughter," Dylan volunteered. "Duncan is one of our wranglers."

"Molly comes to the Triple J during school breaks and summers to earn a little pocket change," Hank said.

"So she's not so old." Kira turned to Hank for confirmation.

"No, ma'am! Fresh and dewy. Hard-working girl—and as smart and as pretty as she is hard-working. You know, Ms. Dodd, I think she has a thing for Dylan. She came up with the idea of driving the horses through Ritter's Cut to impress him. In fact, wasn't it you and Molly who found that pass together, Dylan?"

"Yeah . . . Uh . . . I think so . . . I can't remember exactly how it happened."

"Yeah, sure it was! You two said something about going on a ride together . . . out all day and most of the night, if I recall. . . ."

"You've got a hell of a memory, Hank," Dylan muttered. "Convenient, too."

"Well, I'm certainly impressed," Kira said, settling back in her seat. "I'd like to meet Molly. It'll be nice to have another female, someone close to my own age, to talk to."

"I'm sure I can arrange that. Maybe you and she could hang out during the roundup."

"And compare notes," Kira offered. "I'm sure she could teach me a thing or two about roping and riding a wild stallion."

"Look! Isn't that Baby John over there?" Dylan said, pointing out the window to avert their attention.

Hank burst out laughing. "Sure is. This where they must have set up camp." He honked his horn twice and waved out the window.

"I don't see any horses," Kira said, glancing around her, sounding a little disappointed. She saw plenty of parked trucks and a smattering of camping equipment.

"Don't worry. You will," Dylan promised. "Because they're unpredictable, we don't want to set up the bulk of our gear close to the penning area. If they ever got loose, they could stampede and trample all of it to the ground. We take a few necessities in rolls and tie them to our cutting horses."

"Cutting horses?"

"Horses trained to weed out individual livestock," Hank answered.

"Oh."

"How's it going, Baby John?" Dylan waved to his uncle.

Beside Baby John, Dylan's dog Keeper rose to his feet and barked an eager greeting.

"Hey, there, big fellow. Ready to go to work?" Dylan said affectionately, rubbing the shaggy shepherd over his head.

"Looking real good, Dylan. I know they've spotted at least fifty. Good morning, Miss Kira. You're looking rosy this morning. Here to pick out a horse for yourself?"

"Good morning," Kira said, smiling a little shyly. "No, I just came to watch."

"What good is that if you can't pick out a horse?" Baby John sounded indignant.

"I didn't think I was allowed. What's the point, anyway? I'm only going to be here for a while."

"Who said it wasn't allowed. Did Jimmy or Jesse say you couldn't?"

"No." Kira laughed self-consciously.

"And I certainly didn't. Dylan, you didn't tell Miss Kira she couldn't have a horse, did you?"

"I never said a word," Dylan replied.

"Then it's settled. If you see one you want, you just yell. We'll take care of the rest."

Kira glanced back at Dylan, who simply shrugged. She started to reject Baby John's offer. What on earth was she going to do with a horse? She certainly couldn't take it back to Chicago with her.

As if Baby John could read her thoughts he winked at her and said, "Pick yourself out a good one, Ms. Kira. Might give you a good enough reason to come back and visit us."

"I have a good enough reason," Kira responded.

"Oh?" Baby John asked, glancing over at Dylan.

Kira placed her hands on her hips and said caustically, "You don't think coming back to visit my mother is good enough reason to come back?"

"Certainly is," Baby John said in chagrin.

"How far ahead are the others?" Hank asked.

"I just got a call from Duncan Bell on the cellular. They've got them headed in the direction of Ritter's Cut. Give 'em another hour and they'll have them completely hemmed in."

"Then we'd better move."

"Where's Lightning Blue?"

"Tied off a little ways." Baby John pointed.

Dylan retrieved the saddle from the rear of Hank's truck.

"Come on, Ms. Kira. You join me in my Jeep," Baby John said. "There's another campsite near the mouth of the spring. We can see all of the action from there."

"And where I won't be in the way," Kira said, openly resentful of the implication that she would get into trouble. Dylan heard the resentment in her tone and spun around to respond, "He's just trying to make sure you don't get hurt."

"Like protecting me from the Christmas lights?" she suggested acidly.

"Leave her alone, Dylan. She just wants to be where all the action is," Hank intervened. Dylan shot him an evil look.

"It's all right!" Kira said quickly. "Baby John's right. Since I wouldn't have the slightest clue what to do if things got out of hand, I'm better off out of the way."

"Don't worry, Miss Kira. You won't be too far from the action," Baby John assured her. "Just far enough."

"We didn't let Molly get too close her first time out, either," Hank said, wanting another jab at Dylan for making him back down. "So you're in good company, Ms. Kira."

Molly? Baby John wondered why Hank would bring her up. When he caught the look that passed between Dylan and Kira, he immediately knew exactly why Hank had chosen that moment to interject her into the conversation.

"The Jeep's back that way, Miss Kira. Dylan, I've got

Lightning Blue tied off just beyond," Baby John said. "You two go on ahead. I'll be with you in a moment."

Dylan nodded and followed Kira. Baby John then turned to Hank. "What do you think you're doing, Hank?"

"What do you mean, Baby John?"

"Don't get cute with me. You know what I mean. What's this Molly business about?"

Hank shrugged. "Just wanted to make Miss Kira feel at home. She's looking for some female companionship, just like our boy, Dylan."

"Not that kind. You know damned well that Dylan won't have a thing to do with that Molly Bell. She's as sneaky as a snake and as horny as a goat. Any man with a shred of self-respect wouldn't get within ten feet of her."

"Really? I thought she and Dylan had gotten very friendly."

"After that stunt she pulled with tracking him down and throwing herself at him like a shameless—"

"That's not the way Molly tells it. And Duncan Bell believes her. That's two against one."

"If you listen to the other hands, it's fifty to two. Nobody believes that pack of lies that he asked that girl along on that ride. Everybody knows that when Dylan rides fence line, he does it alone. She tracked him. He's just too much of a gentleman to go against her word."

"Come on, Baby John. You can't believe that he resisted her! That sweet young thing? Not if he has an ounce of red blood in his body."

"If Dylan said he never touched her, then he didn't. And you can count that as gospel. It doesn't help matters much with you spreading those filthy lies about him, Hank, or half truths, or whatever you call yourself doing."

"Just trying to make conversation with Miss Dodd."

"Not another word to Miss Kira. Do you hear me? You keep your mouth shut if you want to keep your job."

"Is that a threat, Baby John? Are you threatening me?"

"No, sir. I don't waste my breath on idle threats. You can take that one as a promise, Hank Darvin."

Hank spread his hands. "All right, all right! I'll button my lip. But if you ask me, something is awfully strange about a man who has a beautiful young woman in his sights and doesn't move a muscle to close the distance."

"They're so far away," Kira said as she scrambled up on the hood of Baby John's Jeep and peered across the shallow waters of Ritter's Spring. "How am I supposed to see anything from back here?"

"They're closer than you think," Dylan said. He sat astride his horse, peering through binoculars at the horses and the ranch hands of the Triple J as they drove the horses closer to Ritter's Cut. "Keep these for me. That should help some."

"Thanks," Kira said, taking the binoculars with a grimace. Dylan laughed softly at her downcast expression.

"I know . . . I know . . . it's not like being there. Trust me, it's not all fun and games."

"But better than standing on the outside looking in," she challenged him. She adjusted the binoculars for her small face and raised them to her eyes.

"You're right. But I'm telling you, it's better this way. Like I said, those horses are unpredictable. We've got to drive them hard enough to get them moving in the right direction, but not enough to be a threat to the lead stallion. If he turns the herd while we're braced for the other direction, there could be real trouble."

"Then I suppose I shouldn't keep you from your work," Kira dismissed him.

"You sure you'll be all right back here?"

"If I move back any further, I might as well be back at the Triple J," Kira complained. "Will you stop hovering over me and get to work!"

"All righty then," Dylan said, shifting in his saddle. The movement, though subtle, caught Kira's attention. It wasn't the creaking of the leather saddle or the impatient whinny of Dylan's horse, eager to join the challenging call of the wild horses. Kira wasn't sure if it was a sound at all that caught her attention. It was, as her mind raced to find the right word, more of a mood—an air.

She glanced up at him. For a moment, she had the oddest impression that he was about to kiss her again. He was certainly close enough to do so.

"Have fun, Dylan," Kira said softly—not backing away, but not leaning toward him, either.

"Thanks," he responded, readjusting his grip on the reins. His hands rested easily on the saddle horn. Yet Kira could almost see the tension in his shoulders as he struggled to maintain his easy air. Baby John chose to appear from beyond the bushes at that moment.

"All set, Dylan, boy?" he asked briskly.

Dylan whistled softly for Keeper and backed his horse away from the Jeep. Kira let out the breath she'd been holding expectantly, quietly, so no one would hear her.

"Ready as I'll ever be, Baby John."

"Then get going. Bring us back some real fire breathers!"

Dylan touched his hand to his hat and wheeled around on Lightning Blue. Moments later he was splashing across the shallow part of Ritter's Spring. Again Kira found herself holding her breath. She raised the binoculars to her eyes and let out a cry of delight.

"See one that you like, Miss Kira?" Baby John grinned at her as he followed the direction of her gaze.

"It's all so beautiful!" Kira murmured. "The sun on the water splashes is making a zillion tiny rainbows. I'm not a nature nut but I think I could get used to this!" She lowered the binoculars for just a moment to grin at him, then immediately raised them to her eyes again. She didn't want to miss a moment of this.

"And the horses! So many horses! Just look at them! Brown ones and black ones and spotted ones! Look! Look, Baby John! There's a baby one. A colt! It looks so funny! His legs are still a little shaky. Is that his mama? He never leaves her side."

"I'd say that was a pretty good guess, Miss Kira."

"This is soooo cool! And I'm not even riding in the thick of them."

"I'm just where I want to be. Let the younger ones do all the work. All we'll have to do is sit back and reap the benefits."

"That's not how I expect a hard-working rancher man to talk, Baby John."

"I work hard," he retorted. "But better still, I work smart. The hard work will come in picking out the horses I want."

"The most work and the most fun," Kira laughed at him.

"What's life if you can't enjoy the thing you do the most. Speaking of which, what do you do for a living, Miss Kira?"

"I'm a teacher, like my mother," Kira said.

Baby John chuckled. "I suppose you could have as much fun trying to corral a classroom full of wild kids."

"It's a satisfying job, but not the same," Kira's sigh was almost wistful.

"Sounds like you need a change."

"You mean quit my job? No thanks, Baby John. I may be curious about this lifestyle, even a little envious, but I'm not that crazy."

"I know you've got bills to pay, expenses to cover, stuff you want to buy. But it's all just stuff. And it doesn't sound like you're having much fun accumulating all of it."

"Even if I did decide to take a break, what would I do?"

"Exactly what you're doing now, exploring an option that you never expected you'd have."

"Unexpected is right," Kira returned. "I've only been

here a while and I've had more excitement than I could honestly say I've seen in a month back in Chicago."

"See? There you go. What more could a woman ask for? Quit your job and come back to live with us here on the Triple J. We can offer you everything you have in Chicago and more—a roof over your head, people who care about you."

"Is that how Mr. Jimmy got my mother to jump ship, enticing her to leave everything she knew behind to come out here?"

"I wouldn't know, Miss Kira. I didn't know anything about Myra until Jimmy sent that postcard saying that he'd met someone and he was bringing her home. None of us did. But I'm glad he did. She's good for him. The best thing that's happened to him in a long time."

"If he's half the smooth talker you are, no wonder she was ready to forget her family."

"She didn't forget her family, Miss Kira. She just added to it." Baby John paused dramatically, then said, "You know there's room for at least one more, don't you?"

Kira cleared her throat delicately and said, "I don't think so, Baby John."

"Oh, I do. And I know someone else who's beginning to think so, too."

"You mean Hank Darvin?" Kira teased, knowing fully well that it wasn't Hank to which Baby John was referring.

Baby John laughed again. "No, ma'am. I don't mean Hank, and you know it."

Kira didn't get a chance to respond. Baby John held up a finger saying, "Hold that thought." He looked inside of his shirt pocket where his cellular phone had begun to ring.

"Hello!" he answered cheerfully; he then glanced at Kira. "Speak of the devil. It's Dylan. He says he's picked out a horse for you already. He said that it fits you to a T."

Kira raised her eyebrows in surprise. "Oh, really? Which one?"

"He wants to know can you see him, Miss Kira?"

She raised the binoculars again. From across the lake she caught him waving and gesturing toward a short-legged, full-rumped chestnut mare.

"Give me that," Kira said, reaching for the phone. "I suppose you think that's funny, Dylan Jolivet!"

She cradled the phone to her ear, trying to hear him over the shouts of the ranchers and the thunder of the horses hooves.

"Just trying to be helpful. You know, make you feel part of the action."

"Oh, yeah? Well, while you're at it, you can pick yourself out a gelding, mister. Because that's what you'll wind up being if you come near me with that potbellied pony!"

Through the binoculars, she saw him flash a grin at her, then disappear into the blurring mass of horseflesh. She then handed the phone back to Baby John.

"You don't think he was serious, do you, Baby John?"

"About the horse? No, of course not." Baby John put the phone away. Serious about Kira was another matter. The fact that he took time out to tease her when he should have been concentrating on those horses was a very serious matter. Anything could have happened during that fifteen-second phone call. His horse could have stumbled, he could have fallen off—but not likely. Or the herd could have changed positions on him, pushing against him instead of flowing with him.

The lead stallion was a crafty old horse, caught several times but never branded. More than once he'd been known to make those chasing him think they had him cornered, only to double back, nearly killing the pursuers as he used every trick at his disposal to get away. If that meant trampling the pursuer under his hooves, so be it.

"What's happening now?" Baby John asked. "It seems a little quiet.

"The horses seem to be calmer now. They're milling around but not really going anywhere," Kira reported.

Baby John nodded in approval. "I guess they've got it handled. If you'll excuse me, Miss Kira, I'm going to make another trip into nature's bounty. I shouldn't have drunk so much coffee without eating a good breakfast."

Kira's own stomach rumbled in answer. "I know what you mean. I barely had time to wolf down a few biscuits myself."

"We've got more food stashed at the other campsite. When I come back, we can make a side trip."

"But won't we—" Kira started to object.

"We won't miss much. The rest is just grunt work. The exciting part, chasing them down, is over."

Kira nodded, then settled down cross-legged on the hood of the Jeep to watch. She turned her head once to wave to Baby John as he disappeared into the woods, but immediately turned her attention back to the horses. Baby John's prediction seemed to be correct. She noticed the change in the ranchers' attitude.

In the beginning of the roundup, they'd been excited, full of nervous energy as they drove the horses closer and closer toward Ritter's Cut. Once they had them penned, their pace slowed to easy, relaxed canters as they circled around the herd.

After sitting still for so long, Kira started to feel sleepy— almost lethargic. She leaned back against the windshield, letting the sun and the breeze blowing off the spring lull her. She tried valiantly to keep her attention trained on the activity going on across the lake. When shouts drifted across, she raised the binoculars to witness the cause of the commotion. But the shouts were coming less and less as the ranchers went on about their business. They seemed to be getting the job done with simple hand signals. The less they could spook the horses, the better. Without the commotion, the motion, or the noise to keep her alert, Kira felt the strain of the past few days settle into her.

Kira didn't realize she'd drifted off to sleep until she was jarred awake by the sound of thunder. She'd curled up on the hood of the jeep, cradling the binoculars in her arms. Sleepily, she cracked one eye open. Was it going to rain? How could it? There wasn't a cloud in the sky.

But there was. Kira frowned. Hovering over her was a big pink-nosed spotted cloud. Followed by a black one, and a reddish one . . . snorting and driving up a cloud of dust that blocked out the sun.

Spotted?

Kira shot up straight, dropping the binoculars in sheer, unadulterated panic as she found herself suddenly surrounded by the herd she'd admired from afar.

"Baby John!" she called out, scrambling to unfurl her legs. She backpedaled on the hood of the Jeep, sliding against the windshield. When her hand contacted the glass, heated by the sun, she cried out again—in pain as much as in fear. She stood up, trying to move away from the source of the heat.

Startled by her cries and the sudden movement, one of the horses reared. Its hooves waved what seemed like inches from her head. Kira froze, in awe of the magnificent animal prancing before her. It was golden brown with a mane and tail the color of corn silk. Kira blocked out everything but the sight, the sound, and the smell of the horse as it neighed and blew a stream of hot air from its flaring nostrils.

A challenge or a greeting? Kira didn't have time to figure it out. One moment she was eye-to-belly with the rearing horse, the next she was dragged off of the hood of the Jeep and jammed into the saddle of another horse.

"What's the matter with you?" Dylan said harshly in her ear. "Didn't you hear me calling to you? Warning you to get into the Jeep? I knew I shouldn't have brought you along! I just knew it!"

"Did you see that?!" Kira said excitedly, unmindful of his scathing comment. "Did you see that, Dylan? He came right up to me!" Kira twisted in the saddle, trying to get another look at the horse.

"She," he corrected. "She came right up to you and almost smashed your fool head in." He pulled against the reigns and backed Lightning Blue away from the Jeep. The horses that had surrounded Kira continued to flow past them, but shifted as the big spotted Appaloosa cut a path through them.

"She was just saying hello," Kira retorted. Then added on impulse, "She's the one, Dylan! She's the one I want!"

"Have you lost your mind? That horse could have killed you, Kira!"

"Maybe I have!" Kira laughed openly, giddily. "But she's the one I want. We were meant for each other. I knew it that moment I looked into those big brown eyes. Please, Dylan. That's the one! Get her for me."

"And what do I get out of it if I do?" he murmured against Kira's ear.

Kira considered the question carefully. She considered every nuance that would make him ask such a question in the way that he had, low and full of timbre, meant only for her ears. She considered the reassuring, and overtly intimate arm he'd wound around her waist when he pulled her from the Jeep and placed her in the saddle with him. She considered the subtle, suggestive rocking motion of the horse as he walked Lightning Blue away from the rest of the horses. She thought about the thudding of his heart that she felt through his chest and the way it made her feel, pressed against her slender back.

"Well, Kira?" he prompted when she didn't respond.

"Catch the horse first and we'll talk about reciprocation later."

"Reciprocation wasn't the word I was thinking of . . . but we can talk about that later, too," he replied.

Dylan then grasped her arm and helped her swing to the ground.

"Wait here. You should be safe enough. If the horses turn again, scramble up that tree. You can climb a tree, can't you?"

"To keep from getting trampled, you bet I could. Is that what happened, Dylan? Why they came across the lake?"

He nodded tightly. "That lead stallion—"

"Tricked you, didn't he? Thought you had him penned?"

"Something like that. He let us get a few of the horses through the cut. Only the older ones, though—the ones who probably only have one or two foals left in them. He got the younger ones to turn and rush us."

Kira chuckled at the idea, then quickly squashed the laughter when she caught Dylan's expression.

"I don't see anything to laugh about. They could have killed you, Kira. Where was Baby John? Why did he leave you alone like that?"

"I don't know. The last thing I remember, he had to go back into the woods and . . . you know . . . handle nature's business."

"I'll handle his business," Dylan threatened.

"That's no way to talk about your uncle, Dylan."

"He should have been keeping an eye on you!"

"I'm a grown woman. I can keep an eye on myself!" Kira flared.

"I'll remind you that you said that the next time you're surrounded by a herd of wild mustangs!" he retorted.

"What makes you think there'll be a next time?" she challenged.

"Oh, that's right. I forgot. You'll be leaving in a week."

"That's right," she said, though Baby John's offer to stay sounded more appealing to her than she wanted to admit.

"So what do you need a horse for?"

When he saw her face fall in disappointment, Dylan instantly regretted that he'd taunted her. To show that he didn't really mean it, he pulled a lariat from the saddle and said curtly, "I'll be back."

By habit, Kira reached for the binoculars, then said, "Uh-oh." They were probably a pile of twisted metal and glass by now. The fact that it could have been her stomped under the feet of those horses sobered her just as much as Dylan's warning.

It didn't take him long to toss the lasso over Goldie's neck, as Kira had come to think of that beautiful horse. She hadn't strayed too far from the Jeep. That was a sign to Kira that what she'd said about what was meant to be rang true.

Panting slightly, Dylan brought the horse up to Kira and handed her the lead rope.

"Here ya go, Kira. But I've got good news and bad news for you."

Kira looked up at him expectantly. "What's the good news?"

"She's a lot tamer than I thought she'd be. She's probably already broken to a saddle."

"And the bad news?"

"She's carrying a local brand. She belongs to one of the ranches around here."

"Oh," Kira said, her face crumpling again. She reached out and tentatively stroked the soft, warm sides of the golden horse. "Maybe it wasn't meant to be, then, Dylan."

"Don't give up yet," he urged her. "I'll tell you what, Kira. Let me ask around. See what I can do. Maybe we can work something out."

"You'd . . . you'd do that for me?"

"Yes, Kira Dodd, I'd do that for you."

"What kind of horse is she?" Kira asked, stroking the warm, velvet flanks.

"A Palomino," he responded.

"She's beautiful. Thank you, Dylan!"

He wheeled around, suddenly uncomfortable by the warm look flooding her face. She'd done it to him again! Made him forget that he was supposed to be upset with her. He should have known better than to bring her out here when anything could happen to her. But she'd looked so happy when he'd asked her along on the roundup. How could he refuse a look like that?

Before he left, he warned, "Hold on tight to her, Kira. And whatever you do, try to stay awake this time!"

Chapter Nine

Kira could barely keep her eyes open. The warm glow of the campsite fire mingled with the full, satisfying meal provided by Manolo had her nodding as she sat on the back of Hank's truck. The conversation was a constant low hum that competed with the sharp trill of crickets. Someone offered her a blanket, and moments later she was stretched out on the bed of the truck—yawning and blinking as she watched the stars wink back at her.

"So, what did you think, Miss Kira?"

Baby John slammed his hand against the truck, startling her as he leaned over the edge. "Did you have a good time?"

"It was a blast!" Kira said, and yawned behind her hand—a yawn that made her jaws ache and her eyes tear.

"Now you'll have a tale to tell your grandchildren. A heck of a lot more exciting than about the time you spent the day finger painting, don't you think?"

Kira laughed and said self-consciously, "Grandchildren?

Aren't you rushing things just a bit, Baby John? I'm not even in the market for a husband."

"Well, don't you think you ought to get to the mall, lady? You're young and you're pretty and you're smart. But that won't last always."

"Thanks, Baby John. I feel so much better now!" Kira retorted.

"I just call 'em like I see 'em. God didn't mean for folks to go through life solo."

"What about you?" Kira turned the tables on him. "Why aren't you married with a zillion kids of your own?"

"I came close to it." Baby John said quietly. "Her name was Carolyn. The most wonderful woman on earth, and for a time, she was all mine!"

A cloud passed over his face, making Kira wish that she hadn't asked him the question. She squashed her curiosity that would have made her naturally ask, "What happened to her?"

Baby John took the initiative and answered the unasked question. "She married someone else and moved away."

"I'm sorry," Kira said simply. She admired the valiant way he tried to hide his pain with nonchalance.

"So was I. But I can't say I blame her. She married the better man."

"Oh, I don't believe that!" Kira said, placing a comforting hand on his arm.

"It's true, Miss Kira. He was everything I wasn't. Rich, successful, and handsome as the devil. But more important to Carolyn, he lived a life that had nothing to do with the dawn-to-dusk dealings with horses, cows, or goats or any other four-legged creature that roam God's green earth. Ranch life was all she'd ever known, all I could ever give her. So, when someone came along who offered her something different, she jumped at the chance."

"What . . . what does he do?" Kira asked, swallowing hard the lump forming in her throat. She didn't know how long ago this happened. But she knew by the pain she saw reflected in his face that the wounds were as fresh as if it had all happened yesterday. Kira tried to imagine the kind of woman that Baby John would consider wonderful.

Baby John shrugged again and said quietly, "Did. He's dead now. They both are."

"No! Oh, no! What happened?" This time she couldn't hold back the exclamation.

"Their plane crashed on their way back from a vacation."

"Back? Back to where? Back here? You don't mean to the Triple J?"

Baby John nodded once tightly.

"Why would they come back here?"

"They didn't have a choice. Before they left, they gave me, Jesse, and Jimmy the chance of a lifetime—the chance to take care of their son while they were away."

"I don't understand," Kira said, thoroughly confused now. What she refrained from saying was how twisted and sadistic it was for this Carolyn to leave Baby John with such a huge responsibility. It must have been torture for him— to know that the woman he loved didn't want him, but had no qualms about leaving her child with him while she went off with another man.

"Don't look like that, Miss Kira," Baby John said, taking note of her expression. "It wasn't like that at all! No, I didn't marry Carolyn, but she was still like family. You see, it was my brother she married, my brother Daniel. The child she left with us was Dylan."

"Dylan," Kira echoed, automatically searching for him around the campsite. She caught sight of him waving a stick over the open flames. She saw him reach into his jacket pocket and pull out a candy bar. When he removed the stick from the flames, he jammed several marshmallows onto the end. Holding the stick in one hand, he ripped open the candy bar with his teeth, then broke off a couple of squares. Kira's mouth watered appreciatively as the sweet, rich chocolate of the candy melted into the slightly charred marshmallows. All he needed now, she thought greedily, was a couple of graham crackers.

"I suppose I never married and had kids of my own because I consider Dylan mine as much as I would if he were my flesh and blood. I can't watch him, or listen to him, or think of him without thinking about my Carrie and Daniel. I have more than their memories to keep me going. I have their living legacy."

"Oh, Baby John! That's the saddest, most beautiful thing I've ever heard!" Kira said, clasping her hands to her heart.

"You think so?"

Baby John's demeanor suddenly changed. He went from the sad, woebegone look of a dejected lover to the jolly old favorite uncle that he'd been since she arrived.

Kira felt as if she'd lived a lifetime since arriving on the Triple J. She found herself caught up in the lives and the loves of the men who ran this ranch as easily as she found herself caught up in her own mother's affairs.

"Glad you think so, Miss Kira," Baby John went on. "Because every word's the truth—except for that little part in the beginning. And maybe some in the middle. Oh, I think I added a little embellishment to make it interesting in the end, too."

"What!" Kira squawked in indignation. "You made it up! You made it all up! The whole story? The love of your life! The plane crash! Everything!"

"Now there's a tale to tell your grandkids." Baby John grinned at her, and rocked back on her heels to avoid the swing she took at him.

Her commotion drew Dylan's attention. He dusted the graham cracker dust from his fingers absently as he headed over to the truck.

"What's going on?" he asked, looking from Kira to Baby John.

"You wouldn't believe the whopper your uncle just told me!" Kira cried out.

Dylan started to grin, knowingly. "He told you that tale about my folks—Daniel and Carolyn."

Kira nodded, her eyes widening.

"He gets all the newcomers to the Triple J with that. Call it an initiation, if you will."

"What I'll call it is cruel," Kira countered. "All this time I was thinking how awful it must have been for you, and how noble you were for taking in an orphan; and it was all a great big joke to you!"

"I thought she had a better sense of humor than that," Baby John said, spreading his hands. He glanced at the stick Dylan carried and said, "Maybe that will sweeten that disposition a little bit. Got enough to share?"

"Sure," Dylan said, sliding onto the back of the truck next to Kira and offering her a sample. "Careful, now, it's still hot."

"Oooh! Ouch ... it is hot!" she exclaimed as she pinched a little off the end and took an experimental sample, followed by, "Ummm, this is so good!" When melted chocolate dribbled down her finger, she stuck it into her mouth.

Dylan quickly averted his eyes. He wished she wouldn't do that. He looked up at Baby John and caught him grinning at him.

"Well, I think I'll go over and take another look at those mustangs. See you back at the house, Miss Kira." Baby John excused himself with an encouraging clap on Dylan's back. He whispered something to Dylan as he passed. Kira wasn't sure, but she thought it sounded suspiciously like, "Merry Christmas."

"So, what was my mother's initiation?" Kira asked as Baby John walked away.

"One of Manolo's concoctions," Dylan told her, then recounted the story of Myra and the *dulce media del fuego*.

Kira couldn't help herself. She laughed, despite feeling a little guilty for laughing at her mother's expense.

"She took it very well," Dylan assured her.

"I'm sure she did. Mama always did have a flair for comedy," Kira said. As she reached for another marshmallow, she said, "So is this how you Jolivet men treat your women?"

"What do you mean?" Dylan asked. What did she mean, their *women*? There was only one woman everyone was concerned about. That was Myra. And she'd made it clear that she wasn't going back to Chicago. That left only Kira. But she couldn't be considered anyone's woman. She was going back at the end of next week. Wasn't she?

"I mean bribing them with food. From the moment I arrived in Murray, I've been tempted on all sides by pecan pies, peach cobblers, steak the size of the original cow, enough salad to feed an army, and now this. . . ."

"Who else has been offering you food, tempting you to stay?" Dylan teased, holding the marshmallow stick out of her grasp.

"Nobody in particular."

"Who?" Dylan insisted, holding the marshmallow just within reach and snatching it away again.

"Just that guy at the gas station," Kira said, reaching around him.

"Eldrick?" Dylan gave a derisive snort. "The motor mouth of Murray? Oh, yeah. I could see where a lady would be really tempted by him." He easily avoided her attempts to take the entire stick away from him.

"I never said I yielded to that temptation," Kira returned, smiling angelically at him. After several near misses, she stopped struggling and folded her hands primly in her lap.

Dylan looked warily at her, wondering what her next plan of attack would be. He never knew what to expect from this woman. One moment she was calm and composed and cute—as she was at dinner the first night she arrived on the Triple J. The next minute she was all claws and fangs, digging into him verbally, viciously—making him draw up to protect himself as carefully as he had from that dog attack.

"Maybe it takes more than a little sweet talk to get to you," Dylan offered.

"Maybe," Kira said coyly. She looked up at him again and smiled when he edged closer to her.

What would it take to get to her, Dylan wondered. Could it be the same thing it took that had helped her get to him? That's exactly what she'd done—gotten to him. It took watching her nearly getting trampled by those mustangs, a wrench to the heart if ever he had one, to realize that.

From the moment he saw her outside of the feed store in town, she'd been on his mind almost every waking moment. What was it about those Dodd women that turned the minds of the Jolivet men to mush? He couldn't eat, think, or even breathe without wondering what Kira would think of him for doing so. Was this what it was like for Uncle Jimmy? Was this what he felt whenever he looked at Myra Dodd?

Dylan tried to picture his Uncle Jimmy on the cruise, head over heels in love with Myra. The gut-wrenching, head-whirling feelings that might have been attributed to seasickness, cured by a double dose of Dramamine, instead were turning into a headstrong, headlong march toward matrimony. Dylan didn't think his Uncle Jimmy could put the skids on even if he wanted to. He was a man totally enraptured by that woman. He didn't want to be saved.

He glanced down at Kira, still waiting patiently for him to share. With a resigned sigh Dylan relinquished the sticky treat to her. Laughing softly in triumph, Kira took the offering and pinched off a portion to cram into her mouth. Munching contentedly, she scooted even closer to him so that her shoulder brushed his. The warmth of her skin, the glow of laughter in her eyes, the temptation of her sweet lips beckoned to him. Casually, Dylan draped his arm around her shoulder. His palm rested easily on her arm, caressing, possessive.

Instead of pulling away, Kira emitted a soft murmur. Sleepily, she rested her head against his chest and closed her eyes. Seconds later, he felt her sigh deepen into long, regular breaths. Her head grew heavy against him. Just that quickly, she was asleep. He couldn't blame her. He was dead tired himself. But, as his uncle Baby John was fond of saying, it was a good tired. They'd made a good find today. Over 70 percent of the mustangs were unbranded. Once the others were weeded out and returned to their owners, the remainder would bring new fire to the Jolivet livestock bloodline.

He especially liked the looks of that Palomino mare that Kira had picked out. He smiled in gentle wonder. It would be more correct to say that the horse had picked her. If he lived to be a hundred, he would never figure out why the horse hadn't knocked her flat. Maybe it was the fact that the horse was tamed that saved her life. The way she'd taken to the Palomino made him believe that maybe there was more cowgirl to Kira Dodd than she realized.

As if she could sense him thinking about her, Kira snuggled closer, resting her palm between her cheek and his chest. Dylan then leaned back against the bed of the truck to make them both more comfortable. He brought his other arm around to embrace her and to shield her from the cooling breeze blowing across the lake. Lying as she was, he could feel the beating of her heart—a strong, steady rhythm that was in marked contrast to the rapid, erratic beating of his own.

She was getting too close. It was getting too hard to consider her an enemy. When he could have been using this quiet, intimate moment to work through a plan to put some distance between Myra and Jimmy, he was instead trying to put as little space between himself and Kira as he could possibly manage. Sitting there, with the prospect of a prosperous winter before him and Kira nestled in his arms, all was right with the world. Dylan rolled his eyes skyward. Heaven help him. He suddenly realized that he didn't want to be saved, either.

"Save some of those for the guests," Myra warned, slapping at Jimmy's hand as he scooped up a handful of mixed nuts and tiny mints that she'd set out. She moved around the family room, laying out the costumes that she'd helped to alter for the pageant participants, queuing holiday music on the stereo, and refilling the snack dishes that Jimmy had emptied.

"But I'm hungry," Jimmy complained.

"Then go into the kitchen and fix yourself something to eat," Myra chastised.

"There's nothing in there that I like. That's why I sent Dylan and Manolo into town."

"I saw the list of junk that you sent them after," Myra said, shaking her head and *tsking* at Jimmy. "I crossed off half of it and put on more fruits and vegetables."

"You're going to be the death of me, woman, with all of this healthy eating."

"Eating better isn't going to kill you." Myra laughed, affectionately patting Jimmy around his midsection.

"Sure it will." Jimmy grinned at her. "I'm going to waste away to nothing."

"You'll be wasting away a long time before that happens," she teased in turn. "But don't get too skinny. I like my man solid so that when I hold on, I can really hold on."

Jimmy grasped Myra's arm and coaxed her to encircle him. "You mean like this?"

"More like this," she corrected, tightening her grip.

"I can handle that," Jimmy said. He began humming

along to the album on the stereo. His voice, soft and low, followed in perfect time to a soulful rendition of one of Myra's favorite songs—the Temptations's version of "Silent Night." Jimmy swept her around the floor, swaying gently back and forth, reaffirming that the woman he held in his arms belonged there. When that record ended and an up-tempo song took its place, Jimmy relinquished his grip just enough to swing Myra out, then snap her back into his arms again.

Laughing until she was almost out of breath, Myra allowed herself to be twirled around and around until her head spun. But she kept time to Jimmy's steps as easily as if they'd been dancing together all their lives.

That's how Dylan found them, laughing, singing, and dancing—unmindful of the preparations still left to complete for the guests who would descend on them this evening. He paused in the doorway, resting his latest purchase against the wall. When the music ended, Jimmy drew Myra back into his arms, bent her over backwards into a dip that belied their years, and gave her kiss—deep and passionate, so that even Dylan shifted uncomfortably. Instead of backing away, however, he cleared his throat loudly to draw their attention to him.

"Do you two partridges in a pear tree want to give it a rest and check out the tree that I picked out?" he demanded, but he was smiling despite himself.

Jimmy and Myra broke apart like guilty teenagers. Myra touched her hand to her hair, trying to restore some order to her holiday hairdo. Jimmy wiped a thin bead of perspiration from his forehead as Myra cleared her throat delicately and indicated the residual lipstick stains on Jimmy's face.

"Cut the cords, Dylan, boy. Let's see what ya got," Jimmy said, helping Dylan to drag the eight-foot Douglas fir to the far corner of the room.

"Put it into the stand first," Myra directed to the metal

red and green tree stand that she had waiting. "Careful, now. Don't let the tree fall."

"We know what we're doing, Myra. We've been doing this for quite a few . . . Watch out!" Jimmy shouted as the tree leaned to one side and then the other. Dylan was quick enough to catch the falling fir before it crashed through a window. Jimmy glanced back in chagrin and said, "Okay, Myra. We've got it now. See if you can tighten the screws around the trunk."

Myra stared dubiously at the two Jolivets as they held a tighter purchase on the tree.

"Don't worry, Mama Dodd," Dylan assured her. He met her gaze openly, communicating the sentiment that he thought simple words could not convey. "We won't let it fall on you. *I* won't let it fall."

"All right," Myra said evenly. Yet she was surprised to hear the heartfelt assurance from Dylan. Since she'd come to the Triple J, he'd been distantly respectful to her— never giving her a direct indication that he didn't want her there, but never fully making her feel welcome, either. If it weren't for the argument between him and Kira that Jimmy had told her about, she would never have any indication of his true feelings for her.

Now, as he held the tree steady while she knelt down to tighten the four screws, she wondered if even that display of temper could be attributed to his true feelings. He'd been obviously angry when he'd uttered those hurtful words, spurred on by Kira's inflammatory accusation.

Since they'd come back from that roundup a couple of days ago, she'd noticed a difference in Dylan's treatment toward her. It was nothing that she could put a finger on, for Dylan was not a man of grand expression. Following in the footsteps of his Uncle Jimmy, Dylan doled out his emotional displays in tight, carefully directed bursts. For the past couple of days, she had more occasion to observe the difference in him because he spent more time around the house.

That, in itself, was a change in his behavior. When she first arrived, Dylan used almost any excuse to keep away from her—taking off on his horse or in his truck at a moment's notice. He worked from sunup to sundown, offering to help anyone with their chores, if his were not enough to keep him occupied, until long past the time when Myra retired for the night. Now, he finished his work in record time and spent the remaining daylight hours finding duties that kept him close to the house.

If anyone remarked on his sudden attachment to home, he insisted that he was only trying to stay close to Sun Morning. It was a convenient enough explanation. Everyone knew that Dylan had raised that mare from a colt. He babied her as he would his own child. He wanted to make sure the birth of the first foal from Sun Morning went without problems. But Myra wasn't so quick to accept that explanation. There were only so many hours in the day he could curry her, only so many times he could check her water and feed bins.

It was Dylan's reaction to Kira that made her think that maybe Jimmy's plan to unite them had a slim chance of succeeding. Too many times she found them standing a little too close, staring a little too long, all the while denying to anyone who would listen that anything had changed between them.

"There, I think that's got it," Myra murmured, crawling out from underneath the tree and brushing a few stray pine needles from the palms of her hands.

"I think it's a good idea letting the guests help us decorate, Myra." Jimmy indicated the boxes of ornaments stacked in the corner.

"I thought it might help get everyone in the Christmas spirit."

"Even Miss Scrooge?" Dylan commented with a nod

toward the ceiling where he knew Kira's room was. "She could use a dose of good cheer." He pulled his knife from its sheath and slit the webbing holding the Douglas fir in place. When the branches remained mashed together, he ran his hands along the sides to even out the squashed branches.

"Don't you two make a lovely couple," Kira commented from the doorway, remarking more on Dylan's preoccupation with the tree than on Myra and Jimmy's arm-in-arm stance. She'd heard Dylan's comment, and in keeping with the charade of caustic animosity, had to respond.

Dylan snapped the knife shut and spun around to face her. He opened his mouth to reply, then thought better of it as the next record fell into place. He glanced over at Myra and Jimmy, already starting to cut a step to Chuck Berry's up-tempo "Run, Run, Rudolf." Myra gave Dylan a barely perceptible wink before Jimmy spun her away from the tree toward the center of the room.

Slowly, deliberately, Dylan approached Kira, crooking his finger at her with a devilish gleam in his eyes.

"Oh, no. Don't you dare!" she mouthed but she was laughing as he grasped her by the hand and pulled her into the middle of the family room floor. "I can't, I don't know how to . . ." Kira began, then fell silent when Dylan's expert guidance brought her into perfect time with the rhythm of the music. With that token protest swiftly out of the way, she fell easily in time with Dylan's light step. He swung her out and back again into his arms, keeping her moving so quickly that she didn't have time to think or worry what everyone must think of her. He kept his gaze locked with hers, so that when that record ended and the next one fell into place, she hardly noticed that transition. Though the artist was different and the tempo had slowed dramatically, she stayed exactly where she was, exactly where she wanted to be. Kira's small hands were eclipsed in Dylan's as he pressed her close, laying her head against his chest like it had been the night of the mustang roundup. She would have been content to stay there all day and all night if the sound of a car horn hadn't broken the moment.

"They're here!" Myra exclaimed with just as much dismay. She flew apart from Jimmy, making one last survey of the room before heading for the front door. "Come on, Jimmy."

Kira hung back self-consciously. Though she'd helped Myra to prepare for this party, she didn't feel quite prepared herself. She'd avoided the trip into town to shop for clothing more appropriate to the occasion. She kept telling herself that any day now she'd pack up her few things and return to Chicago. Every day that passed, she gave another excuse why she didn't have to go into Murray to shop for more things. So far everything she'd worn was perfect for tromping back and forth from the stables and the bird pens. For tonight's affair, she'd put on her nicest blouse and another pair of jeans, but she still felt awkward.

"Dylan, did you bring those packages from Murray?" Jimmy asked in passing as he started to join Myra to greet their guests.

"Oh yeah, I almost forgot." Dylan snapped his fingers in remembrance. "And just so you'll know, I put back on the list some of the stuff that Mama Dodd scratched off."

"Even the extra crunchy cheese curls?"

"Even the extra crunchy cheese curls, Uncle Jimmy."

Jimmy smiled in gratitude, then quickly composed his features when Myra flashed him a disproving look. "That's fine and good, but I asked Manolo to make a special purchase for me."

"Oh . . . that. I left it upstairs in her room."

Kira wondered what special purchase Jimmy had in store for her mother. For a moment she considered that it might be an engagement ring. The thought made her stomach turn flips. When "Jimmy" had been only a name on a postcard, the thought of her mother uniting with him scared her to death. Seeing them together now, how much in love they seemed to be, Kira grew nervous for her mother. This was such a big step, but Myra seemed to know what she was doing. If Jimmy chose tonight to propose to Myra, Kira was certain that she would have nothing but blessings and well wishes for them.

"A surprise for my mother?" Kira asked, probing for information. "Is it bigger than a breadbox?"

"Dylan?" Jimmy prompted, giving him permission to respond.

"I'd say about so big," Dylan replied, spanning Kira's waist with his hands. "And not for your mother. For you."

"For me?" Kira echoed, giving them both a puzzled look.

"Something to put you in a more festive mood, Ms. Dodd," Jimmy said. "I hope it fits. I only had Dylan's say-so on the sizing."

"I think I got it right," Dylan replied, giving Kira's waist a light squeeze before spinning her around and urging her back upstairs. "Go check it out before everybody else gets here."

"I don't know what to say," Kira began. She wasn't sure she should say thank you until she saw the results of their collaboration. The last time one of those Jolivet men tried to surprise her, she wound up with her rental car in the repair shop.

"You don't have to say anything, Miss Kira. Call it an early Christmas present from my family to yours," Jimmy said graciously.

"Thank you, Mr. Jimmy," Kira said, genuinely grateful whether the surprise turned out to be a disaster or not. Jimmy's heart was in the gift, and that's what she took into account. "I'll be down in a sec."

Kira took the stairs two at a time. She pushed open the door to her room. Sitting on her bed was a shopping bag bearing the name of a local boutique. Inside the bag were two boxes—one medium-sized box wrapped in gold foil paper and surrounded by a red bow, and a shoebox decorated in the same manner. Shaking her head, she murmured, "What did those big southern softies do?"

Carefully she ran a fingernail along the edge of the larger box to open it without destroying the festive wrapping. Once she pulled off the top and folded back the tissue paper, she gave a tiny gasp of delight. The box held a black dress made of soft rayon. Simple but elegant, the dress would wear well on any occasion. The shoebox held a pair of black, mid-heeled leather pumps with a selection of clip-on garnishes.

"Thank you," she murmured again. "Thank you so much!" It only took a couple of seconds for Kira to strip out of the blouse and jeans and into the dress. With the new look, she spent more time rearranging her hair.

The sound of caroling and laughter from the family room drifted up to beckon her downstairs. Kira smiled, then softly joined in on one of the familiar songs. She dusted a light covering of powder over her face and applied a smidgen of eye shadow and mascara. Then she pursed her lips to add a shade of lipstick. After dabbing cologne behind her ears and on her wrists, she went downstairs to rejoin her mother.

By now, the sounds coming from the family room indicated a full-fledged party. A chorus of voices competed with the stereo for a heartfelt if not slightly off-key version of "Silent Night." She hovered by the door, working up the nerve to go inside. When Kira stepped through the door, several pairs of eyes swiveled in her direction. The singing stopped; even the stereo was muted. Kira suddenly felt very self-conscious again, even with the new dress. Her eyes swept the crowded room, searching for a friendly face to help bolster her courage. She looked for Jimmy with the intention of thanking him for the present. She also looked for Dylan. Part of her wanted to thank him for picking this dress out for her. Part of her needed to know if he got as much pleasure seeing her in it as he had buying it for her.

"Everyone, I'd like you to meet my daughter Kira." Myra appeared at her side. She grasped Kira by the shoulders and propelled her to the center of the room.

"Hello," Kira said, limply lifting her hand then letting it fall to her side again.

"Kira, this is Danny Ralston and his wife Tessa." Myra used Kira's shoulders to pivot her in their direction. A tall, gangly man, draped in a maroon-colored tunic, stepped forward and offered his hand. His wife, equally as tall, eclipsing Kira with her height, offered her hand.

"How do you do? It's a pleasure to meet you," Tessa said formally, then broke into a wide, open grin. "You look just like your Mom!"

"Nice to meet you, too," Kira said, made uneasy by the comparison. She was not her mother. She didn't know if she would be able to charm the citizens of Murray as quickly as Myra seemed to have. She didn't want to ruin the niche her mother made for herself here. If they didn't like the daughter, would that reflect on how they would treat the mother?

When Tessa Ralston smiled warmly, without a hint of judgment, Kira smiled back and relaxed. The next couple took their cue from the Ralstons and greeted Kira with unrestrained enthusiasm—shaking her hand, kissing her cheek, and offering her a hearty welcome and genuine well wishes. By the time she was introduced to all of the neighbors and ranch helpers, her only fear was that she would forget a name.

"Here you are, Kira. Try this on," Myra suddenly thrust a costume into her hands.

"But I'm not going to . . ." Kira began, then clamped her mouth shut. The annual Murray Christmas pageant was a big event to these townspeople. If she refused to participate, would they take back their welcome? Would they think she was a snob? "Okay, Mama. I'll try on the costume. What could it hurt?"

Myra smiled and nodded. "That's the spirit! When you've gotten dressed, step up on that stool so I can adjust the hem." Myra raised her voice for the benefit of the others. "The rest of you, let me know how your costumes fit. I'll get to you as soon as I can."

Myra moved through the room, tape measure slung around her neck, scissors in one hand, and a tomato-shaped pincushion strapped to her wrist. Someone started a stack of albums to play again. By the time Myra made it to Kira, she and Tessa Ralston were caught up in a duet—with Tessa's practiced alto joining easily with Kira's somewhat rusty soprano.

Myra indicated the stool with a nod of her head without interrupting Tessa and Kira. Grasping the skirt to keep from tripping, Kira stepped up as Myra knelt down with a mouth full of pins.

"Hey, I know what would go great with that costume. With your coloring and the shape of your face . . ." Tessa began, grabbing Kira by the hand. Kira wobbled on the stool, and held out her hands. "Whoa, Tessa!" Kira tried to curb the young woman's enthusiasm.

"Careful, sweetheart!" Myra warned, holding the stool steady. "You can't go anywhere. I'm in mid-pin."

"Sorry, Tessa. Looks like I'm stuck here for a while," Kira gave an apologetic shrug.

"Stay here, then, Kira. I'll be right back."

With his back to the party, Dylan busied himself with trimming a few damaged branches from the Douglas fir. He'd made the obligatory rounds, saying hello to his neighbors and coworkers, then bowed gracefully out of the limelight. This was Myra's party. She'd put a lot of effort into helping to make the annual Murray pageant a success. It was her turn to shine.

The only thing that could drag him away from his private refuge was the sight of Kira in her new dress. That dress! What he had to go through to get it. Of course, he'd never admit to anyone the pains a few pieces of cloth could give him.

When he and Manolo arrived in Murray, he had to work himself up for a full ten minutes before stepping foot into the froufrou frilly boutique that Manolo told him carried the finest quality ladies' clothing.

"How do you know about this place?" Dylan asked, dubiously eyeing the store. Everything about the wholly feminine shop overwhelmed his senses—from the cachets of potpourri set on top of lace doily-covered tables to the partially clad mannequins displaying gossamer gauze lingerie.

Manolo laid a finger on the side of his nose and said, "A gentleman should never kiss and tell, *patrón*. But this is a special occasion, *verdad*? Maybe while you look around for something for the señorita, I'll find something for all of mine."

"All?" Dylan mouthed as Manolo plunged into his shopping task with enthusiasm. Cackling gleefully, he murmured aloud selections for all of the female companions on his shopping list. Dylan had no such list. There was only one woman he was concerned about.

"Let's just get something and go," Dylan hissed when the perky sales assistant trailed him from one corner of the store to the next, offering to model anything he selected. Dylan made sure that he stayed away from the lingerie section.

It didn't take him and Manolo very long to pick out the item they wanted. It had gotten down to two selections— the one Kira wore tonight and a white one trimmed in some kind of glittery gold thread. Manolo had picked that one—saying that it would make Kira look like the *ángelita* she was. Dylan remembered laughing.

"Angel? Tell me, Manolo. Have you ever seen that woman when she's mad? I mean really mad?"

"No, *patrón*. I believe you're the only one who's ever had the pleasure of rousing that kind of anger in her."

"With that wild hair and those blazing eyes . . . I'm here to tell you that 'angel' isn't what comes to mind once she tears into you." Dylan held aloft the black dress. "No, I think this one is more appropriate for our Miss Dodd."

Disappointed that Dylan declined her offer to model the dress, the sales assistant insisted that he watch her parade up and down in a pair of high heels. Manolo quickly dismissed the idea. The shoes the assistant selected were slinky, fragile, useless things that wouldn't last a moment walking across the unpaved sections of the Triple J. He indicated a more sensible pair of shoes and compensated for their plain appearance by adding several selections of decorative clip-ons.

Dylan smiled in remembrance. Between the two of them, they had managed to get Kira ready for this party. He'd intended to march right over to her and gloat over what a wonderful job he'd done guessing her size and her taste. But he held back when he saw that she was immediately swallowed up by half of Murray, curious to meet her.

"Being antisocial again, Jolivet?"

Dylan felt a tap in the small of his back. He straightened from his task of stripping off unneeded branches. "Hello, Molly."

Though irritated at having his reverie and refuge interrupted, he smiled politely in greeting to the daughter of one of the Triple J's wranglers. He quickly swept the room, wondering if Hank Darvin had anything to do with Molly Bell's sudden appearance.

"Where have you been keeping yourself lately? I haven't seen you since the roundup."

Dylan shrugged, picturing Molly as he'd seen her several days go. In her working clothes, covered from head to foot in dust, she didn't look anything like she looked now. She'd traded in her denim for a red velvet dress and heels high enough to put them nearly eye to eye. Dylan started. He'd be darned if those shoes weren't one of the pair selected by that overzealous sales assistant.

Molly's fine, dark hair, usually pulled back into a ponytail, framed her oval face in a sleek cap. She'd applied makeup to accent her olive complexion. Her eyes were made festive with iridescent powder. Her lips were expertly drawn in blood-red lipstick. Dylan was oddly reminded of a little girl playing dress up.

"Working Sun Morning mostly," he answered. "You know she's due to foal soon."

"I know. But everyone says that it's Mama Dodd's daughter that's been taking up your time."

"You shouldn't listen to what everyone says, Molly."

"I'm usually not one to listen to rumors, Jolivet."

Just start them, Dylan thought sourly.

"But I can see where a man gets his head turned around. She's very pretty, if you go for the baby doll type."

"You've turned a few heads yourself, Molly," Dylan remarked.

"Not like the Yankee invasion," Molly contradicted. "That Kira Dodd came down here after her mother and, like a one-two punch combination, laid all of you Jolivets out flat."

"Have you met her, Molly?"

"No, I haven't."

"Maybe you should before you pass judgment."

"I'm not passing judgment. I'm just making an observation," Molly said innocently spreading her hands. When

Dylan flashed her a look of doubt, she quickly changed the subject.

"Nice party. Mama Dodd's done a good job." She took a swig of the eggnog, allowing the thick, creamy liquid to coat her upper lip. Without breaking eye contact with him, she used her index finger to wipe the liquid away and touched the tip of her tongue to her finger.

Dylan resisted the urge to smile. He must have seen Kira perform a similar maneuver over a dozen times. Never once did it occur to him that she'd done it to flirt with him.

"Here, Molly," Dylan said, offering her a paper napkin. He turned back to the tree.

"Look at Mr. Jimmy," Molly said, talking fast to regain his attention. "If his grin gets any wider, he won't be able to get through the door. That's the look of man who's gotten everything he could ever want in a woman." She paused dramatically, then looked down at Dylan.

"That reminds me, Jolivet. I have a present for you. . . ."

Chapter Ten

"For you," Tessa Ralston said with a flourish when she returned to Kira holding a sheer, golden veil in front of her. "Try this on for size." She started to place the veil over Kira, then shook her head as if the idea disagreed with her. "First we'll loosen your hair, like so!"

Tessa removed the barrette from the end of Kira's carefully constructed braid. Without a second thought to how long it took Kira to tame her wild tresses, she pulled the pieces apart with her fingers, then raked through Kira's hair. She fluffed it into a crinkled halo around her face, then whipped the veil over Kira's head. Tucking the extra ends into Kira's costume, Tessa completed the effect by arranging Kira's hair so that the soft, tawny tendrils framed her face and fell to her shoulders.

"Voila!" Tessa said, stepping back to admire her handiwork. "What do you think, Mama Dodd?"

Myra looked up, then let the pins fall out of her mouth as she murmured, "Kira, sweetheart, you look like—"

"An angel!" Tessa said triumphantly. "You sure you

don't want to participate in the pageant, Kira?'' Tessa had asked Kira what part she was playing in the pageant. Kira confessed to her that she wouldn't be around long enough to participate. The pageant began on Christmas Eve. She fully intended to be back in Chicago by then, even if Myra wasn't.

"Thanks for offering, Tessa, but I'm not going to be around for too much longer."

"Now, that's a real shame, Miss Kira. We were all hoping that you would at least be around through Christmas."

Kira half turned to address Hank Darvin. He stood behind her, admiring the view from the rear.

"Hold still, Kira," Myra warned, tugging Kira back into position.

"Thanks for the sentiment, Mr. Darvin. But I didn't expect to stay this long."

"Well, I suppose if you're going to go, it's best if you leave sooner rather than later." Hank heaved a mock sigh. "The longer you stay, the harder it will be to say good-bye to you. You're going to break quite a few hearts when you go." Hank grinned and said, "But I guess some can get over you quicker than I will."

Kira didn't want to know what he meant by that cryptic remark. But she couldn't help following his gaze as he directed her attention with a subtle nod across the room. Standing on the stool, she was barely equal in height to the rest of the guests. Through the press of bodies, if she stood on tiptoe, she could just make out the figures of Dylan and another woman across the room.

Hank stepped close to Kira and whispered conspiratorially into her ear. "Now what do you suppose they're talking about all by themselves over there?"

"I wanted to wait until I could get you alone to give you this," Molly said, opening her hand to reveal to Dylan a black velvet ring box. "But, like you said, you've been so busy with Sun Morning that the moment never came. So, I guess this is as good a time as any."

"What's this, Molly?" Dylan asked

"Open it and see," she said mysteriously.

Dylan felt as trapped as the time she'd caught up to him on one of his rides and had exposed herself to him. He thought he'd been in a quandry then—caught between the instinctual male reaction to take advantage of their solitude and her willingness and his responsibility as her boss and her father's friend. If he refused her present, as he'd refused her offering then, it would be twice that he'd wounded her pride. He was still suffering from the fallout of rumors, innuendo, and bold-faced lies. A woman scorned twice would probably be the end of him.

Gingerly, as if he expected something to leap out and bite him, he took the box.

"Go on, Jolivet. It won't explode," Molly urged laughingly.

Dylan cracked open the lid, then slammed it shut. His face was harsh as he said, "Molly, I mean it, you shouldn't have."

"It's not too dear a gift for you, Dylan," Molly said huskily, moving closer.

"I can't accept this."

"Why not?"

"I'm sorry. I just can't!"

Molly clasped her hand over his, still holding the box. "Take it," she insisted.

"No," he snapped, then looked around, smiling blandly to pacify the few curious onlookers who passed around them.

"Take the gift, Dylan," Molly lowered her voice and her lashes. When she looked up at him again, Dylan saw her eyelashes glittering with the beginnings of tears. Now he really felt trapped. "If not for me, for *her!*" Molly closed his other hand over the box and raised up slightly on tiptoe to press her lips to his.

"A box that small and a kiss that deep says one thing and one thing only to me," Hank observed and laughed raucously. Kira spun to glare at him.

"Kira, hold still!" Myra cried out, her warning a fraction too late. The three-legged stool stood suddenly on no legs at all as it slid out from under her.

The events that followed felt like a scene out of a bad situation comedy. Kira fell straight back, in a jumble of flailing arms and wispy, wafting material. She fell back against Hank, who in an effort to catch her and remain upright, tumbled into another guest. Like dominoes set up in a rally, people, furniture, and serving dishes crashed to the floor. The awful screech of the record player as the needle dragged across the record mingled with the surprised cries of the guests as they were caught unawares by off-kilter tumblers.

"What the . . ." Dylan began, pushing Molly behind him as the undecorated tree went crashing in a *whoosh* of fragrant needles to the floor. He stepped over it and pushed through the crowd to get the center of the commotion.

"Good heavens! Kira, are you all right? Kira, sweetheart, open your eyes!" Myra knelt down beside her daughter.

"Is she all right?" Dylan demanded.

Tessa shook her head. "I don't know. She hasn't moved or said one word since she fell."

"Too embarrassed," Kira groaned from the floor. Her eyes were still closed, but she could hear everything around her with painful clarity.

"Can you stand, Kira? Let's get you upstairs." Myra grasped Kira's elbow and helped her to sit up. Dylan grasped the other elbow and helped lift her to her feet.

Kira bit back an unintentional groan. Her backside ached as if she'd been paddled. She moved stiffly, slowly, biting her lip to keep from crying—as much from embarrassment as in pain. The folks of Murray must think she's a total klutz.

"Sympathy is one way to win over a crowd," Molly Bell commented acidly from behind Dylan. Kira threw her a heated stare, making sure to include Dylan in the visual sweep. If he noticed the look, he gave no indication of it. Instead, he completed her mortification by sweeping her into his arms. "Come on, twinkle toes."

"Put me down . . . ," Kira said through clenched teeth.

"Or what," he interrupted, climbing the stairs and pushing the door to her room open with his shoulder. "You'll yell? Put up a fuss? Make a scene? Too late to be concerned about that."

"I'll be up as soon as I can with an ice pack," Myra called up. Several of the guests gathered around Myra.

"Is the girl all right?"

"She's not hurt, is she?"

"Do you want me to call a doctor?"

"No, I think she'll be all right. There's no need for that. We can handle it," Myra assured them.

"Please, folks, go back to the party." Jimmy took over as host of the party. "There's still plenty of work to be done."

Myra started for the kitchen to prepare an ice pack. Jimmy helped her, crushing the cubes and stuffing them into the pack. When Myra left the kitchen, heading for the stairs again, Jimmy grasped her arm. "Let's not be in too big of a hurry, Myra. Let's give those two a chance."

"Haven't we had enough meddling in their affairs, Jimmy?" Myra warned.

"Trust me this one last time, Myra. If you'd seen those two on the roundup together, you'd know. There's something happening between those two."

"I just wish," Myra sighed, "that I was as confident as you are."

"Here we are." Dylan brought Kira to the bed. He leaned forward, preparing to set her down, but Kira tensed, squeezing his neck involuntarily.

"What is it? What's wrong now?" he asked, noting the nonverbal communication. She nodded at the pillow.

"Oh . . . I see."

Kira shifted and allowed Dylan to place a pillow underneath her as he laid her on the bed.

"How's that?" he asked, gentle in his attention to her.

"How do you think it feels? It hurts like crazy!" she retorted.

"You'll live," he replied. "If there's anything harder than your head, Kira Dodd, it's your backside."

"There's nothing wrong with my backside!" Kira flared.

"So I noticed," Dylan returned softly. His eyes dropped to sweep over her, then glittered as hard as agates as he added, "And so did Hank Darvin."

"What's he got to do with this?"

"I wouldn't be surprised if he pushed you off of that stool to get a cheap feel."

"That's disgusting," Kira snapped. "Hank was only trying to . . ." she stopped in midsentence. What had Hank been trying to do when he directed her attention to Dylan and that woman?

Dylan grasped her chin and tilted it so that she met him eye to eye, gaze for gaze. "Don't shut up now. Keep talking. We really need to talk," he said quietly.

"About?"

"About you . . ." He punctuated the sentence by placing an index finger against her skin at the subtle throbbing at the base of her throat. "And me." Then splayed his hand against his own chest.

"You and me?" Kira mentally gulped, remembering how she'd nestled against that warm expanse of chest the night of the roundup. She remembered how content she'd felt to remain there, how exclusively "his" she'd felt when he danced with her tonight. Her thoughts turned brittle when she remembered the woman he'd kissed downstairs.

Maybe not so exclusive after all. "There is no you and me. Not when you say it like that. There's you, and then there's me. And that's all there is to that."

"Oh, it's like *that* now, is it?" he drawled. Ignoring her disapproving frown and her stiffening spine, Dylan allowed his fingers to trace languidly up and down her bare arm. Sparring for the benefit of the family was one thing. But they were alone now. They could drop the pretenses.

"Yes, it's like that!" Kira retorted, pushing his hand away. "It's bad enough that my mother and your uncle have to go around pawing each other like teenagers with their hormones stuck in overdrive. But you don't have to follow that closely in your uncle's footsteps."

Dylan shook his head incredulously. He couldn't believe what he was hearing. What was the matter with this woman? After all the trouble they went through to make her feel welcome, she had to give him an attitude? Dylan imagined that if he shook the bed, just a little, it would feel just like a retaliatory swat on her backside. He tested the theory, shifting just enough to make the bed creak.

Kira's eyes widened—not because of pain caused by Dylan's movement, but because of the mood he evoked. The almost inaudible creak of the bed as he moved screamed to her of intimacy. Kira didn't know why she reacted so strongly to the sound. It could have been anything that caused the sound—the wind against the wooden shutters, someone walking over a loose floor board, the settling of the old house. Anything! But it wasn't. It was the bed. It was Dylan in her bed, sitting within inches of her.

The bed creaked again, this time to signal the closing of the distance as Dylan's expression and his intentions changed. He could have killed her; instead, he was going to kiss her. He knew it and she knew it.

"Oh, no you d—"

Like the moment Dylan caught her in his arms to dance, Kira's obligatory protest died on her lips when she placed her palms against his chest, presumably to stop his advance. Through the fabric of his shirt, she could feel his heart pounding. She felt him tense. The muscles in his back, chest, and arms rippled as he considered listening to the denial on her lips. He had too much pride to go where he wasn't wanted, no matter how close to the edge he had been pushed. She'd said no, so he would go. He shifted away again, causing the traitorous, telltale bedsprings to creak in protest for him.

When Kira ran her fingers lightly over his shoulders and down his back, drawing him closer, her resistance melted away as rapidly as did the distance between them. He squeezed her tightly, splaying his large hands against her back as if he could draw her into him and through him.

"I want you, Kira Dodd. You know that, don't you?" he murmured against her hair.

Kira shook her head "no." How could he profess wanting her when the lipstick stains of that woman downstairs were still evident on his mouth? "No," she said. Her voice was a hoarse whisper. "No, I don't. I don't know that at all."

"Yes, you do," Dylan said, his mouth quirking into a half smile. "And I know you want me, too." He held her away from him so that she could see the playful teasing in his eyes.

"No, I don't!" she returned petulantly. She felt foolish for responding like a child. But she couldn't help herself. She was jealous of the attention Dylan had given that other woman. She was jealous and hurt.

"Ah-ah-ah!" he chastised, wagging a finger in front of her. "Do you know what happens to fibbers before Christmas, Kira?" Dylan drawled, toying with the folds of her costume. "They get a lump of coal in their stocking."

His hands slipped under the costume and found their way beneath the neckline of her dress. Knowing, skillful thumbs rubbed over her breasts, making her nipples swell and ache for more. Kira imagined Dylan's threat of a lump of coal burning her like a brand. She gasped, arching toward him, unable or unwilling to push him away—though she knew that at any moment someone could come walking through that door.

He lowered his head, kissing her along her jawline, her throat. His lips hovered provocatively over her breasts. Kira could feel the soft air of his breath as he leaned over her. The anticipation of the warm roughness of his tongue against her made her squirm impatiently. She grasped the back of his head, insistently guiding him to a burning that only his mouth could quench.

Kira moaned aloud, leaning deep into the downy pillows. Dylan soon followed, covering the entire length of her as he pressed her deeper into the mattress. She was small beneath him, but so perfectly suited to him. As if he'd known her all of his life, his hands wound their way over the familiar curves of her silky, stocking-clad thighs and the dainty underwear hugging her full hips. A brief, determined tug, and he'd freed her from both. He drew his knee up to nudge her thighs apart.

Kira's hesitation was so slight, he could have easily ignored it. But he didn't. He was sensitive to every throb, every quiver of her body. He could imagine that a million reasons why they shouldn't continue were spinning through her mind right now—only one of which was the compressed time they had known each other.

Common sense should have told them to wait until their hypersensitive emotions settled down before making a commitment this intimate. But Dylan wasn't acting on common sense. He was acting on uncommon sense—his uncanny, unfailing ability that told him when something felt right to him. It must have been the same sensibility that had made his uncle bring home those unseemly birds. It was the same sensibility that had made him bring home Myra. Kira Dodd belonged to him as much as Myra did to Jimmy.

If wasn't the short length of time he'd known her that bothered her, maybe it was his timing. There was a party going on downstairs. People were moving freely through the house. If that's what bothered her, that could easily be remedied by locking the door.

Or maybe timing played a different role in her reluctance. He wanted to make love to her, but not at the risk of bringing an unplanned child into this world. If that was the key to her hesitation, that could be easily remedied, too.

"Kira," Dylan whispered, raising on his elbows and regarding her. Smiling foolishly at what his passion had done to dishevel her appearance, he smoothed his hands over her tousled hair and touched his fingers to her lips made swollen by his kisses. "Kira, I . . . I have something for you," he said, almost bashful in the delivery.

Kira gave a soft snort of amusement and reached between them to touch the evidence of his arousal. "You're telling me?"

"Not that!" Dylan laughed a deep, husky laugh that caused the bedsprings to creak again. "But you're not too far off the mark." He reached into his back pocket where he'd stored Molly's gift to him. When he brought it before her, Kira started. She recognized the black velvet box immediately.

"What is that?" Kira said through clenched teeth.

"A present from me to you," he said cautiously, noting

her hard, glittering eyes and the downward turn of her mouth.

"That's supposed to be for me? I suppose you were just showing this to that woman downstairs to try it on for size?" Kira raised a sarcastic eyebrow at him.

"Try it on for size?" Dylan echoed, shaking with suppressed laughter. "No, this isn't the kind of gift you try on for size. It either fits or it doesn't."

"Are you sure you mean me to have it?" Kira asked. Hank had been so certain that Dylan had meant the gift for that woman. "Are you sure you don't want what's-her-name to have it?"

"Molly Bell," Dylan supplied. "And no, it isn't for her. It never was, never will be. She gave it to me to give to you." For that slight stretch of the truth, Dylan hoped that he wouldn't find a lump of coal in *his* stocking on Christmas morning.

"So that's Molly Bell," Kira mused.

"I don't want to talk about her," Dylan said impatiently. "I want to talk about you and me."

Again, Dylan united them with a touch, emphasizing the invisible but undeniable link between them. "This is for you, Kira. If you want it, take it. If you don't, I'll understand." He pressed the velvet box into the palm of her hand and folded her fingers over it. He then brushed the lightest of kisses on her knuckles, so sweet, so tender, Kira felt a lump forming in her throat. She swallowed convulsively, eager to open the mysterious box.

At that moment, Myra knocked discretely on the door. Careful not to jar the bed and make any more creaking, Dylan backed away while Kira tried to restore her appearance.

"Oh, give it up!" Dylan teased her. "Like she isn't going to notice?"

"Come in," Kira finally called out. Dylan was right. She couldn't hide the passion that had flared between her and

Dylan. Her mother would take one look at her flushed cheeks and her passion-pounded lips, and would know.

"I brought you an ice pack, Kira," Myra called out, cautiously poking her head in the door.

"Thanks, Mama, but you didn't have to. I'm feeling better now."

"It was no trouble," Myra insisted.

"Sorry I ruined your party, Mama," Kira said contritely.

"Don't be silly, Kira. You didn't ruin anything. Everybody is concerned about you, though."

"I'll go down and tell your guests that she's all right," Dylan offered as Kira pulled her hand with the box out of sight.

"Thanks, Dylan. Tell them I'll be down in a minute," Myra said, settling next to Kira as she rearranged the ice pack wrapped in a towel behind her.

"That's not too cold, is it, sweetheart?"

"Mama!" Kira exclaimed in exasperation. "Will you stop fussing over me? I told you that I'm fine. Nothing got hurt but my pride."

"You just gave me a scare when you fell off that stool."

"Get back to your party, Mama. Your guests need you." As much as she loved her mother and was grateful for the extra attention, she was eaten up with curiosity. What was in that small velvet box?

"Good night, Kira. I'll check on you again in a while," Myra promised.

"Yes, Mama," Kira said distractedly as Myra closed the door behind her.

Kira held the box in one hand and gingerly grasped the lid with the other. Slowly she pried open the lid. She'd only opened the box a fraction of an inch, then slammed it shut again, her face burning.

A condom! Dylan had given her a condom as a present. Before she could make up her mind exactly how she felt about such an intimate expression, Dylan gave his distinctive rap on the door with his knuckles and poked his head through the door.

"So, did you get a chance to open the box?" He grinned at her, knowing by the expression on her face that she had. She nodded wordlessly.

"So ...," he drawled. "What did you think of it?"

Kira cleared her throat nervously. She caught her lower lip between her teeth and said, "I think ... I think I'll hold onto it for just a little while longer."

Dylan approached her, his expression guarded. "You sure you don't want to give it back, Kira?"

When he'd headed back to her room, he honestly didn't know what to expect from her. He didn't know if she'd shown the gift to Myra. He didn't know if they'd talked about the implications of such a gift. Would Myra try to talk her out of accepting it? Of accepting him? Or would she come to that conclusion on her own? Would she have second thoughts about the kiss they'd shared?

She shook her head "no" as she clasped the box to her heart. "No, I don't want to give it back, Dylan." Kira paused, choosing her next words carefully. She didn't want the carefully guarded expression on Dylan's face to grow grim.

"But to be honest with you ... I don't think I'm ready to ... uh ... unwrap it, either. Do you understand what I'm trying to say?"

"You don't have to say any more, Kira," he said, resuming his spot on the corner of her bed.

"I just need a little more time, that's all."

"It's all right, Kira. You don't have to explain," he assured her, tracing the worry lines between her eyebrows and around her mouth with his thumbs. He smiled at her to let her know that he understood her decision. And that he was okay with it. "It's all right," he echoed. "Take all the time you need."

Chapter Eleven

"Time to go! Come on, everybody. Let's go. We're going to be late!"

It was Sunday morning and Myra stood at the bottom of the stairs, urging her daughter and the rest of the Jolivet men out of their rooms and into their vehicles. She glanced worriedly at her watch. There was still a full hour before the Sunday service was supposed to begin. She figured by the time she'd assembled everyone, gave each one a personal inspection, and sent them back to correct whatever flaw she found, they would be hard pressed to find a spot in the crowded church.

Jimmy was the first to trudge down the stairs, adjusting his tie as he did so.

"Let me help you with that," Myra offered.

"No, I can do it," Jimmy teased her by fumbling clumsily with the tie. He knew her motivation was spurred more by haste than by an earnest desire to see him properly dressed. When he caught her look of thinly disguised impatience, he deftly tied a double Windsor.

"*Voila,*" he said dramatically.

"Perfect," Myra murmured, indicating a large box of festively wrapped packages near the front door.

"I thought I loaded the last of those gifts last night," Jimmy complained.

"Manolo bought a few more things for me."

"I swear, woman, have you bought out all of Murray?"

"And half of Dellville, too." Myra kissed him on the cheek. "I'd buy up all of Texas to see a needy child happy on this one, blessed day of the year."

Jimmy grumbled, but he couldn't maintain that facade for very long. "Let's go, boys!" he bellowed. He gave a slight grunt as he lifted the box under his arm.

"Careful, Jimmy. Don't strain your back," Myra cautioned.

"Massage it for me later?" Jimmy asked, winking at Myra.

"James Jolivet, we're on our way to the Lord's house. You'd better mind what you're thinking," Myra chastised.

"He knows I've got nothing in my heart but respect for you, Myra," Jimmy said, in a slightly injured tone. He repositioned the box for comfort, then headed out to this car. As he stepped outside, he couldn't help but glance over his shoulder at Myra.

Jimmy didn't consider himself a fanciful man. Working the Triple J didn't leave him much time for idle mind wandering. But as he walked toward his car, he allowed his thoughts to drift. Framed by the warm glow pouring through the doorway and the myriad of lights bordering the porch, Myra looked to him as the heralding angles must have appeared to the simple shepherds.

Jimmy believed that his life wasn't too different from those shepherds of long ago. They must have had the same concerns as he. How do I care for my livestock? How do I tend to my family? How do I live my life each day, being the best man that I can be?

Myra's appearing to him, bringing her warmth, her love,

and her generous capacity for giving was more than one man should keep to himself. He wanted all of his family, his friends, to share in his good fortune. He wanted them to welcome Myra as he had—so they, too, could benefit from her gift of love.

He may have put up a tiny fuss at her shopping spree. He couldn't keep it up for long. Not one of those brightly wrapped boxes was for her. She shopped purely for the pleasure of giving to others less fortunate than her.

By the time he made it back to the foyer, Myra had Baby John, Dylan, and Jesse standing before her. After straightening Jesse's collar, clipping a loose strand from Baby John's blazer, and offering Dylan a shining rag for his boots, she declared them all suitably handsome and dismissed them.

Kira was the last to file downstairs. Tucking her unruly curls under one of Myra's dark-blue, small-brimmed hats, she announced nonchalantly, "I'm ready."

Myra checked her watch again. A thirty-minute drive to Murray. They'd just make it.

"Okay, who's riding with whom?" Myra asked, hustling everyone toward the door.

"With Myra, I've got room for two more," Jimmy said, pointedly staring at Jesse and Baby John. "Kira, you don't mind catching a ride into town with Dylan, do you?"

Kira placed her wrist against her forehead and said with the mock heavy sigh of a martyr, "It'll be a sacrifice, but I think I'm up to the challenge."

Behind their heads, meant for Kira's eyes only, Dylan mouthed "lump of coal" to remind her that he knew the full extent of her feelings for him. That reminder made Kira blush and choke on the blueberry muffin she'd swiped from Baby John.

"Are you all right, little missy?" Jesse asked, pounding Kira more vigorously than necessary in the small of her back.

"Just fine, Mr. Jesse," Kira rasped, stepping away before he crushed her spine.

"Let's not keep the pastor waiting, folks," Jimmy prompted.

When Kira stepped onto the porch and caught sight of Manolo polishing an imaginary speck of grime from the shiny fender of Dylan's truck, she stopped short in mid-stride, nearly making Jesse collide into her. He had to be kidding! Did he expect her to ride in that thing? The monster truck that nearly tore up the streets of Murray?

"Whoa!" Jesse exclaimed, grasping her shoulders to keep from bowling her over. "Time to get those brake lights checked, little missy."

"Sorry, Mr. Jesse," Kira murmured, stepping aside, and moving toward the porch railing.

"Clean as a whistle, no, *patron?*" Manolo said proudly to Dylan. "Just like you asked."

"Looks good, Manolo. Thanks," Dylan said, as he one-handedly caught the keys Manolo tossed at him. He then turned to Kira and asked, "Ready to go?"

"Uh . . . I . . . uh . . ." Kira stammered, stalling for time.

"Where are your manners, Dylan, boy? You're supposed to open the door for the lady on your first date." Baby John gestured toward the truck.

"Who said anything about a date?"

"We're just riding into town together."

Kira and Dylan spoke simultaneously, stumbling over each other in their effort to deny Baby John's declaration.

"Uh-huh," Jesse said, unconvinced. "You're wearing your best Sunday suit, aren't you?"

"You're taking her in your favorite truck, the one you had Manolo wash for you?" Baby John put in.

"And put on a new coat of wax," Manolo reminded them, swiping again at the gleaming chrome.

"And is that a wreath and a big, red bow that I see tied

to the front grill, Dylan, boy?" Jimmy joined in on the teasing.

"You leave Dylan alone," Myra said, coming to his defense. "If he says that it isn't a date, then it isn't."

"What I want to know is what does Miss Kira say," Baby John shifted the attention to her.

Kira glanced helplessly at Dylan. The fledgling, tender feelings she and Dylan were beginning to share were no less precious to her for their newness. She wanted to protect those feelings against anything that would bruise or damage them. If she denied or trivialized those feelings now when they were still so fragile, she didn't know if she could ever restore them. How could she deflect the family's teasing and still let Dylan know what was in her heart? "I say the only date we need to worry about is our date with the pastor of the church. If we don't get moving, we're all going to be late," Kira imitated Myra perfectly, making them all laugh.

"Ready to go?" Dylan prompted.

"Uh . . . yes . . ." she murmured, but she didn't move. She simply held on to the handle of the door with one hand and grasped a hymn book borrowed from Baby John in the other.

"What's the matter, Kira?" Dylan asked.

The dress Kira had chosen from her mother's closet was a little snug. She'd paused at the door, not sure how to go about climbing into the huge truck. If she was wearing a pair of jeans, there would be no problem. She'd simply grab on, scramble up, and strap in. That would be the end of it. But this dress wasn't made for scrambling. It was meant for sitting primly in the pews.

"I . . . uh . . . ," Kira hesitated. She caught another movement from Baby John out of the corner of her eye, then heard Dylan mutter in a tone that bordered on condescension, "Oh, that. Why didn't you say something before, woman?" He stepped around the door, scooped Kira into his arms, then plopped her into the seat.

"What was I supposed to say?" Kira shot back, not having to fake irritation in light of his comment. "That I felt like a refugee from Lilliput trying to climb into this monster truck?"

"Buckle it up, Kira!"

"Excuse me?" she raised her eyebrows, wondering if there wasn't a slight insult hiding in his request.

"The seat belt," Dylan returned. As he climbed into the truck, he pulled off his hat and placed it on the seat between them. He gunned the engine, then called out over the roar as he pulled out of the drive, "We'll see you at the service, folks!"

"If he doesn't kill me in this contraption first," Kira wailed, grasping her hat as a blast of wind whipped through the cab.

"That's not too much air on you, is it?"

They'd been driving for over twenty minutes. It was the first thing Dylan had said to her since leaving the ranch.

"No, I'm fine," Kira responded.

"The gizmo that makes the electric window work on that side is burned out," Dylan explained. "I've been meaning to replace all of the electric windows with hand cranks. I guess I never got around to it. If you get too windblown, let me know. I keep an extra jacket behind the seat."

"The air feels good," Kira insisted.

Dylan took his eyes off of the road long enough to stare at her profile. It seemed to him that the air looked good on her, too. Did he imagine it? Was it the fresh air that put the glow in her cheeks? Or was it makeup? He wasn't sure. She didn't wear much of it. Even last night, she'd used it sparingly.

He cut his eyes back to the road when he realized that if he didn't stop staring at her, the next glow he'd have the pleasure of watching her in would be the glow of ambulance lights after they scraped him off of the highway. Even with that mental warning firmly in place, he couldn't stop himself.

Kira shifted suddenly and made herself more comfortable by crossing her legs. More irresistible than the force of the moon's pull on the ocean tides, Dylan's eyes were pulled along the gradual curve of Kira's legs. *Will you stop it?* he told himself in irritation. *Don't even think about it.* He was supposed to be thinking pure, saintly thoughts, given the direction in which they were headed. Yet the longer the drive lasted, the more he looked. The more he looked, the more he wanted to.

Okay, I mean it this time. Stop thinking about Kira, or else! Dylan gave himself an ultimatum.

"How long have the Jolivets belonged to this church?" Kira asked, breaking into Dylan's thoughts. He glanced at her, wondering whether she had an inkling of what he'd been thinking.

He shrugged in response to her question. "They've had the same church, the same minister for as long as I can remember visiting the Triple J when I was a boy. When I turned sixteen, I joined on my own and became a junior deacon."

Kira chuckled softly.

"What's so funny?"

"I'm trying to imagine you trading in your hat and boots for a minister's robes."

"Choir robes is as close as I'll ever come to standing on the pulpit, Kira Dodd," Dylan snorted. "The only flock I want to minister to comes with four legs."

"Don't you mean herd," Kira said, remembering that for days all Dylan could talk about was the mustangs at Ritter's Cut.

"I mean flock, too," Dylan grimaced. "Uncle Jimmy isn't going to let me get out of taking care of those goofy birds."

"You don't like those birds very much, do you?"

"How'd you ever guess? Let's just say that they don't like me, either. That makes the feeling mutual."

"What's Mr. Jimmy going to do with them?"

"Sell them to some animal processing plant. He's been going on about steaks and boots and pillows and some such nonsense. Frankly I don't care what happens to them as I long as it doesn't involve me."

"Not those poor, defenseless, little chicks?" Kira exclaimed. She couldn't see handing the tiny, squawking chicks that she'd nuzzled over to the chopping block.

"What did you think we were going to do with them? Keep them around as pets?"

"You could," Kira suggested hopefully.

"Don't count on it. Jimmy bought 'em to make a profit. Those things eat their weight in feed. As soon as they're fat enough, off they go!" Dylan made a whistling sound as if imitating a flight plan for the wingless birds.

"There's got to be another way to make money off of them without killing them, Dylan. It doesn't seem fair."

"You're getting way too attached to a potential food source, Kira." Dylan laughed at her. "You weren't this sentimental over that three-inch steak Manolo put in front of you the other night."

"That's because I didn't hold the calf it came from in my hands," Kira retorted. "You're a creative man, Dylan. Why don't you think of a way to save those birds."

"Because I'm the first person who wants to see them leave," he reminded her.

He passed through two of the three signal lights regulating Murray's traffic, then turned down a dirt road lined on both sides with towering pecan trees. When a gust of wind blew over the tops of the trees, the last vestiges of ripening pecans rained down on them, peppering Dylan's glossy finish with dark brown residue. Dylan seemed to grimace as each pecan hull hit the truck.

Kira smiled, patted his hand, and murmured soothingly, "Don't worry, Jolivet. With the extra coats of wax that Manolo put on your baby, those nasty, old pecan hulls wouldn't dare leave a stain."

"It's not the stains I'm worried about." Dylan pulled a long face.

"Then what is it?"

"Every time it rains pecans, the minister's wife sends all the able-bodied people out to pick them up from the church grounds. And with so many folks attending services this time of year, we'll be up to ears in pecan pies, pastries, paste, and candy until next Christmas. You haven't been sick of pecans until you've found them in a stew."

"Pecan stew? Let me guess. That was one of Manolo's concoctions?"

Dylan nodded wordlessly, concentrating on maneuvering the truck into a parking space on the gravel-covered lot. The huge tires crunched into the gravel and drove up a cloud of white, powdery dust that settled over the truck as he backed into a spot, leaving himself plenty of space to pull out again.

As Dylan shut off the ignition, Kira was able to hear the sound of a lone voice through the open, double doors of the church. It was weak but growing stronger, warble out the first line to a familiar hymn. Immediately following the lone singer, the congregation repeated the line, adding volume, depth, and energy to the elderly woman's opening call to worship.

The last of the stragglers climbed the red brick steps, grasped their programs from the attendants, and filed through the open doors. They took their cue from the congregation and joined in on the hymn that was both mournful and uplifting.

Kira didn't notice when Jimmy drove up and parked. But when she heard her mother's clear, strong voice behind her, Kira was even more convinced that her mother belonged in Murray. Myra's voice blended perfectly with the congregation and added to its power.

As Myra walked arm in arm with Jimmy, her face was transfixed with such joy. The image was so pure, so perfect—how could she have ever considered ripping her mother away from the life and the love she'd found here?

Kira swallowed hard, pushing the lump of emotion out of her throat. The emotion rose to settle in her eyes, making them glitter with unshed tears.

"Here," Dylan offered, pressing his handkerchief into her hand. He grasped her around the waist and helped her to the ground. "If I'd known that you'd get this worked up over just the opening hymn, I would have brought along an extra box of tissues."

"She's so happy here," Kira said through a hiccup, and dabbed at her eyes.

"You mean Myra?"

Kira nodded.

"Does that mean that you're not going to try to make her go back to Chicago?"

She bobbed her head again, touching the handkerchief to the corners of her eyes. "I was being selfish wanting her to come back with me. I told myself that I was forcing her to come back for her own good. I even blamed your uncle for tricking her into staying here. I was wrong. I realize that now. As soon as the service is over, I'm going to tell her that. And I'm going to apologize to your uncle, too, for all of the nasty things I've said or thought about him."

Dylan smiled, admiring the courage it took to admit that she was wrong. Then his smile quickly faded. Since day one, Kira had made it known that the only reason she was hanging around was to convince Myra to come back. And during that time, he felt she had gotten close enough to the family that it didn't matter what her reasons were for staying. Now that Myra had swayed her, Kira was left with no more excuses.

"I guess that means that you don't have a reason to hang around Murray anymore, do you, Kira?" Dylan said somberly.

He thought back to last night when Kira had asked for more time. He'd accepted her gentle refusal with good grace, willing to give her all the time she needed. He'd conveniently forgotten that she'd put herself on that stupid schedule. And now, with her agreeing that she didn't need to cajole Myra anymore, their time had just run out.

Kira opened her mouth to speak, then closed it without uttering a word. What more could she say? By repeating what she'd been saying all along, he'd said it all.

Dylan waited for her to announce that she would be staying, too. He waited for her to admit that she really didn't want to leave. Kira shifted uncomfortably, then murmured, "Come on. They'll be shutting the doors soon."

Dylan took her arm and escorted her up the stairs. As they passed through the doors, he took up the congregational song. With her arm resting lightly against his side, Kira felt the rumble of his voice come from deep within his chest and pour from his lips with an intensity that brought a fresh round of tears to Kira's eyes.

Kira had heard of women swooning at the sound of man's voice in song. She'd even seen clips of old rock-and-roll concerts where women were so enraptured that they fell screaming at the balladeer's feet. She never really trusted those clips. She'd always assumed that the young women were acting for the camera or for the singer to get attention. She never imagined that she'd ever allow the sound of man's voice to make her weak in the knees.

But it wasn't only the act of Dylan's singing that affected her so. It was a culmination of the song, his earnest spirit of devotional worship, and his protective hand on her arm that made her turn her face up to him. The wonder and the tenderness she felt for this man shone in her eyes as piercing as the sun's rays. In that instant, Kira knew that she had fallen in love with Dylan Jolivet.

She wished that she could say that she'd come to that decision after months and months of close examination of her feelings, or after a lifetime of binding experiences. She would have given anything to have the wisdom of time guiding her at that moment. But she didn't. All she had was the here and now.

In this moment, in this one, crystal-clear moment when the truth as she believed it to be was revealed to her, all she could do was trust in herself. It couldn't be a delusion, could it? The pounding of her heart, the soaring of her spirit, the deepening assertion that there was no place she'd rather be on this earth than by this man's side—this was no delusion. It was real. She loved him. Heaven help her! She loved him. Kira felt like shouting. She felt like singing. She wanted to throw open the church doors and proclaim to all the citizens of Murray that Kira Dodd was in love with Dylan Jolivet.

In the midst of this ecstatic revelation, Dylan didn't appear to notice. He led her up the center aisle, his somber eyes scanning the crowd to search for a seat. He caught sight of Ellis, the boy who'd helped him to chase down Keeper and Delanie the day Kira arrived. Ellis was waving excitedly, obviously pleased to see them, and pointing to the pews directly behind him. Dylan almost frowned. He supposed that it was fitting that it would be Ellis they wound up sitting with. He was the one who'd literally brought them together. He would also be a part of their separation.

By the time they made it to the seat Ellis indicated, the congregation was in fine form. The choir, the organ, a piano, and an accompanying snare drum had taken the opening hymn to a heightened pitch. The very roof of the church seemed to rattle. Kira smiled inwardly. Even a church as soundly built at this one couldn't contain the joy flowing over and through her. Too happy to hold it in, a moment later, she joined in the song as she slid down to make room for Myra, Jimmy, Baby John, and Jesse.

"Hey, Miss Dodd! Mr. Dylan! Merry Christmas. Did you bring the you-know-what with ya?" Ellis twisted around and whispered loudly.

"What's a you-know-what?" Ellis's sister also twisted around in the pew to ask.

"Mind your own business, nosy!" Ellis retorted, which caused his sister to pinch her older brother. Their resulting squabble caused his mother to hiss, "Turn around and pay attention, Ellis Wyatt, and stop teasing your sister." As Mrs. Wyatt struggled to separate Ellis and his sister, her own motion caused the sleeping baby in her arms to cry.

Frowning and rubbing his arms in sullen protest, Ellis turned around to face the pulpit, but not before Dylan winked at him and gave him the thumb's up sign.

Seated in row upon row of high-gloss pine pews were Murray's inhabitants dressed in their finest. The choir, dressed in white robes trimmed with gold, stood in the risers directly behind the pulpit and offered a song at the minister's request. Once the song ended, the minister thanked them graciously, made special mention of the accompanying musicians, then began the service.

Kira thoroughly enjoyed the minister's fervent sermon—a skillful mixture of scripture and humor that had the congregation laughing, praising, and clapping during the entire service. Several times she caught her mother laughing, only to quickly compose herself when she saw her daughter watching her, and murmur a sedate, "Amen."

Jimmy was more enthusiastic in his appreciation, rising to his feet several times to shout encouragement. Kira sneaked a peek or two at Dylan, curious to know what he thought of both the sermon and his uncle's unrestrained passion. But each time she looked at him, he seemed to be untouched by it all. His expression was cool and distant. His posture was stiff. His knee bounced nervously as if he were impatient for the service to be over.

When the ushers passed around the collection plate, Kira took advantage of the incidental chatter to whisper, "Dylan, is everything all right?"

Dylan shrugged. "Sure. Why do you ask?"

She shrugged in return. "You look a little preoccupied."

"Worried about Sun Morning, I guess. I didn't get a chance to check on her before we left."

"Oh," Kira accepted the explanation and didn't press for more. "I'm sure she'll be all right." She smiled to give him encouragement. He smiled back. That is, he drew his lips back, but his eyes remained flat. Kira assumed that he was more worried about his horse than he was letting on. Though she wondered why he was more worried now than he had been two hours ago. That's how long it had been since they'd all piled into their vehicles and headed for Murray. And during that time, he'd been open, cheerful.

No, it won't be all right! Dylan silently denied. How could it be all right? Kira was leaving him. She was going to get into that rental car of hers and drive back to Chicago. She was going to leave him as if nothing at all mattered. How could she do that? How could she make him believe that she was waiting for him one moment and then was ready to leave him the next?

Dylan glanced up, his attention suddenly focused on the minister. He was making the altar call. Anyone who wanted a special prayer could come to the altar. Anyone could come up to the front of the church and confess what was in his or her heart. Dylan wondered if it would be considered a sacrilege if he went up and prayed secretly, privately for this woman who'd come so unexpectedly into his life to remain in it.

While he debated the morality of wanting to make Kira

want to stay with him, the opportunity slipped away. The next part of the service was mostly administrative. The deacons went into a room behind the choir cove to count the offering. The church secretary took that time to make announcements. After that, they would be dismissed. Everyone would then file out and that would be the end of the service.

He would be hard pressed to get himself and Kira out of there before the curious, gossipy members of the church would come up to him and bombard him with questions—questions that he didn't have the heart to answer. All those who hadn't met Kira the night of the costume party would swarm up to her now—wanting to know about her and Dylan. It had been a long time since he'd openly escorted a lady to church. In the small-town, unofficial code of Murray, that was as serious as bringing a lady home to meet your parents. Dylan sighed. If only they knew. She wasn't hanging around Murray any longer than she had to. Now that she didn't have her mother as an excuse to stay, she was free to go.

"Ready to go?" Dylan rose, nodding toward the door.

"Don't rush her off so soon, Dylan," Myra said, taking Kira's arm. "I'd like to introduce her to Minister Ingram. Besides, don't you have something out in your uncle's car that you could, uh . . . be taking care of?" Myra's voice trailed off as she hinted with raised eyebrows at the young children still milling around the pews.

"Oh, yeah. I almost forgot," Dylan said distractedly. "I'll take care of it."

"Minister Ingram said he'd leave open the back door that leads to the pastor's study. You can leave everything in there."

"As soon as most of the cars have cleared out, I'll help Uncle Jimmy unload," he promised.

"Thank you, Dylan. Come on, Kira." Myra grasped her daughter's arm and tugged enthusiastically toward the minister's pulpit. Kira glanced helplessly over her shoulder at Dylan. She didn't want to talk to Minister Ingram. She wanted to talk to Dylan. She needed to tell him how she felt.

"You sure you don't need any help, Dylan?" Kira asked. "I could—"

"No, I think I can handle it by myself," he said abruptly, turning away from her. Again, Kira felt a definite wave of coolness. She couldn't pass it off as preoccupation with his horse. This time the indifference was directed at her. Her mouth dropped open, wondering what could have happened in the span of an hour to make him turn against her. She watched him as long as she could, until he disappeared entirely from sight.

Unmindful of her daughter's turmoil, Myra pushed her way through the gathering swallowing the popular minister. As they approached, Kira heard him reminding Ellis's mother to set an appointment as soon as possible to arrange for the new baby's christening.

"The weather's been cooperating with us so far," Minister Ingram was saying. "As soon as we're hit with the first good freeze, I know I won't see half the congregation that I had in here today no matter how wonderful and how uplifting you say my sermons are."

That brought an appreciative round of chuckles and denials from his admirers.

"Besides, I want to get this sweet little angel into my fold as soon as possible. Yes, I do. Such a sweet, sweet, little angel," Minister Ingram cooed, leaning his broad bespectacled face over the child. "You get with the church secretary, Mrs. Wyatt. She'll get you on the calendar."

"Yes, Pastor," Ellis's mother said dutifully and nestled the child closer to her when the minister's enthusiastic appraisal brought a sleep-disturbed squawk from the baby.

"Speaking of adding sheep to the fold," Minister Ingram glanced up at Myra standing on the fringes of the gathering, "glad to see you could make it out today, Mrs. Dodd. And you managed to bring all of those Jolivets with you. You must be living clean to have such power over them."

"Oh, I think you're exaggerating my influence just a little bit," Myra said modestly, stepping forward and urging Kira forward with her. "It's your stirring words that gets those Jolivets to their feet."

Minister Ingram smiled and wiped his brow with a hand-kerchief. "Whew! I thought Jimmy was going to start preaching himself. One more 'Amen' from him, and I would have stepped down and let him have the pulpit. Do you think he can keep up that energy when it comes time to gather up the homebound? I need some volunteers to provide transportation to some of our neighbors who want to come to down for the Christmas pageant but don't have a way."

"Say no more," Myra assured him. "Just let us know when and where we need to be and we'll be there."

"God bless you, sister," Minister Ingram thanked her. Her then turned a curious eye to Kira. "And who is this sweet little angel here?"

Kira thought if he tried to tickle her under the chin as he had Ellis's baby sister, she'd bolt for the door.

"This is my daughter, Kira Dodd, Minister Ingram," Myra said proudly. "She came all the way from Chicago to spend some time with me."

Kira looked askance at her mother. She'd come danger-ously close to bending the truth with that introduction. Yes, she'd made a special trip to see Myra. But she hadn't intended on staying or making it a pleasure trip. Just because it turned out to be more fun, more gratifying than she'd expected, didn't mean that Myra could lead everyone to believe that it had been her intention all along.

"Welcome to Murray, Miss Dodd." He gripped her hand, swallowing it in the warm, fleshy folds of his.

"Thank you, sir."

"And so polite, too. I hope you'll be around to help your mother when it comes time for the Christmas pageant, young lady."

"Well . . . uh . . . I'll do what I can," Kira hedged, uncomfortably. As Dylan had pointed out to her, she didn't have her original excuse for staying on at the Triple J. She'd already decided that Myra wasn't making the mistake of her life by choosing to remain with Jimmy. There was nothing keeping her there. Nothing at all.

"God bless you, little sister," Minister Ingram echoed his thanks and excused himself.

"Speaking of blessings, Mrs. Dodd," Ellis's mother began, "Mr. Dylan told me what you did for the kids. . . ."

But Myra made a slight sound as if clearing her throat, then indicated with a raised eyebrow that she shouldn't speak in front of her children. She wanted to see their surprised faces when they opened the presents so painstakingly selected for each child.

Mrs. Wyatt nodded. She understood. She then thrust the baby's diaper bag and the baby into Ellis's arms. "Go to the car and wait for me, Ellis. Make sure everyone is buckled in. I'll be out in a minute."

Ellis grimaced as if he knew he was about to miss out on something of which he wanted to be a part. But he knew better than to argue with his mother this close to Christmas.

"Come on, Ellis," Kira said, seeing this as her opportunity to escape, too. She relieved him of the diaper bag, and on impulse, she took the baby and Ellis took the hands of his sister and brother. "I'll just go along to keep an eye on them," Kira said, making it obvious to her mother that she was deserting her. If the members of the church wanted to interrogate Myra about her daughter, she was on her own.

Kira was down the main aisle and through the double doors before she glanced back at her mother. She shrugged apologetically when Myra flashed her an obvious "I'll get your for this" look. Kira then took a moment to adjust the baby's blanket to protect her face from the bright noon sun. The baby squirmed, protesting the covering. But Kira soothed her back to a drowsy, contented state by murmuring softly and patting her diaper-clad bottom. The baby yawned once—a huge yawn with her eyes closed tight.

Kira touched her finger lightly to the baby's chubby brown cheek, in awe of the velvet texture. In doing so, she caused the baby to respond instinctually to turn her head to that side—her mouth open and eagerly searching for something to suckle. Kira felt an irrational, instinctual, maternal longing spread through her.

"I think she's hungry." Kira smiled, looking to Ellis for confirmation.

"Aw, Miss D, she's always hungry," Ellis complained, rooting through the diaper bag for a bottle.

"What's her name?" Kira then asked, obliging the baby by sliding the bottle into her mouth.

"Camisha."

"You mean your folks didn't name her something that begins with an 'E'?" Kira teased.

"All the boys' names begin with E," Ellis explained. "My dad's name is Everett. There's me and my brother Eldrick. You met him at the gas station. And this is Emil." Ellis lifted the hand of the brother he clung to. "But all of the girls are Cs for my mother. Her name's Cheryl. This is my sister Camille. Say hello to Miss Kira." He propelled them forward. The four-year-old Emil just stared back at her with large, round eyes. He stuck his index and middle fingers into his mouth, then turned his face to rest against Ellis's chest. But Camille spoke up with all the wisdom of a seven-year-old, "You have to burp Camisha when she's about half finished with the bottle, Miss Kira. If you don't, she'll just spit it back all over you."

"Thanks for the warning," Kira said, accepting a small

white cloth diaper from Ellis to place over her shoulder. By the looks of Camisha's enthusiastic pulls on the bottle, it would only be a matter of minutes before she'd reached the halfway mark.

Getting the bottle out of the infant's mouth proved to be more difficult than getting her to accept it. She protested loudly, blowing bubbles of the milky formula from her lips.

"Yes, I know," Kira soothed, placing the baby over her shoulder and patting her gently to bring up the air bubbles. The resounding release of gas from Camisha's lips followed by the satisfied gurgle brought a round of laughter from Kira, Ellis, and his siblings.

"We'd better get you to the car like your mother wanted," Kira said, hushing the children when a few churchgoers threw disapproving stares in her direction. She started down the stairs, anxious to get away from the unwanted attention. "Where's your car, Ellis?"

"Over this way." Ellis canted his head to indicate the direction. Kira made a small sound of dismay when she noticed that he was leading her very close to where Jimmy had parked his car. If they came up on Jimmy and Dylan while they were transferring packages for the children into the church, it would ruin the surprise. Kira slowed her steps, pretending to be fussing over the baby. She hoped that either Jimmy or Dylan would look up, see them approach, and quickly hide the "evidence." They didn't appear to notice her. Their backs were to her. And Jimmy was just seconds away from opening the trunk of the car.

Kira needed a diversion. She couldn't let the children see the packages in the car. She knew Ellis was old enough to know the truth about Santa. He knew by his secret sign with Dylan that something would be waiting for him at the church on Christmas morning. But Camille and Emil were little more than babies themselves. If their parents wanted to end the magic for them, that would be their decision.

But to find out like this, so close to Christmas, would be unfair.

She had to think fast. As Jimmy fit the key into the truck of the car and started to raise the lid, she quickly plucked the bottle from the baby's mouth, causing her to cry out again.

Jimmy glanced up, then slammed the trunk shut. "Rug Rats at six o'clock," he warned Dylan out of the corner of his mouth. Dylan spun around, leaning nonchalantly against the trunk of the car. His posture shifted abruptly when he saw Kira approaching with the baby in her arms. She was busy calming the child, coaxing a near-empty bottle back into her mouth. Her face was obscured by the hat and the strands of caramel hair, which had worked themselves loose.

The timeless image of woman and child burned into his mind and touched off an explosion of wildly conflicting emotions within him. Dylan thought that he would never see anything as beautiful as this woman at her most nurturing. It didn't take a grand leap of imagination to replace the current child in her arms with his own. The thought of planting *his* seed into Kira Dodd, seeing her grow heavy with *their* child, and bringing *their* child into this world filled him with a deep longing. He knew he would make a wonderful father, so loving, so attentive—and a model husband, too, he mentally added, staring dutifully at the church. That's how he knew it had to be right. He and Kira together had to be destiny. Would he have been given a vision so wonderful, so perfect, if it weren't meant to be? Could the Good Lord be so cruel?

Dylan's face clouded. He wouldn't, but he thought that Kira would. Not knowing the depth of his feelings for her, she would soon pack her little bags and scoot back to Chicago faster than he could get down on one knee. Now that she'd confessed that she was ready to leave him behind, he didn't dare confess the turn his heart had taken.

Simply knowing that he was attracted to her hadn't been enough for her. She'd shown that at the party by kindly but firmly refusing to sleep with him. All she'd done was admitted that she was as attracted to him as he was to her. He understood now that the feelings he had for her went beyond sexual. This was the first woman he'd ever seriously considering offering his name to.

"You all right, Dylan, boy?" Jimmy touched a hand to his nephew's shoulder when he didn't respond to a question he'd asked three times.

"I'm fine, Uncle Jimmy," Dylan said distractedly, finally catching Kira's gaze over the heads of the children. She nodded approvingly at the closed trunk, then continued on to the Wyatt family car.

"Those Wyatts are poppin' up like mushrooms," Jimmy commented. "If they keep having babies every year, pretty soon they'll have enough for their own football team— offense and defense."

"Uh-huh," Dylan grunted, following Kira with his eyes long after she'd passed them.

"Looks like the coast is clear. We should drive the car around to the back to unload."

"Uh-huh," Dylan repeated.

"What's on your mind, son?" Jimmy prompted.

"I'm in love with her, Uncle Jimmy," Dylan blurted out before he could recall the words. He couldn't tell Kira, but he had to tell someone.

Dylan thrust his hands deeply into his pockets and leaned dejectedly against the trunk of the car. Jimmy blew out a small sigh. He tucked his hands in his pockets as well and mirrored Dylan's stance.

"I know, Dylan, boy. I know," he said sympathetically.

"How did this happen to me? This wasn't supposed to happen to me. Not like this."

"It never happens like you imagine it will," Jimmy said sagely. "How'd you figure it would be for you?"

"I was supposed to fall for some local woman, someone I've known all my life ... someone who knows me better than I know myself. That's the way it's supposed to happen. We're supposed to marry and have enough kids to rival the Wyatts," Dylan exclaimed, sounding both angry and amazed at the same time.

"Sounds like you have it all figured out."

"Had," Dylan corrected. "I had to fall for the one woman I can't have. She's leaving. She told me that she's not going to try to take Myra back so there's no reason for her to stay," Dylan said bitterly.

"The way I see it, you've only got two choices. You can let her go—" Jimmy began.

"I don't like that option at all." Dylan interrupted him.

"If you don't like it, then take the other choice. Make her want to stay."

"How do you expect me to do that? Hog-tie her? Slap one of those bird leg bands on her so I can track her down if she ever tries to skip out on me?"

Jimmy chuckled at Dylan's attempt to hide his desperation with humor. "Either one you choose, I have only this to say ... if you love her, son, if you really love her, don't let yourself do without her. Wherever she goes, you go. Do you understand what I'm trying to say to you? Don't go through this world alone, Dylan. I've tried it both ways, and I'm telling you, sharing your life, your love with someone is better than being alone."

"She's gonna leave me, Uncle Jimmy, and nothing on this earth is going to stop her."

Chapter Twelve

It was time for Kira to leave. There were no more excuses. The two weeks she'd agreed to give Myra were up. Hank Darvin and Baby John had already returned her car in perfect working order. She'd done all she could to help Myra prepare for the annual Murray Christmas pageant. Costumes were altered and distributed. Presents for the children were all labeled and delivered to the church. There was nothing more she could do. If she wanted to be home in time for Christmas, if she wanted to be with her sister Alicia, her grandmother, and her Aunt Galen, she had to leave now.

She sat on the edge of the bed, gathering her courage and her spirits. It was no easy task. The ride back from church with Dylan had to be the most depressing ride of her life. Neither was in the mood to make pleasant conversation. Anything that came out of their mouths was stilted, forced, as if they had become strangers all over again. Kira didn't think the artificiality of the conversation would have hurt so much if the Jolivets hadn't bent over backwards to make this as much her home as theirs. It was her quiet, empty apartment that seemed foreign to her now. When she went back there, she knew there would be no more rowdy wakenings the Jolivets treated her to each morning as they set about their chores, no more delicious smells of home-baked goodies luring her out of bed. No more good-natured teasing as she sat at the dinner table. Instead of the piles and piles of mouthwatering morsels conjured up by Manolo and Myra, she'd have to be content with going back to her prepackaged, frozen meals.

Kira smiled ruefully, thinking about the pound or two she'd gained since coming here. Maybe she could stand to miss a meal or two. But there was so much else she couldn't stand to miss. No more waking to glorious sunrises. No more tender, timid chicks nestling in her hands. No more golden horses on heart-stopping roundups. No more Dylan! Kira pressed her fingers to her eyes to squeeze back stinging tears. *No more Dylan.* . . . She wasn't gone, yet she'd already lost him. After the service, he'd gone out of his way to avoid her.

After dinner, when Dylan still didn't show, Kira cornered Baby John and asked him about Dylan's absence.

"Well . . . uh . . . Miss Kira . . . you know . . . the horse . . . and, you know how it is."

He tugged on his lower lip. Kira knew by now that meant he was deep in worry.

"Yeah, I know how it is," Kira had echoed. Maybe he didn't want her as much as she thought he did—not enough to fight for her. She'd thrown one tiny roadblock in his path, and what had he done? Run to the barn with his tail tucked between his legs. Sure she'd said a thousand times that she had to go back. Did he think she really meant that?

"Maybe it's best if I leave, Baby John," she'd told him last night. "It's a blow to my ego to compete against a horse and wind up second."

She'd waited all night for Dylan to come to her. She'd waited all night for the opportunity to open up the black velvet box. When he hadn't come, she was all the more convinced that she should go. She didn't want to make things any more awkward between them.

She automatically searched under her bed for Delanie, then remembered that she'd agreed to Mr. Jimmy's request to let her remain behind. She was free to run to her heart's content on the Triple J, and it would be cruel to separate her from Keeper when it was obvious that they would be the proud parents of poodle/shepherd puppies—the little shoodles, as everyone had affectionately begun to think of them.

"Good-bye, Mama's little angel," Kira whispered. Then she hefted her suitcase and started down the stairs. "Mama?" Kira called to Myra as she closed her bedroom door behind her.

Myra stood at the bottom of the stairs, making no attempt to put on a brave face. Mr. Jimmy stood behind her, his hands resting lightly on her shoulders. He squeezed encouragingly.

"Are you sure you won't stay just a couple of more days, Miss Kira? It's so close to Christmas," he urged. He asked as much for himself as he had for Myra's sake. Together, these two women had brought more love and laughter into this house than he'd seen in a long time. He was desperate to buy a little more time to hang onto those precious feelings for as long as he could.

If Kira stayed a few more days, maybe she could be convinced to stay a few more after that. By that time, maybe she would decide that she really didn't want to leave at all. Maybe by that time, she'd decide that she could make Murray her home. Maybe she would accept the fact that she was needed and loved here as much as she was anywhere. So many maybes. It would take a miracle to get them all going the way he wanted—the way he knew Dylan wanted.

"I wish I could. But I can't," Kira said earnestly. "I have duties, responsibilities, family that needs me back . . . back in Chicago." Kira surprised herself. She'd started to say "back home," then found that she couldn't bring herself to do it.

Her apartment, her first home away from home, used to be her pride and joy. She'd painstakingly chosen every stick of furniture, every color-coordinated accent. It surprised her, and saddened her, to think that she could quickly come to think of a place this far away as her home, too.

"You always have a place here," Jimmy said. "You have family here, too. People who love you . . . who need you . . . You know that, don't you?"

"I know," Kira murmured. "You don't know how much it means for me to hear you say that after the way I acted."

"You were just trying to take care of your mama."

"Well, Mr. Jimmy. Now it's your turn. You take care of my mother for me. And yourself," Kira said as he took the suitcase from her.

Jimmy opened his mouth to say more, then quickly shut it. There was so much more he could say, but he didn't. Was it his place to? Could he speak for the conspicuously absent Dylan? Jimmy stalled for time, hoping that his nephew would step on that stubborn pride and confess his love for Kira.

When Kira had announced last night that she was heading back in the morning, Jimmy had seen a mask of indifference slam down on Dylan's face as effectively as if someone had pulled a hood over his head. He'd excused himself abruptly from the table and made himself absent for the rest of the evening. Jimmy had wanted to say something then.

"Go after him!" he'd wanted to encourage Kira.

"Don't let her go!" he could have shouted at Dylan.

What was the matter with those two? Were they blind? Insane? If they gave up now, when they were so close to finding true happiness, they would never be truly happy again. No matter where they went, no matter who they wound up with, there would always be the nagging doubts in the back of their minds. What about the one they let get away? Had they had the chance for love and foolishly let it slip away?

Jimmy had not slept all night. His mind was troubled, his heart heavy with indecision. Kira and Dylan were adults, capable of making up their own minds. But he loved them both, and didn't want to see them make a mistake. He roused himself out of bed early, before any of the others. He was going to say something, do *something*, to get these two together at the risk of making them both angry at him.

He went up to Dylan's room and poked his head in. The bed hadn't been slept in. Jimmy shook his head. Looked like he wasn't the only Jolivet up all night. He must have spent all night in and around the stables.

He turned around, ready to head for the stairs, but Myra stopped him.

"Where do you think you're going?" She'd just come from peeking in on Kira herself.

"You know where I'm going."

"Oh, no you don't, James Earl Jolivet," Myra warned him. "Enough is enough. You leave those two alone."

"But they love each other, Myra. I'm as sure of it as I am of my love for you."

"If they do love each other, then they'll find out for themselves."

"Somebody needs to shake some sense into those two."

"It won't be us," Myra insisted. "We tried playing Cupid and it didn't work. We were selfish to push them together. Just because we wanted everybody to accept us, we tried

to force fit our families. Well, it didn't work. Let them
alone. Let them heal."

Now, watching Kira preparing to leave, Jimmy held his
tongue and hoped that divine intervention would stop her
from going.

"You have a care, Miss Kira," Jimmy murmured, then
headed outside to give mother and daughter a moment
alone.

"I'll call you as soon as I get back to Chicago, Mama,"
Kira said stoutly.

Myra drew her daughter to her. Her throat was too
constricted to do much more than hold her close and rock
her.

"I'm going to miss you so much."

"I'll miss all of you, too. Don't be a stranger to us, Mama.
Call often. Come back every now and then."

"You know I will. I'll be there for the birth of my first
grandchild. I wouldn't miss that."

"I know you won't. It's just that Ally's so nervous. We
may be grown and living on our own, but we still need
you, Mama. She wants you to be there."

"And I will be," Myra insisted.

"Then, I guess there's nothing more to say but good-
bye." Kira tried to sound brave.

"Be careful on the road, Kira."

"I will, Mama. I'll call you as soon as I get there," Kira
promised, reaching for the doorknob.

"Where do you think you're going?"

"*¿Adonde vas, ángelita?*"

Jesse and Manolo stepped through the door carrying
the suitcase that Jimmy had taken out to her car.

"I told you last night at dinner," Kira said, forcing an
air of cheerfulness into her voice. "I have to go back."
She reached for her suitcase, but Jesse snatched it out of
her grasp.

"Who do you think you're trying to fool, little missy.

You don't want to go. Your home is here," Jesse said, pointing at the floor for emphasis.

Kira looked helplessly at her mother for backup. Jesse was such an imposing figure, glowering down at her through those burning eyes and scraggly eyebrows. No one argued with Mr. Jesse.

"What Señor Jesse is trying to say, *Angelita*," Manolo stepped between her and Jesse and soothed, "is that it isn't safe for you to be on the roads right now. *Esta muy peligroso*. Very, very dangerous."

"What are you talking about?" Kira asked. "What do you mean, dangerous?"

Baby John and Jimmy came in at that moment. "Looks like you're going to have to delay your trip back for a few days, Ms. Kira," Baby John said, grinning.

Jimmy elbowed him in the ribs, clearing his throat gruffly. "We started up the car for you and heard the national weather report on the radio."

"There's a front blowing in from Canada. It's a real humdinger." Baby John shook his head and *tsked*. "Snow drifts ten feet high and ice sheets that stretch on for miles. Folks as far south as Tennessee are feeling the effects. That means it will get to Murray before too long. We might even have a white Christmas."

Kira pinned Baby John with a hard stare, trying to bluff him into pulling on his lower lip. If she could do it, it would mean that these Jolivets were probably pulling her leg. Or rather, hanging onto it to get her to stay.

"If you set out now, you might not make it. It's only a matter of time before the roads leading out of Texas get bad, too . . . It's the ice, you know, makes for very treacherous driving," Jimmy warned her. "You'd be snowed in at some strange place, probably some greasy spoon truck stop or seedy motel, far away from either home, far away from family. You don't want that, do you, Kira?"

Kira stared suspiciously at all of them, her arms folded

resolutely across her chest. "An ice storm? Yeah, right. It's just a little bit too convenient for me."

"You don't believe us?" Baby John said incredulously. "Frankly, I'm hurt."

Jimmy jabbed Baby John again and muttered out of the corner of his mouth, "Don't overdo it."

"I knew the weather was going to turn," Jesse pitched in. "Felt it in my feet this morning. Toes started cramping like the devil himself was stamping on them."

Kira withheld a small groan at the image.

"If you don't believe us, ask Dylan. He heard the reports first thing this morning, too," Jimmy said quickly.

"Then why didn't he say something?" Kira demanded. "Why'd he let me get all packed up and ready to go?"

Jesse shrugged. "Go ask him yourself."

"Where is he?" Kira faltered. She was hurt that he wasn't there to say good-bye. At the same time, she dreaded the moment that he would come trudging from the horse pens. Then she would be forced to say good-bye to him.

"You *know* where he is," Jesse said in his gruff manner. "Fooling around with that mare." He held the door open for her and canted his head in the direction of the stables.

"All right, then. I will ask him," Kira said, pinning each one of them with a disbelieving glare. *Ice storm!* It had to be seventy degrees out there. How gullible did they think she was? She tromped down the stairs, back straight, arms placed resolutely on her hips.

Then again, maybe it wasn't too much of a stretch of the imagination. It was winter. She'd almost forgotten that in the nearly tropical warmth that had settled over Murray.

As she headed across the yard, Jesse called after her, "And while you're at it, why don't you ask that boy to marry you!"

"Jesse!" Baby John exploded, punching his brother on the arm. "You're about as subtle as a freight train."

"I was only saying what everyone else around here has

been too chicken to say. It'll be next Christmas before those two get around to seeing the truth."

"And just what truth is that?" Kira spun around and demanded.

"That instead of making tracks, you and that boy should be making babies," Jesse said bluntly.

"After a grand, hometown wedding, of course," Baby John put in.

"For which I will cater the reception afterwards," Manolo offered. "I can see it now, a wedding cake ten tiers high with each layer more *delicioso* than the last!"

Myra looked at Manolo, then laughed as they chimed in unison, *"Dulce media del fuego!"*

Kira huffed and rolled her eyes skyward. Well, she'd asked. . . .

He should have asked her to stay. He wanted to, but held back. If her own mother couldn't get her to stay, what could he do to change her mind?

Dylan sat on the stable floor, his back propped against a bale of hay. He sat directly across from Sun Morning's stall, tossing bits of apple at her. He carved a chunk for her then sliced another for himself. As he munched, he realized that this was the first thing he'd eaten since breakfast yesterday. After it was certain that Kira was leaving, he'd lost his appetite.

Sun Morning leaned her nose over the gate of the stall and demanded another apple treat.

"Here you go, lady," he soothed, standing to place half an apple between her teeth. He rubbed behind her ears and underneath her thick, red-gold mane. Her mane was the reason he'd given her the name Sun Morning. The streaks of mingled red and gold perfectly matched the look of the early morning sky over the Triple J's east horizon. The sky had looked like that the day he'd invited Kira along on the roundup. He almost wished that day had never happened. That was the day when he knew for certain that he was in love with her. When she'd fallen asleep in his arms, he thought he'd never known such contentment. He couldn't imagine sharing that feeling with anyone else—sharing that part of himself with anyone else.

"Let it go," he muttered aloud. "Just let it go." He leaned his head against Sun Morning.

Kira slipped through the entrance of the stable. She leaned against a far wall, regarding horse and rider with as much tenderness as Dylan had experienced Sunday morning when he saw Kira and Ellis's infant sister together. She didn't think that she'd made any noise as she entered, but Dylan's head whipped around as if she'd shouted at him.

Dylan stepped away, embarrassed that she'd caught him in an unguarded, tender moment coddling his horse. "What are you doing down here?" he demanded, then softened his tone and added, "I thought you'd be on your way to Chicago by now."

Kira pressed her lips together. That coward! He had been avoiding her.

"My bags are packed. The car's warming up," she told him. "But your uncles said I should talk to you first."

"Did they?" Dylan said blandly. He wondered what those three were up to now. If they'd thought of a good reason, some plausible excuse that would keep her from leaving, he wished they'd let him in on it. "If it's my permission you're waiting for, you can roll out now, Kira."

His reticence stung her. It pierced her heart and brought stinging tears to her eyes. She started to turn away, to head back to the house, but a movement seen out of the corner of her eyes made her halt—something she read in his stiff-backed stance and in the automatonlike brushing motions. There was no joy in the tending to his horse. Something in the disconnect between the pleasure he derived from caring for his horse and the forced, unnatural motions after he'd dismissed Kira spoke to her, even through his silence.

Dylan could feel the pinpoint of Kira's gaze on his back. He didn't dare turn around. He'd heard the catch in her breath when he told her to go, and knew that he'd probably made her cry. He didn't dare turn around to show her how close she'd brought him to breaking. So he stood, brushing Sun Morning, and silently pleading that if she was going to end it, she would do it now. The longer the silence grew between them—the longer she stood there regarding him—the more he strained to maintain his air of indifference.

When Kira saw the clenched-jawed muscles in his lean face start to quiver, she let out a slow breath. She wasn't going anywhere. Not just yet. She clasped her hands behind her back and casually strolled around the stable. She noticed more of Dylan's currying tools hanging from various hooks in a section of the stable set aside for tack. "May I?"

"Go ahead." Dylan stepped aside. Kira picked up a stiff-bristled brush, looped the heavy, corded handle around her hand as she'd often seen Dylan do, and slowly approached Sun Morning. Dylan held the gate open for her and allowed Kira to enter.

"How's she doing?" Kira asked, gingerly touching the mare's swollen belly.

"Any day now," Dylan predicted.

"I'll bet you can't wait to be the proud papa of a . . . what kind of a horse is Sun Morning?"

"Pasofino," Dylan supplied.

"Pasofino pony," Kira continued. She moved around to Sun Morning's opposite side while Dylan calmed the horse from the other. "Nice, easy strokes," was all he said for several minutes while Kira brushed Sun Morning's mane, down her back, and over her roan flanks.

"She's so beautiful," Kira murmured. "So perfect."

"Yes, she is," Dylan caught and held Kira's gaze.

She cleared her throat, then asked, "What do you want, Dylan, a boy horse or a girl horse?"

"Stud or mare," Dylan corrected automatically. He then grinned at her when she shot him a look of mild annoyance. "It doesn't matter, Kira, as long as it's healthy."

"I think you're going to make a wonderful papa." Kira sought out his gaze. She wasn't necessarily talking about the horse. Though when it came to the horses, she'd seen him at his most tender. He cared for Sun Morning as diligently as any father would his child. She had also seen him at his toughest. When the mustangs at Ritter's Cut had stampeded, she'd watched him move masterfully among them as if *he* was their leader. She had no doubt that if he ever became a father, he could be as disciplined as he was doting.

She imagined Dylan, sitting in the middle of the floor, playing with a chubby-cheeked, dark-eyed, caramel-haired child. Kira swallowed convulsively. His children would be dark-haired like himself. *Their* children, however, might not be.

Kira ducked under Sun Morning's head. Dylan moved back, allowing her to continue with her currying.

"Like this?" Kira asked, deliberately shortening her brush strokes. Sun Morning snorted and swung her narrow head around to stare at Kira as if to say *"Amateur!"*

"No . . . it's more like this. . . ." Dylan closed the distance between them, then clasped his hand over hers. Kira trembled as he wrapped the other arm around her waist, drawing her back against him. She could feel his heart, pounding steady and strong, through the cotton fabric of her shirt. She knew he could feel her heart, too, as he brought his hand up to unfasten the top buttons of her blouse and rested his hand possessively between the valley of her breasts.

"Ohhhh," she let out a long breath. She didn't care if he heard the tremor in her voice. She wanted him to know how she felt. She wanted him to know that she wanted him. She needed him. "So that's how it's done."

"Not quite," Dylan murmured against her hair. He plucked the brush from her hand and tossed it carelessly to the stable floor. He drew his lips lightly across her hair. How he loved the smell of her hair—light and floral. He loved the way it felt against his fingers, like coils of silk slipping and sometimes catching against his roughened fingers. He nuzzled her at her cheek, then breathed a kiss into her ear, causing a shiver to run the length of her rapidly melting spine. Kira leaned against him, relying on the broad expanse of his chest and the protective arms encircling her for support. She arched her back and reached behind her—interlocking her fingers behind Dylan's neck. She had to hang on. The way she felt now, as light as gossamer, if she didn't hold onto him, she'd drift away.

"Hold me, Dylan," Kira pleaded softly. "Don't let me go."

That was all he needed to hear. She wasn't going to go back to Chicago. He wouldn't let her go. He spun her around, crushing her body to him with silent desperation. He would hold her like this, warm and shielded in his arms, until the last tie tugging her back faded into nothingness.

"Stay with me, Kira," Dylan said raggedly. "Stay with me." He buried her face in a flurry of kisses that literally left her no breath to speak.

When she dragged her lips away from his, she was panting, "I . . . I don't want go, Dylan."

"Then don't! You don't have to go, Kira."

"But what about my family . . . my friends? They need me," she said helplessly casting around for excuses.

"Nobody—nothing—back there needs you more than I do, Kira Dodd."

Kira looked up at him with doubt in her eyes. Could it be that simple? What about her family back in Chicago? What about her job? Her friends? Her apartment? Could she let go as easily as Myra? No. She couldn't do it. It just wasn't in her to be so impulsive.

Dylan saw the decision reflected in her eyes. "I can't let you go, Kira," he said fervently. She was slipping away from him. Dylan took a deep breath, making one, last, heartfelt bid. "Please don't go, Kira. I love you."

"What . . . what did you say?" Kira unclasped her arms and dropped to the ground. "What did you say, Dylan?"

"You heard me, woman."

"You . . . you love me?" Kira echoed, a smile lighting her face. If there was anything she had learned at her stay on the Triple J, it was that the Jolivet men were proud men of their word. Dylan would not say it if were not so. "Say it again, Dylan. Tell me you love me." She placed her hand against his heart. She wanted to feel the words coming from his heart.

"I love you, Kira! Do you want me to shout it to the rafters? Is that what you want from me? Do you want me to beg you? I will, you know. I'll get down on my knees and beg you to stay. Is that what you want? To see one of the proud, Jolivet man reduced to begging?" He clasped his arms around her waist and slid to his knees. He pressed his cheek against her breast.

"No, Dylan, for heaven's sake, you know that's not what I want. Get up from there!"

"Then tell me that you're going to stay."

"I can't!"

"I'm not going to let you go, woman." Dylan squeezed tightly, eliciting a gasp from Kira.

"Dylan, you're crushing me," she croaked.

"You'd better say it, Kira. You'd better tell me you're going to stay." He looked up at her, his dark eyes twinkling with mischief. Kira recognized that look, then squirmed to free herself from his grasp. She couldn't stand it when he looked at her that way. She couldn't resist him.

"Kira," Dylan warned, his voice rumbling deep in his throat. He swept his arm around her knees and pulled toward him. Kira's knees buckled, sending them both sprawling onto the haystrewn floor. "Come on, sweetheart. Tell me that you're going to stay. You know you want to. You know you belong here."

"But what about my family back in Chicago?"

"Send them a postcard," Dylan teased, remembering that the biggest and most blessed upheaval in their lives had started with a postcard.

"That's not funny, Dylan. My sister Ally is going to have a baby. I don't want to miss out on the birth. I have to be there."

"And you will," Dylan promised. *"We* will, if that's what you want." He remembered the advice Jimmy had given him on the church grounds yesterday. If she had to go back, for whatever reason, for whatever length of time, she would not go back alone. He would be with her, every step of the way, reminding her of home and of the life they had waiting for them here.

"Yes! Oh, yes!" Kira exclaimed. "I *do* want."

"Then say you'll stay," he urged.

"I'll stay," she echoed, nodding vigorously.

"Now keep nodding," he murmured against her ear. Brushing away her soft curls, he whispered, "Say that you love me, too."

Kira squeezed him tightly against her. "I love you, Dylan."

Filled with emotions too deep to express, he didn't trust himself to speak. Instead, he pressed his cheek to hers and began to hum, soft and low. . . .

"I'll be home for Christmas. . . ."

Epilogue

One Year Later . . .

Kira woke up and found that the temperature had dropped considerably since she'd gone to bed. She rolled over and squinted out the window. It was still pitch black. Rain was falling in steady sheets and turning to ice as it hit the windowpane. She shivered and drew up her knees.

She considered jumping out of bed and throwing on an extra layer of clothing, but she didn't want to lose the warmth she'd already generated. Careful not to disturb the covers too much, she leaned her head over the bed and called softly.

"Here, Delanie. Here, girl. Want to climb in bed with Mama?"

Delanie yawned sleepily and whined. A deeper snuffle and several answering whines let her know that Delanie wasn't exactly suffering for warmth. Keeper and the litter of seven little shoodles were with her. Their combined body heat, coupled with the sheltering fringe of the blanket falling over the side of the bed, left them a cozy nest that made Kira jealous. She didn't blame them. She wouldn't want to come out, either.

She sighed and settled as best she could under the covers. Moments later, a soft tap at the door made her raise up on one elbow.

"Yes?"

"Kira, are you awake?" Myra poked her head in the door. She carried a thick quilt in her arms.

"Mama? What time is it?"

"It's three o'clock in the morning. Looks like we got that cold front that Jesse told us about."

"So I noticed," Kira grimaced, clutching her knees to her chest. "Jesse and his telltale arthritic toes. If someone had given him that rubbing alcohol when he'd first started complaining, we'd probably still be in the eighties now."

"Here, sweetheart. Get under these," Myra spread a quilt over Kira. It smelled faintly of mothballs, cedar chips, and potpourri. "Jimmy's checking on the furnace. It should be warmer in here in a little bit." Myra tucked ends of the blanket under the mattress as she used to when Kira and her sister were little girls. "Better?"

"Umm-hmm," Kira said sleepily. "What are you doing up, Mama? You haven't been baking again, have you?"

Myra laughed softly. "No, not yet. Those Jolivets are already stirring around. I got up to put on some coffee. They're checking on the bird pens. Dylan said he was going to make another check on the horses while he was out."

Kira flung the covers back and reached for her jeans. "Goldie!"

"Kira, where do you think you're going?"

"My Goldie is going to have her baby today. I can feel it. I wouldn't miss this for all the quilts in Murray!" Kira declared. The horse that Dylan had caught for her on the roundup a year ago was pregnant with her first foal.

She pulled on a flannel shirt over her pajamas.

"Kira, it's nasty out there. You shouldn't be out in this weather."

"I don't want to miss it, Mama. I won't be out long. I promise," Kira said, slipping her feet into her tennis shoes and taking the stairs two at a time. She moved more slowly through the kitchen, taking a moment to soak up the warmth before darting outside. It was only forty yards from the rear of the house to Goldie's pen. It seemed like forty miles as she avoided slick patches of ice.

She flung open the door to the barn, panting slightly, and blinking in the bright glow of the portable lanterns.

"D-d-did I muh-miss it?" she chattered, pulling the door closed behind her.

"Good grief, woman! What are you trying do? Give yourself triple pneumonia?" Dylan chastised, noticing her soggy shoes, hastily buttoned rain-drenched shirt, and sopping hair.

"Goldie's colt? Did I miss it?" she repeated, hurrying over to the stall. The palomino stood in the far corner—calm but alert. Except for an occasional whinny, the only evidence Kira saw that indicated the mare was in labor were the periodic convulsive ripples along her flaxen flanks.

"No, you didn't miss it," Dylan said, tossing his flannel jacket over her shoulders.

"How long do you think it'll take?" she asked.

"Can't say. Maybe minutes. Maybe hours. All we can do now is wait. Come over here, Kira. Let's give her some privacy." He moved a thermos of coffee and patted a blanket tossed over a bale of hay. Kira settled next to him. He placed his arm around her, as much for warmth as for companionship. When she leaned her head against his shoulder, he lightheartedly complained about her damp hair.

"Sorry," she murmured, grasping a fistful of her hair and twisting it on top of her head out of the way.

"Maybe this will help." Pulling a faded blue bandanna from the pocket of the flannel jacket, Dylan swabbed at Kira's dripping hair. He ran the bandanna under her bangs, down her neck, and inside the collar of her shirt. When a droplet of water squeezed from the bandanna and trickled down over the swell of Kira's breast, Dylan leaned forward and touched her with the tip of his tongue to trace the droplet's path.

"Cut that out, Dylan, Jolivet! That's for the baby!" Kira playfully chastised, pushing him away.

Dylan grinned, and leaned his ear against her abdomen. Almost five months along in her own pregnancy, Kira's abdomen was just starting to protrude. Dylan removed his gloves and wormed his warm hand possessively against her skin. He planted a tender kiss on her navel. Then, cupping his hand to his mouth, he whispered, "Are you ready to come out and face the world, little fella? Huh? Daddy's waiting for ya, little man," he encouraged.

"She says it's too cold to come out and *she'll* just wait for the summer," Kira countered.

"Just in time to take *him* riding the fence line with me," Dylan said smugly.

"Are you really hoping for a boy first, Dylan?" Kira asked.

"It doesn't matter, Kira," he insisted, searching out her gaze to impress her with his earnestness. "As long as the baby's happy and healthy."

"Speaking of babies, Ally said they should make it down for Christmas."

"Good. That means we can put one of our own in the arms of the pageant's Mary and Joseph instead of another one of Ellis's siblings."

Kira chuckled appreciatively. Poor Ellis. If he got another sister or brother, he'd be hanging around gas stations to raise extra money for Christmas presents for the rest of his life, she thought.

"Not a bad tradition to start, eh, Mama Jolivet? A baby for the pageant every year," Dylan murmured. His continuous caress turned from tender to tantalizing as he warmed her skin. Kira caught her lower lip between her teeth—reveling in the sensation but wondering about his timing. "Dylan, shouldn't you be concentrating on my horse?"

"Let nature take its course, Kira," he responded, moving over her. Kira opened her shirt and the flannel jacket to him. When he'd settled over her, pressing her back into the prickly, crinkling cushion of hay, she brought the huge folds of the blanket around them, cocooning them in its warmth.

"Seems like that's how I got in my condition in the first place," she teased, lovingly tracing her fingers over the deep laugh lines of his cheeks. "Listening to you and your . . . nature."

"Are you complaining, Kira Jolivet?" Dylan raised an eyebrow at her.

Kira Jolivet. As happy as she was at becoming Dylan's wife, she still wasn't quite used to the sound of her new name, her new life. "Who, me? Complain?" Kira said innocently, smiling up at him. "Of course not. Getting in this condition was half the fun."

"Only half fun?" Dylan asked huskily. The blatant, heated intention in his eyes made her forget the sheets of ice forming just outside the barn door. His hands, familiar but ever new in the feelings he invoked in her, made her forget that in just a few hours she would help act as hostess to the pageant participates waiting for their completed costumes. His kiss, deep and all-consuming, made her forget that in a few hours she along with the other, more fortunate members of Murray would spend most of this pre-Christmas week delivering food, blankets, and gifts to those less blessed. She would deal with the busloads of children coming to visit the emu chicks at the new Triple J petting ranch later.

For now, there was only her and Dylan. And when he came to her, filling her with the miracle that sparked the life within her, Kira knew that there was no place she would rather be. She was home. And she was loved.

ABOUT THE AUTHOR

Geri Guillaume is the psuedonym for an author who lives in Texas. A technical writer, she is also the mother of two children and raises horses.

Coming in December From
Arabesque Books . . .

THE LOOK OF LOVE by Monica Jackson
1-58314-069-7 $4.99US/$6.50CAN
When busy single mother Carmel Matthews meets handsome plastic
surgeon Steve Reynolds, he sets her pulse racing like never before.
But he and Carmel will have to confront their deepest doubts and
fears, if they are to have a love that promises all they've ever
desired . . .

VIOLETS ARE BLUE by Sonia Icilyn
1-58314-057-3 $4.99US/$6.50CAN
Arlisa Davenport's impoverished childhood never hurt more than
when she caught Brad Belleville, her young love, mocking her. A
decade later, when her pregnant sister is kidnapped, she must turn to
Brad for help and soon discovers that their desire is far more alluring
than she'd ever imagined.

DISTANT MEMORIES by Niqui Stanhope
1-58314-059-X $4.99US/$6.50CAN
Days after realizing her Hollywood dreams, Racquel Ward finds herself
tragically disfigured and near death. With her abusive ex-husband at her
bedside, she places her fragile trust in Dr. Sean KirPatrick. Now they
must both overcome overwhelming obstacles to believe in the power of
love . . .

SPELLBOUND by Deirdre Savoy
1-58314-058-1 $4.99US/$6.50CAN
Ariel Windsor is insistent that heartache will never crush her again . . .
until she meets irresistible Jarad Naughton. He is intrigued by her
beauty and by the rumor that she's the last in a line of witches who
can make men fall in love with them in six days . . . now, they're
both playing for keeps.

Please Use the Coupon on the Next Page to Order

Coming in January from Arabesque Books . . .

SECRET LOVE by Brenda Jackson
  1-58314-073-5 $5.99US/$7.99CAN
When Hollywood star Diamond Swain decides to hide out at a remote ranch, she never expects to meet rugged Jake Madaris. Burned by a bad marriage, Jake is wary but it isn't long before they're both drawn into a whirlwind secret romance that just may create a love to last a lifetime.

MESMERIZED by Simona Taylor
  1-58314-070-0 $5.99US/$7.99CAN
Talented businesswoman Sean Scott is devoted to her work until Christian Devine, her ex-fiancée, unexpectedly arrives as her new Operations Manager. Soon, under the threat of danger, their smoldering passion erupts and they are given the chance to finally trust in each other again.

SAY YOU LOVE ME by Adrianne Byrd
  1-58314-071-9 $5.99US/$7.99CAN
After years of playing second-best to her husband's successful company, Christian Williams breaks his heart by asking for a divorce. With all they've built hanging in the balance, the two must rediscover the desire they once shared—and the passionate dreams still waiting to be fulfilled.

ICE UNDER FIRE by Linda Hudson-Smith
  1-58314-072-7 $5.99US/$7.99CAN
Champion figure skater Omunique Philyaw overcame tragic loss to become an Olympic hopeful. But when her new sponsor, business mogul Kenneth Maxwell, ignites an irresistible attraction, they must brave distrust and dangerous opponents if they are to have a love worth winning.

Please Use the Coupon on the Next page to Order

Celebrate the New Year with Arabesque Romances

__SECRET LOVE by Brenda Jackson
1-58314-073-5 $5.99US/$7.99CAN

__MESMERIZED by Simona Taylor
1-58314-070-0 $5.99US/$7.99CAN

__SAY YOU LOVE ME by Adrianne Byrd
1-58314-071-9 $5.99US/$7.99

__ICE UNDER FIRE by Linda Hudson-Smith
1-58314-072-7 $5.99US/$7.99CAN
